Her lips
lured Paul's attention

He was too far away to hear what she was saying, but not too far to recall the way her mouth had felt one afternoon in the greenhouse, seemingly ages ago, when he'd stupidly believed a relationship could develop between her and himself. The kiss they'd shared had been so dazzling, so rich with promise....

Remembering that kiss put Paul in mind not of what had actually occurred at her house a couple of nights ago but of what he wished had occurred. He wanted to make love to her, properly, sensitively, passionately. He wanted to love *her*, not some undefined fantasy figure in a flashback nightmare. He wanted her to give herself to him not in charity but in ecstasy—and he wanted to give her everything she gave him, and more.

ABOUT THE AUTHOR

Herself a survivor of the 60s, Judith Arnold has always believed in the healing power of love. In her latest novel, she tells a story of healing, forgiving and making peace.

Judith lives with her husband and two sons in Sudbury, Massachusetts.

Books by Judith Arnold

HARLEQUIN AMERICAN ROMANCE

149—SPECIAL DELIVERY
163—MAN AND WIFE
189—BEST FRIENDS
201—PROMISES*
205—COMMITMENTS*
209—DREAMS*
225—COMFORT AND JOY
240—TWILIGHT
255—GOING BACK
259—HARVEST THE SUN
281—ONE WHIFF OF SCANDAL
304—INDEPENDENCE DAY

*KEEPING THE FAITH SUBSERIES

HARLEQUIN TEMPTATION

122—ON LOVE'S TRAIL

Don't miss any of our special offers. Write to us at the following address for information on our newest releases.

Harlequin Reader Service
901 Fuhrmann Blvd., P.O. Box 1397, Buffalo, NY 14240
Canadian address: P.O. Box 603,
Fort Erie, Ont. L2A 5X3

SURVIVORS

JUDITH ARNOLD

Harlequin Books

TORONTO • NEW YORK • LONDON
AMSTERDAM • PARIS • SYDNEY • HAMBURG
STOCKHOLM • ATHENS • TOKYO • MILAN

To Freddy and Greg—
may all your wars be make-believe.

Published February 1990

First printing December 1989

ISBN 0-373-16330-4

Prologue

May, 1969

"No," said Paul. "I'm not going."

Around him swirled the nocturnal sounds of the forest: the incessant screeching of crickets, the distant hoot of an owl, the electric hum of a cicada, the syncopated patter of raindrops that penetrated the dense foliage to strike the muddy ground beneath his feet. To the south lay the village—quiet and dark at night, but Paul had been in country long enough to know that quiet and dark didn't mean safe.

"If you wanna talk back to me, Private, this isn't the time," said Macon in a hushed, intense voice. "I just gave you an order."

Paul held his ground. Intuition was more important than orders, and this time his intuition was strong. He knew trouble was waiting on the other side of the hill. "Shove your order," he said. "I'm not going."

"Come on," Swann whispered, giving Paul a friendly nudge. "It's just over one little baby hill, and then we get to go back to camp. Ain't nobody gonna mess with us."

"I've got a feeling," Paul whispered back. He wouldn't have wasted his breath explaining to Macon, but Swann was his friend. "It just doesn't feel right to me."

"This ain't sniper territory," Swann reminded him.

"The whole damned countryside is sniper territory."

"Let's just go and get it over with," Rigucci snapped impatiently. *"We stand around here, we're sitting ducks."* He was hyper, fidgety, probably on speed. Lots of the grunts took it when they pulled night patrol. It was better than nodding off, losing concentration and getting blown away.

Paul had considered taking something to get him through the night, but now he was glad he hadn't. His nervous system was working overtime, telling him things, sending out signals he might have missed if he'd had a buzz on.

"I'm not going," he insisted, staring down the trail through the eerie layers of fog that snagged on the vines and branches like vaporous cobwebs. Something awful was waiting for them on the other side of the hill. He didn't know what, but his gut told him it was going to go down bad if they patrolled over there.

Macon clamped an iron hand around Paul's upper arm and gave him a sharp tug. Off duty, the sergeant was a nice enough guy, but when he was pulling rank he could be a real hard-ass. *"You march over that ridge with us, Tremaine,"* he growled, *"or you're going to get brought up on charges."*

"What charges?"

"Failure to obey a direct order."

"I don't care," Paul said. He did care—his heart was ricocheting around in his chest and his back was drenched in a cold sweat. But the possibility of a court martial didn't scare him half as much as going over that ridge.

"I think he's nuts," Swann said to Macon. *"I think he snapped or something."*

"*Tremaine isn't a loony, Swann. He's just being stubborn. You're his buddy—tell him to get it in gear or he'll ride out the rest of this war in jail.*"

"*You heard the man,*" Swann murmured. "*He's gonna hang you out to dry.*"

"*I'll take my chances.*"

"*It's gonna go on your record, man. You might wind up doin' hard time.*"

"*I'm doing hard time now,*" Paul muttered.

"*I'm gonna do you hard time with my boot on your butt,*" Macon snarled, trying to yank Paul back onto the trail. His eyes were hard and round in his camouflage-painted face; his helmet rode the back of his skull. His neck was leathery and large dark circles stained his shirt under the arms. "*Now get moving, or I'm bringing you up on charges.*"

Paul wrenched his arm free. "*Go to hell, Macon.*"

"*Come on,*" Rigucci muttered, starting down the trail. "*I can't stand still any longer.*"

"*I'll be back for you.*" Macon jabbed a thick, threatening finger at Paul, then hiked his rifle higher on his shoulder and turned to join the others. "*Your days are numbered, Tremaine. I'll be back for you.*"

Paul stayed where he was, partially hidden behind a mesh of rain-slick vines, watching as Rigucci, Swann and Macon fell into step on the trail. He listened to the crunch of their boots on the loose-pebbled path and the clank of their canteens against their belts as they headed up the hill, vanishing into the eddying folds of fog.

Chapter One

Like most of the back roads in Northford, Carpenter Road was a twisting, hilly strip of asphalt barely two lanes wide, bordered by tall trees and massive outcroppings of granite. Cruising down Carpenter Road—especially when one drove fast and tight, the way Paul did—required a fair amount of concentration. He had the pickup's windows open, the radio cranked up and a few sacks of cedar chips in back. His eyes were on the double yellow line and his mind was on the six-pack chilling in his refrigerator at home. As soon as he dropped off the cedar chips back at the nursery, he planned to head for his house, pop open a beer and unwind. He worked most Saturdays, so he felt no compunction about leaving the nursery early Friday nights. And tonight he had no date, no plans, no obligations.

Lost in the pleasure of driving, he almost didn't see the boy standing just beyond a sharp bend in the road, his head turned to stare over his left shoulder and his right thumb stuck out in silent supplication. His hair was scruffy and tawny-colored, his jeans were torn at the knees, and his feet were encased in oversize leather hightops. He was tall and stringy in build, with peach-fuzz cheeks and squinting eyes.

Paul slowed to a halt, shifted into neutral and turned down the volume on the radio. Then he leaned across the seat toward the passenger window. "Where you headed?" he asked.

The boy peered into the cab of the truck. Paul saw that behind his squint he had gentle hazel eyes, almost feminine in their beauty. "Fair Hollow Lane," the boy said, his voice twanging and cracking the way male voices did during early adolescence.

Fair Hollow Lane was on the southern end of town, well out of Paul's way. But if he didn't give the kid a lift, someone else might—some creep, maybe. Tall though the boy was, he lacked the heft to defend himself. "Get in," Paul said, straightening in his seat.

"Thanks." The boy gave him a broad, toothy smile and climbed into the truck.

Paul waited until his passenger was settled before he shifted into gear. He drove for a minute in silence, keeping his speed down and contemplating whether he should offer a lecture along with the ride. He didn't like being lectured, himself, but this kid appeared too innocent, too trusting. He ought to be more cautious, given how many sick people there were in the world. "You know, hitching isn't safe," he said, hoping he didn't sound judgmental.

The boy shot him a quick look, then shrugged. "This is a small town. It's not like I'd hitch in Lowell or Boston or anything."

"Small town or not, you run a major risk getting into a stranger's car. You're lucky I came along. I'm sane. A lot of folks aren't."

The boy eyed him, his expression a blend of impatience and edginess. "Yeah, well . . ." He turned his gaze to the windshield. The thick, shaggy locks of his dirty-blond hair blew back from his face in the spring-tinged breeze that gusted in through the open window.

"What's your name?" Paul asked.

The boy gave him another toothy grin. "Shane Hudson. What's yours?"

"Paul Tremaine."

"Yeah, I noticed that on the outside of the truck. Tremaine Nursery."

Paul nodded. "It's my uncle's business," he said. "I just work there." That was an understatement; Uncle Steve had already started the paperwork to transfer half ownership of the operation to Paul. But as much as he enjoyed the myriad tasks of running the farm and its retail nursery—and as good as he was at it—he didn't like viewing himself as an entrepreneur. It sounded so white-collar.

"So, what, you sell plants and stuff?" Shane asked.

"We grow them, we sell them, we plant them. Wholesale and retail. Shrubbery is our middle name."

"Huh?"

Paul glimpsed Shane and realized that his joke had flown over the boy's head. "Never mind." He braked at the stop sign, then turned right, heading south into the center of town.

Symptoms of civilization began to proliferate around them. The road grew straighter and wider and the number of houses increased: fewer rambling old farmhouses, stone-walled mansions and derelict mobile homes, more neat Cape Cods and Colonials. The closer to town they traveled, the tidier the yards and the greater the preponderance of white clapboard in the architecture.

The heart of Northford was its rectangular green. The streets bordering it held the Congregational church, the

Methodist church, the town hall, the post office, a couple of stores and the fenced-in playground of the elementary school. Pristine sidewalks crisscrossed the green beneath the leafy boughs of several ancient maple and oak trees. At the east end of the green stood a granite obelisk bearing a plaque that read: In Memory of the Brave Men Who Gave Their Lives in the Service of Their Country.

Paul was familiar with that monument. He knew every name carved onto its four sloping faces: those lost in the Civil War, World War I, World War II and Korea. Some had been born in Northford; some had resided in Northford just prior to their deaths. What mattered was that they'd died in war and the town of Northford had wanted to honor them.

What also mattered was that the obelisk didn't have room on it for Paul's war.

The knoll where he wanted to put a new memorial was at the western end of the green, a good fifteen yards from the nearest oak tree. He'd made his proposal at the town meeting a week ago, and while the idea hadn't automatically been approved, at least he hadn't been booed out of the room. The councilmen had expressed their gratitude that Paul was willing to donate ten thousand dollars of his own money toward the project, and they'd said they would review the budget to see what monies the town might contribute. Providing a small parcel of land on the town green would be no problem, they had assured him.

In fact, as far as Paul could tell, the only problem his memorial faced was the objection of that belligerent schoolteacher who'd risen to her feet and declared that she thought it would be downright scandalous to spend thousands of dollars in a celebration of the nation's militaristic blunders when the elementary school couldn't even scrape together the funds to update its library. The councilmen had listened to her as respectfully as they'd listened to Paul, but he suspected they were on his side. Who was she, after all, but some recent arrival, someone without any real roots in the town? Paul's father had grown up in Northford, and so had he. His uncle, who had never lived anywhere else, was currently managing fifty fertile acres and paying taxes on them. The Tremaine name meant something in these parts.

Sooner or later, persnickety schoolteacher or no, Paul was going to erect his memorial. Then he'd be able to put the past to rest.

"Make a right here," Shane was saying, indicating the intersection at the southwest corner of the green. "It's a great shortcut to my house."

"Are you in a hurry?" Paul asked. It occurred to him that not ten minutes ago he'd been in a rush to drop off the extra sacks of cedar chips at the nursery and head for home. For some reason, he wasn't quite as anxious to race home now as he'd been before. The boy wasn't exactly scintillating company, but Paul was enjoying the drive and the balmy May dusk.

"Well...I don't want to get in trouble with my mom."

"How old are you?" Paul asked.

"Fourteen, almost."

"That's an unusual name—Shane."

The boy shrugged. "My father loved that old movie, you know, with Alan Ladd."

"I know the one," Paul said, wondering why Shane had referred to his father in the past tense. "Mysterious stranger passing through, saving the settlers. It's a classic."

Shane turned to him. "You like old movies?"

"I like new ones better. They've got more—" He almost said "skin," but he caught himself in time. "More grit," he said instead.

"You know what really burns me up?" Shane complained. "Here in Northford, you've got to drive to another town just to see a movie. Like, you can't even get cable TV here—even though my mom probably wouldn't let me have it, anyway. She thinks TV makes your mind rot. But you can't just walk to the movies. I mean, like, you've got to get someone's mom to drive you."

"I take it you're not a native of Northford," Paul surmised.

"We moved here almost three years ago. We used to live in *Cambridge*," Shane said, his emphasis implying that Paul was supposed to be impressed. He wasn't. Cambridge was an academic enclave, fun in small doses and a mecca if you happened to be an old movie buff, which left Paul out. Nor did he like exotic and overpriced cuisine, overweening intellectualism, used-book stores or city congestion.

"Cambridge, huh," he grunted. "Clean air must be a novelty to you."

"I guess my lungs have gotten used to it by now," Shane said solemnly.

Paul cast him a quick look and realized he was kidding. They shared a grin. "So tell me, where's this shortcut of yours?" he asked.

Shane pointed. "Right there—Pond Road."

"Are you nuts? That mud hole?"

"It's not so bad. My mom drives it all the time."

"What does she drive, a Sherman tank?"

"She's got a Subaru," Shane said. "If she can handle it, I bet this truck can."

Paul laughed. "You're missing the point, kid. If the mud splatters up onto the door panels and covers up the nursery name, we lose our free advertising."

"If it splatters up, I'll clean it off for you."

Paul admired Shane's spirit. "You've got yourself a deal," he said, wrenching the steering wheel to the left and veering off the smoothly paved main route onto the potholed and rutted back road. They bumped along, Paul deftly steering around loose rocks and deep pits, dodging puddles whenever he could. "So help me," he muttered, "if I need a new alignment after this—"

"It's not so bad," Shane insisted. "I'll tell you what's real nasty—doing it on a bicycle. Me and my friend Matt do this strip all the time. Back in March, during the thaw, Matt wiped out on a mud slick and went flying. He landed about fifty feet from his bike."

"That must have been fun," Paul grumbled. He was smiling, though. There was something refreshing about a teenage boy who thought wiping out on a bike was more exciting than ingesting drugs or getting a girl into bed.

The front right tire hit a deep rut and set the truck bouncing. "Nice suspension you've got on this thing," Shane observed.

"Nice suspension I *had*. How much longer before we get off this road?"

"It runs right into Fair Hollow. Then you make a right, and my house is right there."

"I can't wait." Paul maneuvered around another deep rut and grinned when the truck remained level. Overhead the tree branches met, forming a canopy of dense leaves that sifted the sunset's golden light. To the right extended a marshy lake, and to the left a few houses were visible.

Paul spotted a break in the trees. After steering adroitly around a bowling-ball-size rock, he accelerated toward the smooth pavement at the intersection up ahead. "Is that Fair Hollow Lane?"

"Yeah."

Allowing himself a private smile at having emerged from Pond Road relatively unscathed, Paul stopped at the intersection and then turned right. "Which house?"

Shane pointed to a small gray two-story house set back from the street at the end of a gravel drive. A front porch extended nearly the entire width of the house beneath the roof's overhang; two bentwood rocking chairs sat welcomingly beside the railing. A star-shaped crystal hung from a thread in one of the front windows, catching the slanting sunlight and tossing it at Paul in rainbow-colored glints.

He cruised slowly up the driveway. The front lawn, he noticed, needed watering, but the flower bed abutting the porch was flourishing; red tulips shared the loamy soil with yellow daffodils, and an azalea bush at the far end of the bed was dappled with tiny pink buds. A gnarled crab apple tree shaded the lawn near a hedge of evergreens. Closer to the driveway stood a dogwood tree that appeared to be dying.

"Nice place," he said.

Shane scowled. "I wish it had air conditioning."

"If you're tough enough to navigate Pond Road on your bicycle, you're tough enough to go without air-conditioning," Paul joked, slowing to a halt and turning off the engine.

As Shane shoved open his door, the shadowy figure of a woman materialized at the screened front door of the house. She stepped onto the porch, lifting her hand to shield her eyes from the sun's glare. "Shane?" she called. "Is that you?"

Paul's mouth fell open in surprise as he stared at the woman on the porch. She was the schoolteacher, that pompous lady who'd sounded off about militaristic blunders at the town meeting last week. He shouldn't be so shocked; in a town as small as Northford, people frequently ran into each other in a variety of contexts, but still... Paul hadn't yet gotten over his resentment of her attack on his memorial, and now here she was, the mother of this nice kid.

If he got out of the truck, would she recognize him and resume the argument where they'd left off last week? Should he throw courtesy to the wind and tell her he thought she had a hell of a nerve trying to block his memorial with the claim that a few Dick-and-Jane readers for the kindergartners were more important than honoring the young men who'd bled and died so people like her would have the freedom to stand up and sound off at town meetings?

Or should he give her a smile and ask her if she'd like to discuss the memorial over a drink some evening? Sure, she was a mother and, her son's use of past tense notwithstanding, there was an Alan Ladd fan in the picture somewhere, but... damn, she was pretty.

Her beauty hadn't registered on Paul at the town meeting—probably because he'd been too focused on the memorial and too angry with her for voicing her opposition to it. She'd been sitting way to his left at the other side of the room, and he'd caught only brief glimpses of her as she yammered away on the subject of the underfinanced school library.

Now, however, as she stepped off the porch and approached the truck, he took the opportunity to admire the straight ash-blond hair that dropped past her shoulders, silky and long, and then her fresh face, unadorned by makeup, and her tall, slim body clad in a gauzy white blouse and a denim jumper. After reaching her leather-sandaled feet, his gaze ran back up again, surveying her slender calves, the curves hinted at beneath the loose folds of her jumper, her graceful arms and finally her face. She had a strong chin like her son's, elegantly hollow cheeks, a narrow nose, a severe forehead and glittering hazel eyes as pretty as Shane's—although, in her case, their effect on Paul was dazzling.

"Shane, what's going on?" she asked, her gaze flicking from her son to the truck. The slight movement of her head caused her hair to shift, revealing gleaming gold hoop earrings. "Where's your bike?"

"It got a flat," the boy said as he jumped down from the seat. "I left it at Matt's."

Frowning, the woman turned fully to the truck. "Are you a friend of Matt's?" she addressed Paul through the open window.

Taking a deep breath, he opened the driver's door and climbed out. Common decency required that he reassure her that her son had been safe with him. He only hoped that, once she realized who he was, she wouldn't light into him. "I gave Shane a lift," he said, walking around the front of the truck with his hand outstretched. "Paul Tremaine."

She glanced at his hand and then lifted her gaze. Her hazel eyes locked with his, piercing in their clarity, and she smiled thinly and shook his hand. "How do you do?" she said before pivoting back to her son. "How did you happen to get a lift from Mr. Tremaine?"

"I hitched," he confessed, showing no remorse. "He picked me up."

"Hitched! Shane, that's dangerous! How could you? You don't know who this man is—"

"You told me you and Dad used to hitch all the time when you were my age," Shane retorted, squaring his shoulders. He stood as tall as his mother, yet he still seemed to be looking up at her.

She planted her hands on her hips. The motion drew Paul's attention to her fingers. They were long and slim, with clean oval nails. His own hands were soiled with telltale dirt—he'd come upon Shane shortly after delivering a load of yews to one of the new subdivisions in Bolton. He shoved his hands into his pockets so she wouldn't notice them.

Not that she seemed particularly aware of him. "First of all," she admonished her son, "when your father and I used to hitchhike we were much older than you are now. But more importantly, the world was a different place twenty years ago. There weren't so many weirdos."

Shane poked at the driveway's loose gravel with his toe. "You always say that, but I don't believe it. I bet there were just as many weirdos then. More, I bet. Anyway, Paul isn't a weirdo."

Shane's mother eyed Paul dubiously. He shrugged and gave what he hoped was a reassuring grin. "I gave him the same speech when I picked him up."

She almost smiled. "Thanks. For all the good it did," she added under her breath. Turning back to her son, she said, "If your bike had a flat tire, you should have asked Matt's mother to give you a ride home."

"She wasn't there. She was getting her hair done or something."

"Then you should have called me. I would have come and picked you up."

Shane smirked. "Yeah? Well, I knew what's-his-name was here, and you always tell me not to interrupt you when he's here."

What's-his-name? Paul glanced toward the house as Shane did, and saw that a ruddy-faced young man with bright red hair and a matching beard had emerged onto the porch to observe the squabble. Whoever he was, he couldn't be Shane's father or even his stepfather, or Shane wouldn't have called him "what's-his-name."

A boyfriend. The kid's parents must be divorced.

"I've always told you not to wake me up earlier than nine o'clock on a weekend," the woman pointed out to her son. "But if the house was on fire, I certainly hope you'd get me out of bed, regardless of the time. And if you're stranded all the way across town without a functional bike, Shane, I certainly hope you'll give me a call."

"Okay," Shane grumbled.

"No more hitchhiking."

"Okay." He didn't sound as if he meant it.

"Now please go do your homework."

"Haven't got any."

The woman looked skeptical, but she didn't question him further. Giving his shoulder a firm nudge, she angled her head toward the house. "Why don't you go call Matt and find out if we can pick up your bike after dinner."

Shane brightened, obviously sensing that his mother was done chewing him out. He loped across the yellowing grass to the front porch, gave a friendly nod to the bearded man and then bounded inside.

The woman rotated to face Paul. "Thank you for bringing him home in one piece," she said earnestly.

His hands still in his pockets, he leaned against the front fender of his truck and gave her a leisurely assessment. At first glance, she hadn't looked old enough to be the mother of an almost-fourteen-year-old, but when Paul studied her more closely he noticed the faint crow's-feet fringing the outer corners of her eyes and the lines bracketing her mouth. A light breeze tangled through the hair framing her forehead, and he saw a few strands of silver interspersed with the blond. "I didn't catch your name," he said.

She moved her lips, as if unsure whether to introduce herself. But her eyes were unwavering, gloriously radiant. "Bonnie Hudson," she told him.

He gave her a lopsided grin. "We may as well get acquainted. Know your enemy and all."

She returned his smile, evidently willing to acknowledge their previous encounter. "We aren't enemies, Mr. Tremaine. We happen to disagree on the matter of a statue, that's all."

He almost blurted out that it wasn't merely a "statue," but rather was his way of atoning, his gift to a universe that had chosen, for whatever reason, to spare him and not others. He had promised to do something for his fallen friends, and he would do it, and no schoolteacher, no matter how pretty she was, was going to stand in his way.

Instead, he said, "Your son's a good kid."

"He's the best kid in the whole world," she said, stating it as a simple fact even as her smile widened. "I really appreciate your having brought him home safely. And telling him that hitchhiking is dangerous. He's more apt to listen to you than to me."

"He's at that age," Paul commented.

Grinning wistfully, she nodded. Her eyes were a jewellike mixture of silver and emerald and gold. She smelled like fresh daisies.

"I guess you ought to get back to your guest," he said, motioning with his head toward the red-haired man on the porch.

She looked at the man, sent him a modest smile and turned back to Paul. "Thanks again, Mr. Tremaine," she said, taking a step backward, and then another.

"Paul," he corrected her.

"Paul," she echoed, still smiling as she continued toward the porch. "Think about what I said at the meeting last week. Books are alive. They're useful. They're educational. Who ever learned anything from a carved rock?"

Again he checked the impulse to argue with her. If he thought about what she'd said at the town meeting, he'd dwell less on her ardent endorsement of books—he personally had nothing against books—and more on her disparaging remarks about military blunders. Yes, the war had been a mistake, a tragedy, a waste and a folly. But that didn't diminish the pain it had inflicted on so many people. That didn't mean that those who carried its scars ought to forget it ever happened.

A carved rock would teach people about the cold, unyielding finality of death. It would stand on the green, a constant presence, reminding people of what wasteful follies too often led to. It would be beautiful and solid and real. He'd make sure of it.

This transplanted teacher from Cambridge wasn't going to stop him. No matter how attractive he found her, she wasn't going to change his mind.

"I'M SORRY," she said to Kevin as she climbed onto the porch and opened the screen door.

He smiled amiably and held the door for her, then followed her inside. "Forget it. Things are bound to crop up when we're at your house. I don't mind."

She entered the living room, sank into the overstuffed cushions of the easy chair, pulled off her sandals and tucked her feet under her. Kevin resumed his seat on the sofa, fussed with his tape recorder and lifted his pencil and pad. Closing her eyes, she tried to remember what they'd been discussing before they were interrupted.

All she could think of was Paul Tremaine.

She'd been vaguely aware of the fact that he was handsome when he'd risen to his feet at the town meeting and made his proposal regarding a Vietnam war memorial on the green. But she'd paid more attention to his words than to his looks. She'd become indignant when he started pandering to the patriotism of those present, waxing sentimental about that ugly war. Of course men had died, and she wasn't suggesting that anyone forget about them. But the real heroes of that era, to her way of thinking, were those brave men and women who had held fast to their principles and raised their voices in protest, who had dared to stand up to their government and say, "Enough is enough. We refuse to be a part of this war."

Bonnie wasn't asking anyone to build a memorial to people like her husband—although, she had to admit, that was more or less what Kevin McCoy was planning to do with his book about Gary Hudson and the Cambridge Manifesto. A book was the perfect memorial, she believed. Let Paul Tremaine write a book about his fallen comrades. That would suit her just fine.

At least that was what she'd thought last week, before Paul had picked up her son and brought him home safely. That was before she'd actually talked to Paul and seen his ruggedly chiseled face, his dark, deep-set eyes, his thick black hair and his surprisingly sensual mouth.

She wasn't attracted to him. He was a big, tough, macho war hero. Besides, he was probably married, or otherwise attached.

Even so... for all his wrongheadedness, he was a remarkably good-looking man, and she wasn't above appreciating that.

"We were discussing Tom Schuyler," Kevin broke into her thoughts.

Bonnie narrowed her gaze on Kevin, who had stopped flipping through his notes and had his pad open to a clean page. Eight years her junior, he was on leave from a staff position at the Boston *Globe*. It had been his idea to write a book about the Cambridge Manifesto, which had been born of her late husband's opposition to the Vietnam War. Gary, Tom Schuyler and their associates had organized rallies and demonstrations against the war, had practiced civil disobedience, had counseled undergraduates on ways to evade the draft. When the war finally ended, they'd turned their energies to disarmament issues. Gary had published pamphlets, given lectures nationwide, testified before a Senate committee and written guest columns for newspapers. Some of the people who had known and worked with him said that if he hadn't died he'd probably be serving in Congress by now.

Bonnie wasn't so sure of that. Politics was a corrupt enterprise, and Gary had always been ethical in the extreme. Even if he hadn't gone into politics, however, he would have been serving the country in some way. He'd been a leader in his twenties, and he surely would have continued to be a leader if he were alive today.

But he wasn't. All that was left were his notes, his successes, a war ended, in large part, because people like him refused to support it. And his son, Shane. And the enduring memories of his widow.

She twisted in her chair to gaze at the framed photographs lined up on the mantel above the fireplace. She herself appeared in some of the photos, an infant Shane in one, Tom Schuyler in a couple and the whole Cambridge crew in one. Gary was in all of them, naturally. She had laughingly told Kevin that the photographs were her shrine to her late husband.

Standing, she crossed to the mantel and pulled down the photos featuring Tom Schuyler. "He was Gary's most trusted ally," she told the reporter as she passed him the photos. "He was brilliant. A graduate student in mathematics at M.I.T."

Kevin studied the photographs for several seconds, then handed them back to her. "You weren't crazy about him, I take it."

Bonnie smiled crookedly, surprised that her voice had betrayed her. Placing the photographs back on the mantel, she shrugged. "He was an excellent tactician and a good sounding board for Gary. But personally... I always felt he was a lecher. He was always surrounding himself with groupies."

"Groupies?"

"Back in those days," she explained, reminding herself for not the first time that Kevin was from a different generation, "prominent antiwar activists were idolized just like rock stars. Gary wasn't interested in groupies, but Tom courted them at every opportunity. When he wasn't busy hammering out strategies he was bed-hopping and notching his belt."

Kevin wrote furiously. "And Gary never succumbed to temptation?"

"Gary," Bonnie said firmly, "loved me as much as I loved him."

She heard the heavy clomp of footsteps on the stairs and spun away from the mantel, bracing herself for yet another interruption courtesy of Shane. He appeared in the living room doorway, smiling sheepishly. "I just got off the phone with Matt," he reported. "He says we can come over any time after dinner to pick up the bike."

"Did you tell him you hitchhiked home?" Bonnie asked.

His grin expanding, Shane nodded.

"It was a stupid thing to do," she said, aware that she was nagging but unable to stop. Her anger arose partly from a genuine fear of the tragedies that too often befell youngsters who hitchhiked nowadays, and partly from the frustration of knowing that the world had changed drastically since her own youth, that strangers could no longer trust one another, that everybody had to practice a certain self-protective paranoia, that life would never be the same as it had been during those idyllic few years when she and Gary had been together, when they'd loved each other and married and had a son, when anything had seemed possible if you believed hard enough.

She felt the sting of tears forming in her eyes and averted her face before Shane or Kevin McCoy would notice. Most of the time she was strong; most of the time she didn't miss Gary in a conscious way. He was a part of her, an eternal flame burning in her memory, and she was content.

But today, as she stared at the photographs of him lining the fireplace shelf, she felt bereft. It wasn't fair that he'd died and abandoned her. It wasn't fair that he was smiling in so many of the pictures, when his life would be ending so soon.

It wasn't fair that, for the first time in the ten years since he'd been killed, Bonnie could look at his pictures and find herself thinking not of him but of the tall, dark-eyed man who wanted to build a monument to everything her husband had abhorred, everything he'd fought against. It wasn't fair that one brief encounter with Paul Tremaine could make Bonnie so painfully aware of how very alone she was.

Chapter Two

Emerging from one of the greenhouses, Paul spotted Shane loitering near a row of cherry trees at the edge of the parking lot, sitting astride a ten-speed bike. Paul wiped his hands on a rag, stuffed it into the hip pocket of his dungarees and sauntered over. "How's it going?"

Shane turned and grinned, then shoved an errant lock of sandy-blond hair out of his eyes. "Hey, Paul."

"I see you got the tire fixed," Paul observed, inspecting Shane's bicycle. It was old and weather-beaten; the crossbars were speckled with mud, the saddle was worn and the chrome no longer gleamed.

Shane twisted to glance over his shoulder at the rear wheel. "Yeah. I patched it this morning."

Paul studied the boy for a moment, recognizing the oversize high-tops and artfully torn jeans as the same items Shane had had on the previous day. He was also wearing a baggy T-shirt and a necklace of braided leather. His neck and forearms showed preliminary signs of mature fullness, but his face was still young and innocent, his complexion fair and his eyes sparkling with facets of silver and gold.

Just like his mother's.

Not that Paul needed anything to remind him of Bonnie. He'd been thinking about her ever since he'd driven away from her house yesterday: her iridescent eyes, her magnificent hair, her stubborn chin and gaunt cheeks and her tall, slender body. He'd been thinking about her bearded friend on the porch—trying to figure out what his relation to her might be—and about her fatuous little speech on how books were alive, and about her sweet, apologetic smile when she made that speech, as if she'd known she was coming across as a sanctimonious prig and hoped Paul wouldn't hold it against her.

"How's your mom?" he asked Shane with deceptive nonchalance.

The boy's smile faded and he turned to examine one of the cherry trees. "Don't ask," he muttered. "She's really steamed at me."

"Why?"

Shane gave a how-should-I-know shrug, then proceeded to prove that he did know, quite well. "Well, first because I hitched, and then because I got the flat tire when me and Matt went riding down through Breaker Gorge. There's lots of major hazards there. That's part of the fun, you know? But she got real ticked off about it. I probably should have lied to her about where we were riding, but . . ." He offered another eloquent shrug. "So then we had to drive to Lowell this morning to get a patch kit for the tire, and that screwed up her grocery shopping, and . . ." He drifted off. "I don't know. I guess I really blew it."

Paul regarded Shane, wondering whether he should risk fishing for information about Bonnie. "What does your dad think about your hitchhiking?" he asked.

Shane turned back to him. "My dad's dead."

It took Paul a full minute to digest the news that Bonnie Hudson was a widow. The concept of young widowhood usually put him in mind of sobbing black-clad women with babies on their hips, poor and stranded and helpless. He sensed nothing helpless about Bonnie, however. His reflexive pity was supplanted by a healthy measure of respect. She had a career, a nice home, a healthy teenage son and a flinty disposition. She wasn't the sort of woman a man should feel sorry for.

Nor did her son seem to be in need of sympathy. "I'm sorry," Paul said because it was the right thing to say. "That's a tough break."

"Yeah, well..." Shane mumbled, apparently embarrassed. "Anyway, so my mom's been real crabby. It's like everything's rubbing her wrong. What I thought was—" he gazed hopefully at Paul "—maybe I could give her a tree."

"A tree," Paul repeated uncertainly.

"Yeah." The idea obviously invigorated Shane. "A new tree for the front yard," he explained. "Like, there's this dead tree in front of our house."

"The dogwood," said Paul with a nod. "I noticed."

"Yeah, well, it's been dying since we moved into the house. Mom says it's supposed to have flowers on it, but it's never had any. This year it didn't even get any leaves. I mean, the thing's defunct, you know?"

Paul grinned at Shane's choice of words. "It certainly didn't appear to be in the best of health."

"So anyway," Shane continued, "I was thinking maybe it would cheer her up if I bought her a new tree to take its place."

Paul shook his head in amazement. At Shane's age, he would never have come up with such an idea. "I bet she'd like that," he said, trying to keep his astonishment hidden. If Shane realized what an extraordinary gesture such a gift would be, he might back off from it.

"Yeah, well, I've got about fifteen bucks," Shane told him. "These trees are really nice, Paul. How far would fifteen bucks go?"

"Not far enough." The prices on the nursery's adult cherry trees ran upward from a hundred dollars.

The boy's expression fell. He stared longingly at the lacy pink blossoms dappling the lush branches of the tree nearest him, then sighed and shaped a brave smile. "Well, like, what would fifteen bucks buy?"

An honest answer might crush him, so Paul didn't bother with one. "Why don't you check out those white birches over there?"

Shane's gaze followed Paul's outstretched arm to the rows of slender white birch trees already wrapped for sale. The smallest among them were priced at fifty dollars, but Paul wasn't above taking a loss on one to help Shane out.

Shane dismounted from his bike and walked it across the lot to the birches. He read the price tag wired to one of the branches and grimaced. "I haven't got that kind of money."

An idea took shape inside Paul's head. "I can lend you the difference," he suggested. "And then you can work off the debt."

"Work it off?" Shane looked intrigued. "How?"

"Odd jobs here at the nursery. Coiling hoses, sweeping the greenhouse floors, whatever." During his teens, Paul had worked weekends at the nursery helping his uncle. The chores had been tedious, but he'd enjoyed the money his uncle paid him, and the job had kept him out of trouble. "We'll figure something out. Are you interested?"

"Yeah," Shane said enthusiastically. "Yeah, sure. That'd be cool. I'd have to check with my mom, though."

"Of course." Paul would have to check with Shane's mom, too. He would have to present himself as a reputable employer, someone who would treat her son well. He liked Shane, and knowing that the kid had no father made Paul feel protective toward him. If Bonnie agreed to let Shane work at the nursery a couple of hours every weekend, a lot of good could come out of it.

Not the least of which was that she'd have a beautiful white birch tree taking root in her yard, instead of a dying dogwood—and Paul would have an excuse to get to know her better.

THE CRUNCH OF TIRES against the gravel driveway distracted Bonnie from her reading. The May afternoon was warm and sunny; after she'd finished putting the groceries away and straightened up the house a bit, she'd settled on one of the porch rockers with a tall glass of lemonade and a book. She was dressed in her standard weekend attire—jeans and a baggy man-tailored shirt with the sleeves rolled up to her elbows and the tails tied in a knot at her waist. She'd pinned her hair back from her face with a tortoiseshell barrette, but a few fine ash-blond strands had escaped from the clasp and drooped against her cheek.

Brushing the stray hairs back from her face, she spotted the green Tremaine Nursery pickup cruising up her driveway. This time, she knew, Paul wasn't delivering her hitchhiking son. Shane had arrived home on his bike over an hour ago, mumbled that he had something he wanted to discuss with her later and then vanished upstairs into his bedroom.

Her gaze traveled to the rear of the truck, where she noticed several leafy branches of an otherwise invisible tree protruding above the tailgate. Looking back at the cab, she saw Paul Tremaine swing open the door.

She braced herself against the sudden ripple that coursed down her spine at the sight of him. The man made her uncomfortable, not only because he wanted to construct a second war memorial on the green when one was more than enough, but also because there was something about him, something so disturbingly... male. It wasn't as if Bonnie hadn't known any men in the years since Gary passed away; it wasn't as if she'd lived a cloistered life. But Paul Tremaine could make her want him, and that frightened her. She didn't want to want anybody—certainly not him.

Relax, she admonished herself, acknowledging him with an impassive smile as he ambled around the truck and across the front lawn. Just because the blue denim of his jeans clung to his legs and hips in a way that hinted provocatively at the athletic contours of his physique, just because the collar buttons of his Tremaine Nursery shirt were undone, displaying his strong neck, and the sleeves were rolled up to reveal the traces of dark hair along his sinewy wrists and forearms, just because his jaw was hard and his lips were thin and firm, and his eyes seemed able to pierce her defenses, and his hair was so very black and thick, curling over his ears and collar...

She slid a bookmark into the pages of her book, closed it and balanced it on the railing. "Hello, Mr. Tremaine," she said in an impressively calm voice. "What can I do for you?"

He arched his eyebrows, and one corner of his mouth quirked upward in a lopsided smile. "You could call me Paul, for starters," he said, his deep, sonorous voice sending another hot shiver down her spine and making her resent the hell out of him for having this ridiculous effect on her.

"Paul," she obliged, refusing to shift her eyes from him.

He propped one foot on the edge of the porch and rested his arm across his knee. All that separated him from her was the railing and a few feet of space. Bonnie focused on the sharp line of his nose; it seemed safer than meeting his penetrating gaze. "You ought to do something about the grass," he commented.

She wondered whether he had driven all this distance to sell her some lawn-care product or service. "What ought I to do about it?" she asked warily.

"Water it, for one thing. Your lawn's dying of thirst."

"Watering the lawn is Shane's job. Unfortunately, he doesn't always remember to do it, and I don't always have it in me to get on his case about it."

Paul surveyed the wilting grass, then stared for a minute at the lifeless dogwood tree next to the driveway. When he turned back to Bonnie, his smile seemed suspiciously friendly. "I've come to talk business," he announced. "Have you got a minute?"

"If you expect to change my mind about your stupid memorial—"

"Not that business," he cut her off, his grin waning. "It's about Shane."

"Shane?" She peered toward the front door, grateful for the excuse to turn from Paul. "I think he's in his room. Should I get him?"

"No, don't bother."

She turned back to Paul. "What happened? Did he damage your truck yesterday?"

To her surprise, Paul laughed. "No—although that's something of a miracle. The directions he gave me to get here included a roller-coaster ride down Pond Road. That road ought to be barricaded until somebody repaves it. I was sure I was going to crack an axle on it."

Bonnie permitted herself a smile. "Shane and I are used to it," she said. "In fact, we view it as one of life's great challenges."

Paul's laughter faded into a warm, blessedly unthreatening grin. She liked the way it gentled the harsh lines of his face and infused his eyes with warmth. "What I wanted to discuss with you is the possibility of Shane working for me."

"Working for you?" She was astounded. "Doing what?"

"Odd jobs, helping out at the nursery. I was figuring, maybe three hours every Saturday morning—"

"Of course not. Absolutely not." Frowning, she rose from the rocker, pleased by the height advantage the porch gave her. "He's only thirteen, Paul. He's much too young to take a job."

"He's already got a job," Paul pointed out. "Watering your lawn."

"And you can see for yourself how irresponsible he is about it. No, Paul—I'm sorry, but a job at your nursery is out of the question." She tried to convince herself that her adamant rejection of the job offer was solely for Shane's sake, that it had nothing to do with the man for whom he'd be working.

Paul turned away to glimpse his truck. He exhaled and turned back to her. "Then we've got a real problem, Bonnie," he drawled. His lips cut a grim line, but she detected amusement in his eyes.

"What problem?"

"You see that tree in the truck?" He angled his head toward the leafy branches peeking out over the walls of the truck bed. "Shane bought it for you."

"What?"

"He came by the nursery this afternoon and bought it. He said he wanted to replace your dead dogwood. He thought that would cheer you up."

Bonnie closed her eyes. Shane was full of surprises these days; to her dismay, most of them were bad. Yesterday he'd surprised her by hitchhiking. Tomorrow, she was certain, he'd spring some new horror on her: piercing an ear or asking her to pick up some condoms at the drugstore for him, or something equally dreadful. Surprising Bonnie seemed to be one of Shane's greatest talents.

But to go out and buy a tree for her...

A few tears filtered through her lashes. Swallowing, she gazed past Paul at the tree in the truck. "Where on earth did Shane get the money to buy a tree?" she asked, hoping her voice didn't sound as scratchy as it felt.

Paul tactfully didn't comment on her weepiness. "That's the thing of it, Bonnie. He didn't have enough money to buy it. He and I got to talking, though, and I told him that if it was all right with you, he could work off the cost of the tree. I'm figuring, maybe five or six weeks, just a couple of hours every Saturday morning, and we'll call it even."

She turned to Paul, her eyes round. "That's awfully kind of you." She contemplated his explanation, then frowned slightly. "Is it legal?"

He shrugged. "It's a barter, Bonnie. I don't think we need to file papers with Social Security." He could tell that she was still unpersuaded. "I'm not going to have him doing anything dangerous or difficult. It's mostly just picking up around the place, sweeping up the dirt and carrying sacks of fertilizer to the customers' cars. I used to do the same stuff when I was his age.'' He gave her a moment to consider, then continued, ''It's all pretty straightforward. He works eighteen hours, and the tree is his.''

''But—but you've already brought it here.''

''Think of it as a loan. No sense waiting for that dogwood to keel over. We'll plant the birch now, and after Shane's put in his eighteen hours, it'll officially belong to him.''

She struggled to clear her mind. Paul's offer was much too generous. She couldn't believe that a mere eighteen hours of minimum-wage labour would pay for a birch tree. ''Shane is young,'' she repeated, thinking out loud. ''I don't know whether he's ready for this sort of re-sponsibility. I can't even get him to help me around the house.''

''You're his mother. You say black, he says white. I think it'll be different with me.''

She considered his boast presumptuous, even though he was probably right. Perhaps Shane would behave dif-ferently with Paul; perhaps he would rise to the occa-sion. Perhaps a little structure in his life would do him some good. If he was willing to sacrifice a few hours each week to pay off a debt, Bonnie shouldn't discourage him.

''I tell you what,'' she said, hedging. ''Why don't we take it one week at a time and see how it goes? If Shane can't handle the job, I'll pay you whatever he owes you on the tree.''

''He'll be able to handle it,'' Paul said confidently. He lowered his foot to the ground and straightened up, grin-ning. ''Why don't I dig up the dogwood and get the birch into place?''

"Right now?"

"Sure, right now." He started for his truck.

"But—you'll need a shovel, or something—"

"I've got everything I need in the truck."

Her fingers curling around the railing, she watched as he jogged to the rear of the truck and lowered the tailgate. "Do you want some help?" she called to him, feeling utterly useless as he heaved the sturdy white tree out of the truck bed and propped it against the side of the truck.

"Sure," he called back. "Is Shane around?"

She'd meant that she, not Shane, would help him. But it made more sense for Shane to be Paul's assistant. She reluctantly turned from the railing, gathering her book and her empty glass on the way, and stepped inside the house, calling for her son to come downstairs.

Within five minutes Shane was hard at work beside Paul, digging the point of a spade into the grass and loosening the soil around the dogwood's roots. His enthusiasm for hard physical labor surprised Bonnie. Was this the same kid who groused whenever she asked him to take out the garbage or scrub the dried blobs of toothpaste from his bathroom sink? A tiny flame of indignation burned inside her as she spied on Paul and her son through the living room window. Why was Shane so excited about helping a near-stranger and not his own mother?

Because she was his mother, that was why.

Pulling back the lace-trimmed linen drapes, she gazed wistfully past the decorative crystal hanging in the window. Simply observing the man and boy at work forced her to admit that maybe, especially now that he was entering adolescence, Shane needed a male role model in his life, someone he could work with and look up to.

She didn't want that man to be Paul. He was a war hero—Laura Holt from the town council had told Bonnie as much after the meeting. "He served a tour of duty and came home with a chest full of medals," the gossipy gray-haired woman had jabbered. "Funny thing was, until he submitted his proposal for a memorial to us a couple of weeks ago, you couldn't get him to talk about his war service. He's the strong, silent type. I'll bet he killed dozens of enemy troops over there."

Wonderful, Bonnie had thought bitterly at the time. What a marvelous accomplishment.

She didn't want some strong, silent he-man who had killed dozens of people to be her son's role model. She wanted Shane to model himself on his own father, a man of peace. But that option was no longer available.

She watched as the two of them gripped the trunk of the dogwood, twisted it and freed it from the soil and then lifted it up and out of the hole. They worked well together, their movements smoothly coordinated, Shane beaming proudly in response to Paul's words of encouragement. She was troubled by the camaraderie developing between them.

Maybe, as good a mother as she tried to be, she was no longer enough for Shane. Maybe he really needed a man in his life.

If she continued to think along those lines, she might find herself wondering whether she needed a man in her life, as well. So she put the notion out of her mind and wandered into the kitchen to begin preparing supper.

Chapter Three

"*Isn't he cute?*" *Marcie whispered.*

Bonnie stared at the young man addressing a crowd of students from the top step of the Widener Library, at the heart of the Harvard University campus. His dirty-blond shoulder-length hair was held off his face with a red bandanna tied into a headband, and his lanky body was clad in low-slung denim bell-bottoms and an Army surplus shirt with a black arm band around one sleeve. In spite of the heat he wore leather work boots, and a peace-symbol pendant hung around his neck. He was speaking into a portable microphone connected to a pair of huge speakers, his voice rich, musical and all the more persuasive for his lack of histrionics and hyperbole.

"In 1961, President John F. Kennedy told us to ask not what our country could do for us but what we could do for our country," he said, holding the microphone below his chin so as not to obscure his face. "Well, my friends, what your country is doing to you today is drafting you and your brothers and boyfriends and sending them halfway around the world to fight in a war that has no justification, no meaning and no legal standing. And what you can do for your country is to stop the

madness." He raised his fist into the air and repeated the words, "Stop the madness!"

Entranced, the crowd raised their fists high and echoed, "Stop the madness!"

"I told you he was cute." Marcie sighed, uncurling her fist and letting her arm fall.

Bonnie gave her friend a tolerant smile and then turned back to watch the man on the library steps. As calm and reasonable as he seemed, there was something hypnotic about him, something about the electrifying glow in his silver-gray eyes and the defiance in his posture that cut through Bonnie's soul. "Cute" seemed too trivial a term to describe him. The man was riveting.

"What's his name?" she asked Marcie.

Marcie tugged her embroidered drawstring bag higher on her shoulder and said, "Gary Hudson. He's the teaching assistant I told you about, in my American history course. Rumor has it he's dropping out of grad school so he can devote himself to the cause full-time."

"Dropping out of graduate school?" Given how hard it was to get into graduate school—to say nothing of one as selective as Harvard—dropping out would be an incredible sacrifice. "He must be awfully dedicated to the antiwar movement," she murmured respectfully.

"One day in class he told us he felt guilty attending graduate school when so many of his colleagues had lost their student deferments. The guy's really into it. But it's not like by dropping out he's going to lose any status," Marcie noted. "I mean, if you're going to make a name for yourself in the movement, now's the time to do it. If he spends too much time vegging out in graduate seminars he's going to miss the boat, you know?"

Bonnie chuckled. "You ought to go into public relations," she teased her friend.

"*PR for peace. I could hack that,*" Marcie happily concurred. "*See that guy fiddling with the volume control on the speaker?*" She indicated a dark-haired man with a scruffy mustache and soulful eyes. "*His name's Tom Schuyler—grad student at M.I.T. Suzanne Plunkett slept with him.*"

"*No!*"

"*Not only that, but Nancy Curtiss told me Suzanne hitched to New York City and got a prescription for the pill.*"

"*No!*" For not the first time since she'd begun her freshman year at Radcliffe last September, Bonnie felt like a hick. She shouldn't have—she'd grown up only ten miles away, in the Boston suburb of Newton. But sometime between her last year of high school and her first year of college the universe seemed to have turned upside down. A war that had once been little more than black-and-white images on the living room television was suddenly real and dangerous. Boys on this very campus, boys she might have danced with at mixers or debated with in class, were walking around with low lottery numbers and the shadow of the draft darkening their lives. Boys who might have gone to high school with her were overseas, deploying antipersonnel bombs and defoliating deltas, slaughtering peasants and burning villages. Her contemporaries were killing and getting killed, and it was wrong, so very wrong.

"*If my parents knew I was at this rally right now instead of studying for finals, they'd murder me,*" Marcie muttered. "*I can just hear my father: 'I'm spending three thousand dollars to send you to that fancy college, and all you do is sit around listening to drug-crazed radicals!'*"

"He doesn't sound drug-crazed to me," Bonnie said, continuing to watch the clear-eyed man speaking into the microphone. "As a matter of fact, he sounds brilliant."

"Tom Schuyler's supposed to be the brilliant one," Marcie informed her, gesturing toward the man with the mustache, who had sprinted down the stairs and was now distributing fliers to the assembled students.

"Yeah?" Bonnie checked him out as he wove through the crowd to their right. He winked at a pretty girl as he handed her a flier, and then whispered something in her ear. "If you ask me, he looks like he's hot to score."

"Suzanne Plunkett would know," Marcie said with a giggle.

"Is she really on the pill?" Bonnie asked.

Marcie nodded sagely and leaned toward her. "She even gave me the name and number of the gynecologist she used down in New York. You interested?"

Bonnie shook her head. How could anyone think about birth control when there was a war raging in Southeast Asia, when young American boys were losing their lives? All she could think about were the fiery exhortations of Gary Hudson, urging his audience to petition Congress, burn their draft cards and refuse to serve. She was spellbound by his words and dazzled by his single-minded adherence to principles, by how very much he was willing to give up for those principles.

"This war is a travesty," he was saying, his voice resounding through the brisk spring afternoon. "Those who participate in it—who don't do everything in their power to bring it to an end—are part of the problem. Refuse to go. Refuse to serve. Fight this evil with everything you've got, my friends. Stop the madness!"

Bonnie flung her fist up into the air. "Stop the madness!" she cried.

"HEY, MOM!" Shane hollered through the screen door. "Come on out and have a look!"

Bonnie dried her hands on a dish towel and left the kitchen. Shoving open the screen door, she stepped out onto the porch and gazed across the lawn. Where the barren dogwood used to be the birch now stood, all eight grand, sturdy feet of it, its straight white-barked trunk spreading into a generous teardrop-shaped cloud of green leaves. Paul was kneeling beneath it, patting a circular mound of dark soil into place at the base of the trunk, but he rose to his feet at Bonnie's approach.

"It's beautiful!" she exclaimed, descending from the porch to examine the tree closely.

"You like it?" Shane bounced around her like a hyperactive puppy.

"It's lovely," she murmured, circling the tree slowly to assess it from every angle. "Thank you." Her eyes met Paul's, and for a brief, strange moment she felt drawn in by their profound darkness. She quickly shifted her gaze to Shane. "Thank you both," she said.

Dusting off his hands on his dungarees, Paul scanned the tree critically. "Have you got a hose?" he asked, shoving his hair back from his perspiration-damp forehead. "We ought to wet down the soil."

"Of course. In the garage." She glanced toward Shane, about to ask him to fetch it, but before she could make her request he was already at the garage door, sliding it open and then ducking inside.

"He's a terrific helper," Paul remarked.

"Not always," Bonnie muttered, then succumbed to a wry smile as she recalled what Paul had said earlier. "With you, maybe. But I'm his mother."

She lapsed into silence, wondering whether she should give voice to the idea she'd been tossing around in her head ever since she entered the kitchen fifteen minutes ago. Without consciously acknowledging what she was doing, she had calculated how far the chopped beef would stretch, how much lettuce she'd need for an extra portion of salad, how many jars of spaghetti sauce to pull down from the pantry shelf. She'd scanned her meager wine collection and rummaged through the cabinets in vain for something that could pass for dessert.

"Would you like to stay for dinner?" she finally asked.

He stared at her, the late-afternoon sunlight slanting across his face and throwing his eyes into deep shadow. "I'm kind of messy," he said, spreading his hands for her inspection. Obviously he detected her ambivalence toward him, and he was offering her a way to back out of the invitation if she'd offered it only out of some obligatory sense of etiquette.

"I've got soap."

He scrutinized her upturned face. "Are you sure you have enough food to go around?"

"I'm making spaghetti," she told him. "I can make as much or as little as we need."

He meditated for a moment. "I'll need a lot," he finally said, smiling tentatively.

Bonnie returned his smile and headed back to the house. "Then I'll make a lot," she called over her shoulder. Back in the kitchen, she pulled out her largest pot, filled it with water and set it on the stove to boil.

After a few minutes, she heard Shane's voice through the open window above the sink. "We'd better use the back door—she busts a gasket whenever I track dirt through the living room."

Rolling her eyes at his exaggeration, she greeted Shane and Paul with a grin as they trooped into the kitchen through the mudroom. "There's the bathroom," she said, gesturing with a fistful of dry pasta. "The towels are clean, so help yourself."

Paul nodded. "Thanks," he said before disappearing into the lavatory.

Shane straddled one of the chairs at the kitchen table and presented his mother with a self-satisfied smile. "So?" he asked. "You like that tree or what?"

"I love it. And I love you." She dumped the pasta into the bubbling water and then gave Shane a smothering hug, which he quickly wriggled out of. To spare him further embarrassment, she backed off and said, "Why don't you go upstairs to wash? I could use a little help getting dinner ready, but your hands are filthy."

"Paul's staying, right?"

"That's right."

"You gonna have wine?"

She eyed her son with feigned impatience. "Yes, and you can have a taste. Now go wash up."

"I'd like my own glass," he requested, springing from the stool and starting toward the stairs. "I'll take a juice glass, say, a couple of inches full—"

"Git!" She shook her cooking spoon at him in a mock threat, then laughed.

She wound up permitting Shane a half inch of Chianti in a wine goblet. She served the garlic bread in a napkin-lined straw basket, and she made certain all the plates and silverware matched. She even gave some thought to using the dining room table, but it was covered with the book reports she'd brought home to grade over the weekend, so she set the kitchen table, instead. That was where she and Shane always ate; she believed they'd feel more comfortable there.

"This looks delicious," Paul said, once they were all seated.

"It's about as good as it gets," Shane warned him. "My mom's a lousy cook."

"Thanks a heap," Bonnie said, although she was unable to suppress a chuckle. She had never aspired to be a great cook. Back in the old Cambridge Manifesto days, the women who cooked well always ended up doing just that—cooking—while everyone else sat around on the living room floor hammering out proposals and creeds and planning disruptive demonstrations for the group to stage. Thanks to her ineptitude in the kitchen, Bonnie generally ended up at Gary's side in the living room of the old Victorian house on Avon Street that had served as both headquarters and a communal dwelling for the inner circle, while poor Marcie, who had once made the mistake of boasting that she knew how to bake phyllo-dough pastries, invariably found herself in the kitchen brewing tea and slapping together sandwiches for the hungry strategists.

"My friend Matt, his mom has every kitchen gadget you can think of," Shane informed Paul as he dug into his spaghetti. "Go ahead and guess. Food processor, blender, pasta maker, microwave, yogurt maker, she's got it."

"Has she got an ice cream maker?" Paul asked.

"Yeah, she's got one. And last Christmas Matt got her a butter melter."

"I've got one of those," Bonnie joked. "I call it a pan."

Paul eyed Bonnie and laughed. "Funny—I always thought the best way to melt butter was to leave it out of the refrigerator for a few hours."

"Right," Bonnie chimed in. "That's my favorite kitchen gadget—air."

"Great stuff, air," Paul confirmed, lifting his wine-glass in a salute to her before he drank. "Most kitchens come with it these days, don't they?"

"I believe so. But you've got to pay extra if you want it warm."

Shane obviously didn't share his elders' sense of humor. "Maybe if I had some more wine I'd know what you guys were laughing about."

"Sorry," Bonnie said. "Have some more bread, instead."

Shane finished his dinner without talking. Every now and then, his sullen gaze would shuttle between Bonnie and Paul, who continued their amiable banter. Bonnie wanted to include Shane in the conversation; she knew he felt left out and probably resented her for monopolizing Paul's attention. But if she deliberately steered the discussion to a topic Shane might enjoy, he would sense that she was patronizing him. And if she reached out and gave his shoulder a loving pat, he'd probably punch her in the nose. So she let him bolt down his dinner and didn't question him when he said he would have his dessert while he watched television in the den.

"He told me you think television rots the brain," Paul commented once Shane had poured himself a glass of milk and stomped off with a bag of chocolate chip cookies.

"I do," she confirmed. "But I don't mind if he tunes in to a ball game every once in a while." When Paul peeked through the doorway to the den, she said, "You can go on in and watch, too." She knew Shane would enjoy sharing the game with a like-minded male like Paul.

Paul remained at the doorway for a minute, gazing into the den. Then he pivoted and returned to the table to gather up a few dirty dishes. "Shane isn't angry with me, is he?"

Bonnie shot him a quick glance, then busied herself filling the sink with detergent. "What makes you ask that?"

Paul shrugged. "I don't know. He was so bubbly all afternoon, and now he seems kind of sulky."

The fact was, Shane could very well be angry with Paul for choosing to socialize with his mother. But if Bonnie told Paul that, he might feel bad. "Shane gets into moods sometimes," she explained vaguely. "He's a teenager. You never know when something's going to rub him the wrong way."

"We worked well together today," Paul noted, locating the dish towel and positioning himself next to Bonnie. She handed him a clean plate and he dried it. "He seemed awfully eager to please."

She didn't doubt that he was eager to please Paul. "Maybe you're right, maybe this job at your nursery will be good for him," she granted, handing Paul another plate to dry. "I just hope he's old enough to handle the responsibility."

"I'm sure he is." Paul placed the dry plate on the stack. "I think the experience will do him good."

She cast Paul a swift, probing look, wondering how much she should open to him. He'd been unexpectedly easy to talk to over dinner, but they hadn't discussed anything of significance. Still, if Paul wanted to take Shane under his wing, he ought to do so with his eyes open. "Shane's father is dead," she said.

"I know. He told me."

Bonnie wondered how Paul and her son had hit upon that particular subject, but she couldn't think of a discreet way to ask. Sorting her thoughts, she scrubbed another plate, rinsed it under the tap and handed it to Paul. Her gaze lingered for a moment on his strong hands. His fingers were blunt, toughened from physical labor, yet they moved with a certain economical grace, wiping the plate and stacking it without any wasted effort. His nails were short and clean; his left pinkie had a scar on it.

They were sensuous hands, and for a fleeting instant Bonnie tried to imagine what it would feel like if he brushed a knuckle against her cheek, if he slid his fingertips along the hollow of her throat. Disconcerted by the direction in which her imagination had wandered, she turned away and groped in the sudsy water for the silverware.

"I mention Shane's father only because..." She swallowed the faint catch in her voice. "Sometimes I worry that Shane might need a man to share things with. You yourself have noticed that he's moody. He's at a tricky age, and I'm sure he's got things on his mind that he doesn't feel comfortable talking about with me."

"Sex, you mean?" Paul asked.

Bonnie felt her cheeks turn crimson. She yanked out the drain plug and rinsed the sponge. "I was thinking more along the lines of baseball," she said tautly.

Paul put down the towel and laughed. "Do you want me to discuss box scores with him? No problem."

"Thank you." She did her best to ignore his teasing undertone. "Would you like some coffee?"

"I'd love some."

She busied herself with the percolator, keeping her back to Paul until she was sure her complexion had returned to its normal golden-pink shade. She considered herself open-minded; indeed, she'd gotten through more than a few awkward birds-and-bees dialogues with Shane without becoming unduly rattled. Some basic sex education was a part of the fourth-grade curriculum, and Bonnie usually had less trouble than any of the other teachers in covering the topic with her students. She had always viewed sex as a natural part of love. She wasn't a prude.

But discussing sex, however obliquely, with Paul was...different.

"I haven't really got any dessert," she said, "but—" Abruptly aware of the room's unusual silence, she glanced behind her and discovered that she was alone.

Paul must have gone into the den to watch the game with Shane. Sighing—with relief, she tried to convince herself—she stacked cups and saucers and the percolator on a tray and carried it to the doorway. Shane was seated on the floor of the den, leaning back against the couch and wolfing down cookies, his gaze riveted to the television screen. Paul wasn't with him.

Frowning, Bonnie continued through the dining room to the living room. She found Paul by one of the front-facing windows, staring out at the new birch tree, his hands in his pockets and his posture relaxed. "Is it still standing?" she asked, setting down the tray on the table in front of the sofa and joining him at the window.

"It better be," Paul replied. "If I couldn't plant a tree that would stand for more than an hour, I'd be out of business."

"It's beautiful," Bonnie said. "I know I'm repeating myself, but thank you."

Paul dismissed her gratitude with a shrug. Turning from the window, he eyed the tray for a moment, then lifted his gaze to the mantel. "Is that your husband?"

The shrine. "That's Gary," she said, for the first time feeling self-conscious about the abundance of photographs lining the shelf.

Paul crossed the room to study the photos more closely, and Bonnie turned on one of the lamps so he'd be able to see better. "The blond guy, huh," he guessed, observing that one particular individual figured prominently in all the photos. She wondered what Paul thought of Gary's shaggy hair, his black arm band, his peace-sign necklace, his raised fist. She wondered what he thought of the photo in which Gary's arm was wrapped possessively around her shoulders while she cradled an infant Shane in her arms, whether Paul could see the love shimmering in Gary's eyes and in hers.

"What was he, a hippie?" Paul asked, a faint tinge of sarcasm coloring his voice.

"A lot of people were hippies back then," Bonnie pointed out, unconsciously sweeping a hand through her unfashionable flower-child hair. "But you shouldn't judge him by his appearance. He was a very principled man, not some pot-smoking freak." She was aware of the self-righteousness creeping into her tone, and she pressed her lips together to silence herself.

Paul continued to study the photographs as she poured the coffee. "Who are all these other people?" he asked.

She glanced over her shoulder and saw that he was holding one of the group photos. "Friends and colleagues. It was a group Gary organized to figure out strategies to end the Vietnam War. They wrote a famous position paper called the Cambridge Manifesto, which was widely published. After a while the group itself took that as its name."

Paul examined the photograph for a minute longer, then put it back in its place and crossed to the sofa. "The Cambridge Manifesto," he repeated, not bothering to hide his distaste. "It couldn't have been that famous. I never heard of it."

Bonnie didn't want to lecture him, but she couldn't smother the pride she took in Gary's achievements. "It was famous enough that someone is writing a book about it."

"A book?" Paul looked less than overwhelmed.

"A lot of books have been published lately about the big political movements of the late sixties and early seventies," she said. "A reporter from the Boston *Globe* has been interviewing me and some of the other Cambridge Manifesto participants for a book he's writing about Gary's group and what they accomplished."

With a nod of thanks, Paul took the coffee she offered him and sat on the couch. His gaze traveled back to the mantel, then to her. "Why do you say 'they,' Bonnie? Weren't you a part of it?"

"I played only a small role," she said modestly. "I was pretty young at the time, just a freshman in college when I met Gary. He was a graduate student, and most of the other people involved in the Cambridge Manifesto were all in their twenties, too. I contributed ideas every now and then, but Gary was the real genius behind it."

"Genius?" Paul appeared skeptical.

Bonnie bristled. Hearing anyone mock her husband, however mildly, set her nerves on edge. Hearing Paul do it vexed her even more. "He *was* a genius," she insisted hotly. "He was totally committed to the cause of peace. He wasn't a show-off; he didn't go out of his way to get arrested or have his picture featured on the cover of *Life*. He worked quietly but effectively, and people responded to him. He was an amazing man." Her voice broke slightly and she took a sip of coffee.

Paul twisted on the sofa to face her. "I'm sorry," he said, evidently sensing the depth of her loyalty to Gary.

He eyed the mantel one last time, then observed, "You haven't got any recent pictures of him."

She understood what he was asking. "He passed away ten years ago."

Paul frowned. "That must have been tough, with Shane so young."

"Actually, I think I was lucky to have a young child at the time," she said. "Taking care of him kept me busy and focused. It didn't matter how depressed I was— Shane still had to be fed. I don't know how I would have survived without him."

"How did your husband die?"

"He was murdered."

"Murdered." Wincing, Paul cursed under his breath. "That's terrible."

Bonnie nodded. It was terrible.

"Did they catch the guy who did it?"

"Well..." She sighed. "He was struck and killed by a car, and the police recorded his death as accidental. But two of his colleagues witnessed the accident, and they said it was a deliberate act."

Paul digested what she'd said. "That's a heavy charge, Bonnie. There's a big difference between being killed accidentally and being murdered."

"I know. I also know that the driver fled from the scene, and he didn't come to his senses later and turn himself in. He knew exactly what he was doing. He went after my husband and ran him down. Gary's friends saw it happen. They had no reason to lie to me about it."

"Of course not," Paul said gently.

Bonnie felt her defensiveness ebbing. Paul's concern appeared to be sincere. "It happened in Fresno," she told him. The words came easily; simply speaking them seemed to have a calming effect on her. "Gary and Tom and Marcie were touring California, giving lectures at some of the state universities. I used to travel with Gary a lot before I had Shane, but after he was born I usually stayed at home with him while Gary and the others toured." She sighed and glanced up at the array of photographs above the fireplace, feeling a fresh stab of pain at the sight of Gary smiling so confidently, looking so healthy and whole.

"While he'd been speaking on campus, there had been a counterdemonstration at the auditorium, some reactionary group that thought Gary was a Communist or some such thing. According to Tom, the protesters had been awfully menacing. And then, later that evening, when they were leaving the campus, the car ran Gary down." She drifted off for a moment, staring at the white swirls of vapor rising from her coffee.

"The irony is, Gary would have been the first to support a person's right to conduct a protest against him. He believed that all voices should be heard. And they cut him down for it," she concluded bitterly.

"You don't know for an absolute fact that one of them did it," Paul noted.

"I do know it," she retorted. "Some things you just know."

Paul remained silent, absorbing her words and nodding. "Yeah," he said, half to himself. "Well, you've done a fantastic job with Shane, considering."

She gave him a smile of thanks.

"We don't have to talk about it if you don't want to."

"No, I don't mind." She honestly didn't. In spite of the pain generated by her memories of Gary, she wanted to tell Paul about herself and her past. She wanted him to understand why men like Gary opposed the war, why they rebelled against it, why they died for what they believed in. She wanted Paul to comprehend why she considered it obscene to build public monuments to commemorate the waste of life Vietnam represented.

"So, how did your husband stay out of Nam?" Paul asked, failing to keep his voice neutral. "Did he burn his draft card?"

Bonnie chuckled. "Didn't everybody?"

"No," Paul said grimly. "Some of us didn't."

She hadn't meant her comment literally. But Paul's reaction made her feel guilty for having joked about it. "I understand you were quite a hero during the war," she said, hoping she didn't sound critical.

"Who told you that?"

"Laura Holt, after the town meeting the other day."

He took a long sip of coffee. "She was wrong," he said flatly.

"Were the people you want to build your memorial for heroes?" she asked. A warning alarm inside her head blared that she ought to change the subject, but she couldn't seem to stop herself.

"No. They weren't heroes. It wasn't a very heroic war." He scowled. "At least they weren't cowards," he added, sending a quick glance toward the mantel.

"My husband wasn't a coward," Bonnie asserted. "He loved his country as much as you did. And he had the courage to stand up and tell his country it was doing the wrong thing."

"Yeah. My buddies and I were risking our lives overseas so your husband would have the freedom to stand up and tell the country."

"If more men had done what my husband did," she declared fervently, "there wouldn't have been a war at all. Remember the old saying, 'What if they had a war and nobody came?' If all the soldiers had had the courage to refuse to fight, there wouldn't have been a war.''

"Sure," Paul said sarcastically, setting his cup on the tray. He rose to his feet. "I'd better be going."

"No." Bonnie stood, too, and reached out to hold him back. He looked down at the place where her slim fingers arched around his forearm. His skin was warm, the hair unexpectedly soft. When he lifted his gaze he offered a contrite smile. "I don't want to fight with you, Paul. But you asked about my husband, and I told you."

His smile was also apologetic. He slid his arm through her fingers until his hand met hers. He gave her hand a gentle squeeze and then released it. "We all did what we felt we had to do back then. Let's just hope Shane never has to face the kind of choices your husband and I did."

Bonnie felt her eyes growing misty as Paul's words resonated inside her. It was all so long ago, both the war in Southeast Asia and the war at home. She found it paradoxical that the soldier had survived and the pacifist had died—but that didn't matter. What mattered most was creating a peaceful future for Shane's generation.

That Paul should share her sentiments regarding Shane was no reason to start crying, but she couldn't will her tears away. Abashed, she turned away and pressed her hand to her eyes.

Paul hovered behind her, as if not sure what to do. "Hey," he said softly, patting her shoulder. "I'm sorry if I made you cry."

"Don't apologize."

"You still miss your husband, don't you."

Wiping her eyes, she nodded. "He was an incredible man."

"I'm sure he was." Paul let his arm drop. "I really should be going, Bonnie," he said, gently this time. "I appreciate the dinner."

"I appreciate the tree." Sniffling away the last of her tears, she smiled. "What should I do for it? Does it require any special care?"

"No, just the usual. Birches are hardy. I'd do something about watering your lawn a bit more, though, if I were you."

"Do me a favor and tell Shane," she said, her smile widening. "If I mention watering the lawn to him one more time, he'll nominate me for nag-of-the-year honors."

Paul smiled, as well. He opened his mouth to say something, then closed it and started toward the den. "I'll go say goodbye to him," he said.

Bonnie watched him stroll into the den. She heard the low rumble of his voice and Shane's mingling with the animated patter of the sports announcer from the television. She was grateful to Paul, not only for forging a friendship with Shane but for treading so carefully around her tender emotions, for retreating from their argument about the war before it could escalate out of control.

She didn't want to be grateful to him. She'd been independent for too long, strong and confident and steadfast in her convictions. She hardly ever cried, and that was the way she liked it.

Her feelings for Paul frightened her. Not that he could undermine those convictions, not that he could sap her of her strength and independence, but she honestly didn't want to like him so much.

"I DON'T CARE," said Paul. *"Do whatever the hell you want, Macon. Bring me up on charges if you want. I don't care."*

Rain had started to fall more heavily, now, the drops warm and fat. He focused on the raindrops, the vines, the rumble of what his brain told him was thunder and his soul told him was gunfire somewhere to the north of where they were standing. Crickets shrieked and the clouds hung low and ominous.

"Do you know what kind of trouble you're getting yourself into?" Macon asked. *His voice was knife-sharp, cutting through the oppressive humidity.*

"We'll all be in trouble if we go over that hill," Paul countered. *"I just know it, Macon. Some things you just know."*

"Come on," Rigucci called. *He was already heading back to the trail. "Come on, let's get this gig over with."*

"No!" Paul thought he was whispering, but his voice emerged in an anguished scream. *"No! Don't! Damn it, don't go!"*

PAUL'S EYES FLEW open in panic and he bolted upright, struggling for breath.

The dreams hardly ever came to him in his own bed. When he first returned from Vietnam, he'd had them every night, no matter where he was. But now he was bothered by them only when he was sleeping in an unfamiliar place. It put a crimp in his social life, but that was the way it was.

Tonight, however, as he climbed into his bed after a quick shower, he'd felt uneasy, besieged by memories. He recognized the softness of his sheets, the smell of his pillows, the exact arrangement of the toiletry items on his dresser. The position of the window, the closet door, the easy chair. The shadowy texture of the carpet and the silver stripes of moonlight that seeped through the slats of the vertical blinds to strike the opposite wall.

Some things you just know.…

His pulse slowed and he started to breathe more regularly. He raked his fingers through his sweat-damp hair, shoving it back from his face, and fought off a shiver. It was over now. He was going to be all right.

Flashback dreams were a common affliction. His mother had told him that to this day his father still occasionally fought the Battle of the Bulge in his sleep. John Slinger once confessed, after a few beers, that his nightmares about Nam had gotten so out of hand his wife had made him see a therapist for a while. "It wasn't for my sake," he explained, "but for hers. She said I was keeping her up all night, screaming and throwing punches."

Paul wasn't that bad. Not once in the six years of his marriage had Kathy demanded that he seek therapy. Of course, it hadn't been her style to admit that anything could be wrong. She had turned a blind eye to his dissatisfaction with his work, his restlessness in their marriage and his fitful sleep habits. When he tried to talk about his unhappiness, she'd refused to listen. "Things are fine," she'd argue. "I don't know what you're complaining about."

He gazed at the pattern of light the moon cast against the wall. Why was he thinking about it? Why was he thinking about the jungle nights, the fear, his ill-fated marriage?

Bonnie.

He settled back against the pillow and closed his eyes, this time laboring hard not to drift toward sleep. Instead, he forced himself to picture her magnificent hair, her poignant smile, her clear, beautiful eyes. He used to become enraged when some holier-than-thou antiwar maniac started sounding off—and his initial reaction to Bonnie's description of her husband had been to pick a fight with her. But that reflex had faded when he'd realized how sad she was, how lonely and grief-stricken her husband's death had left her.

He'd wanted to gather her into his arms, to whisper that he'd also lost people he'd loved. He'd wanted to give comfort, and receive it. He'd almost kissed her.

Some things you just know.

He heard the words in her hushed voice and felt for a moment as if he understood everything there was to understand about her.

She wasn't the sort of woman he ought to get involved with. She had a son; she was still in mourning for her husband. She despised the things Paul had done with his life in the past, just as he despised the things she'd done with hers. Merely spending an evening in her company brought back the dreams.

Ten years after becoming a widow, she was still living with too many memories.

So was he.

Chapter Four

Bonnie leaned against the chain link fence and stared across the street at the town green. Behind her, a hundred third- and fourth-graders romped in the school yard; the air was filled with happy shrieks and giggles and the scuffling sounds of sneakers as the children darted from the swings to the slide, from the jungle gym to the jump ropes. After spending three hours indoors at their desks, they had surplus energy to burn, and they were making the most of their recess period.

She listened for calamities and heard none: no whining, no sobs, no howls of pain or anger. A quick scan of the playground revealed nothing out of the ordinary, and she returned her gaze to the green. Shoving up the sleeves of her cardigan, she rested her arms on the fence and surveyed the rolling rectangle of lawn, the stately trees shading it, the sidewalks spanning it, the formal New England architecture of the buildings surrounding it. At the far end stood the old war memorial, a stark ten-foot spire of stone on a concrete pedestal.

Twenty-five years ago, the United States hadn't needed another war. And today, Northford didn't need another memorial.

"You look like a lady deep in thought."

At the sound of the intruding voice Bonnie turned to find the school librarian, Claire Collins, sidling up to the fence beside her. "Not terribly deep," she admitted. "I was just thinking about how many books you could buy with the money Northford wants to spend on a stupid military statue."

"Don't I know it," Claire grumbled, her gaze paralleling Bonnie's across the street to the green. "I just got word this morning that my budget's going to be trimmed by ten percent again this year. Meanwhile, Mike tells me his men are all gung ho about the memorial. They're setting up a collection to raise money for it." Claire's husband, Mike, was the town's police chief.

"I always thought that when they took up a collection, it was for a police widow or some child in the hospital."

"Guess again. Rumor has it that the town council's going to start soliciting bids on designs and costs for the memorial. The guys at the police station figure that if they contribute something toward it, it's more likely to get built. And then, of course, with Paul Tremaine kicking in so much money out of his own pocket, there's no way the thing isn't going to happen."

Bonnie sighed. She'd spent a great deal of time since Saturday thinking about Paul's generosity regarding the birch tree he and Shane had planted for her. She wondered whether he was the sort to throw his wealth around on a whim—whether, for that matter, he was especially wealthy. "Do you know Paul Tremaine?" she asked Claire, trying not to sound too interested.

Claire grinned. "After living in this town for eighteen years, I know everybody."

Bonnie gazed across the street, attempting to picture what the green would look like adorned with not one but two monuments to death. "Do you know why he's so eager to have a new memorial built?"

Claire meditated for a moment. "He's a private man," she said, leaning against the fence beside Bonnie. "Northford sent maybe fifteen boys to Vietnam, and three didn't make it back. I don't know that any of them was a particular intimate of Paul's, so I doubt that's what's motivating him."

"What's your guess?" Bonnie pressed her.

Claire shrugged. "Beats me. He didn't come straight home after the war. He only moved back to town maybe ten years ago. People talked about how he'd been a big hero over there, he'd seen a lot of action and so on, but you can't believe everything people say."

"Laura Holt told me she thought he must have killed lots of enemy troops," Bonnie muttered, grimacing.

"A lot of men did a lot of things back then," Claire remarked philosophically. "Paul Tremaine seems like a nice fellow, what little I know of him. From what I gather, he sometimes has a couple of beers and shoots pool down at Max's with some of the guys from the police station, but he mostly keeps to himself."

"Is he married?" Bonnie asked. Given that he'd accepted a spur-of-the-moment dinner invitation from her, she assumed he wasn't, but it didn't hurt to get confirmation.

Claire shook her head. "I've heard tell he got married after the war, but as far as I know he's living alone these days. He doesn't date much, either—at least nobody local. I can think of a few women who wouldn't mind getting him into bed, but if he's dating anyone she must live somewhere else." She eyed Bonnie curiously. "Why do you ask?"

"Know your enemy," Bonnie answered, echoing what Paul had said the first time they'd met.

She didn't really think of him as her enemy, though. Quite the contrary, she was delighted to learn he was single—although her delight unsettled her. She had no ambition to become yet another local woman who hoped to get him into bed. "So, how serious are these rumors about the bids?" she asked, choosing to concentrate on the issue that would always come between her and Paul.

The air was riven by the shrill peal of the school bell announcing the end of recess. Claire and Bonnie turned to watch the children gravitating sluggishly toward the school door. "I imagine the only way to find out is to talk to someone on the council," Claire answered.

"I will," Bonnie resolved. As long as she remained focused on the memorial, she wouldn't have to worry about succumbing to Paul's allure. "Do me a favor, Claire, and put together some library budget projections for me—before and after the ten percent reduction. I'd love to march into town hall with a list of books the school desperately needs and can't afford. Maybe that'll make them realize how ridiculous their priorities are."

"Dream on, Bonnie," Claire murmured under her breath as she and Bonnie joined the students at the door. "Dream on."

BONNIE LEFT the town hall two and a half hours later, a copy of Claire's library budget tucked unread inside her briefcase and Councilman Edwin Marshal's platitudes ringing in her ears.

He'd been oh, so cordial, clearing his desk and listening attentively while she explained her sentiments to him. He'd told her that, while her passionate speech had given everyone at the meeting a lot to think about, the budget for the memorial was totally separate from the school library budget. With or without the monument, the library budget would still face a ten percent reduction. Then he'd told her that his neighbor's daughter was one of her students and that he'd heard she was an excellent teacher, and he'd asked her to call him Ed.

She stood in the parking lot behind the town hall, reviewing her encounter with him. She hadn't made a dent in his opinion, she conceded grimly. If only Gary had been around to present her position, the silver-haired councilman would have been moved to rethink his position. Her husband had been so forceful, so articulate. Compared to him, she was utterly inept.

The closest she'd gotten to undermining Ed's certainty was when she'd said, "If Paul Tremaine weren't putting up so much of the money, Northford wouldn't be so enthusiastic about the thing." After squirming for a moment in his massive leather chair, Ed had gone on about how he and Paul Tremaine's father had been classmates together in the very same elementary school where Bonnie now taught. He'd pointed out that the Tremaine family had deep roots in town and that most folks were darned glad that, after so many years away, Paul had chosen to return home. He'd been a hero in the war; he'd served his country with honor and he deserved this small token of the town's appreciation.

"If he wants a memorial, we'll do whatever we can to find the funding for it," Ed had declared.

Apparently, local support for the project had less to do with dollars and cents than with small town allegiances, Bonnie concluded as she climbed into her car and shut the door. The only way to get the memorial concept dumped was to get Northford's local hero to back away from it.

It wasn't that she wished to enter into combat with Paul. All she wanted was to convince him to see things her way so they wouldn't be on opposite sides of this matter. If only he agreed with her, she would be free to...

To what? Venture into a romance with him? Follow through on her mind-boggling attraction to him? No, of course not. She had no interest in engaging in a superficial affair with him, and anything deeper than an affair was unthinkable. He wasn't Gary; she could never love him.

Her sole aim, she assured herself, was to prevent the creation of a war memorial. The only way to accomplish that would be to get Paul to withdraw his support for it. That would be difficult, but not impossible. They did share some common ground, after all—they both cared about Shane. She remembered the warmth of Paul's hand closing briefly around hers, and his pensive smile when he'd said that he hoped her son would never have to confront the horror of fighting in a war.

For Shane's sake. That was why Paul should abandon the idea of a memorial.

Tremaine Nursery was located in the eastern part of town on a rural road that bordered a couple of pastures and an old tobacco farm. Bonnie had never had any reason to do business there—given her meager salary, she had considered replacing the sickly dogwood with a new tree beyond her means—but she'd driven past the nursery numerous times while taking a shortcut to Lowell. Now that Shane was going to be working at the nursery, she imagined she ought to get acquainted with the place.

The broad gravel parking lot was crowded when she arrived. The air smelled even cleaner here than in town, redolent with the fragrance of damp earth and greenery. From a forest in the distance came the melodic chirping of birds, offering a lilting counterpoint to the nearby rumble of a tractor. On the other side of the parking lot stood row after row of trees and shrubs for sale, their roots wrapped in burlap and their branches adorned with price tags.

Shoving her hands into the pockets of her cardigan, Bonnie entered the greenhouse. Plants were displayed on long, neat tables, many of them with identifying tags or illustrations. People browsed among the tables, fingering the leaves and squinting at the prices. Bonnie searched the crowded shop for Paul, but she didn't see him.

A woman was posted by a cash register not far from the entrance, wearing a Tremaine Nursery shirt like the one Paul had had on both times he'd been to Bonnie's house. "Excuse me," Bonnie said. "Can you tell me where I might find Mr. Tremaine?"

"He's in the garden center," the woman said, nodding her head toward a double-door entry into an adjacent warehouse.

Bonnie thanked her and wove among the tables to the warehouse, which contained a vast assortment of garden equipment for sale. She spotted a cluster of men engaged in a lively discussion near a row of power mowers, but Paul wasn't among them. One of the men was wearing a shirt like Paul's, but his hair was streaked with white and his face was lined.

She wandered over to the group and waited until the man was done expounding on the many features of a particular mower. He glanced at her and smiled. "Can I help you?"

"I was told I'd find Mr. Tremaine in here," said Bonnie, offering the other customers a contrite smile for having interrupted them.

"I'm Mr. Tremaine," the man said. "What can I do for you?"

He was too old to be Paul's brother and too young to be his father, especially if Paul's father had been a classmate of Ed Marshal's. Yet the man's dimples reminded her of Paul's. "I'm looking for *Paul* Tremaine," she clarified.

The man nodded. "He's probably in one of the other greenhouses. Would you like me to page him?"

Bonnie hesitated. She didn't want Paul dragged away from important work in order to be subjected to one of her diatribes on the necessity of setting peaceful priorities for the next generation. If there was any chance that he might agree to withdraw his plan for a memorial, Bonnie suspected that he'd be more likely to change his mind in private.

"Don't bother paging him," she replied. "I'm sure I'll be able to find him."

"Those greenhouses aren't open to customers."

"I'm not here as a customer," Bonnie explained. "It's a personal matter."

As soon as she spoke she realized her mistake. The man's eyebrows shot up, and one of the customers nudged the other in the ribs. The dimpled man chuckled and gave her a wink. "In that case, ma'am, I don't suppose there'd be any problem, as long as you don't mess with the merchandise." He shoved open a back door and pointed her toward the greenhouses behind the warehouse. "Check the one on the left first—I think you'll find him there."

"Thank you," Bonnie muttered, trying to ignore the flush of embarrassment that warmed her cheeks. She hurried outside, picked her way across a dirt lane carved with tractor treads and pulled open the door of the greenhouse.

This greenhouse was much smaller than the main one; the interior was warm and humid, the concrete floor damp and the roof steeply peaked. Shelves lined the outer walls and a narrow table bisected the long room. Every square inch of horizontal space was covered with potted seedlings.

Paul stood at the far end of the greenhouse with his back to Bonnie, spraying the seedlings with mist. She watched him manipulate the heavy black snake of hose along the narrow aisle, his shoulders stretching the cotton of his shirt smooth across his broad upper back. He had on his uniform shirt and a pair of faded work dungarees; she could discern his lean, well-proportioned hips and legs through the weathered denim. His hair curled along the collar of his shirt, and droplets of water trapped in the hair of his exposed forearms glistened beneath the fluorescent overhead lighting. The muscles at the base of his spine flexed visibly as he leaned across the table to spray the plants adjacent to the glass wall.

What he was doing wasn't exactly strenuous, but it struck Bonnie as remarkably physical. Feeding seedlings was a gentle, nurturing activity, yet when Paul did it it seemed supremely manly, the very opposite of Gary's cerebral theorizing.

Why was she comparing the two men? Another blush heated her cheeks as the obvious answer came to her. Clearing her throat, she shouted above the hiss of the water, "Paul?"

He shut off the nozzle and turned. He seemed to exert himself not to appear startled by her unexpected intrusion, but she sensed his surprise in the subtle widening of his eyes and the smile that whispered across his lips. Setting down the hose, he pulled a dark blue handkerchief from his pocket, dried his hands on it and then shoved his mussed hair back from his brow. "Hi," he said, wiping his right hand a second time before he extended it to her.

She accepted it, cautioning herself that if his enveloping grip seemed a bit too possessive, it was only her imagination. When he released her hand she hid it safely within the pocket of her cardigan. "I've just met a man who said he was Mr. Tremaine," she told him, pleased by her light tone. "Is he a relative of yours?"

"My Uncle Steve," Paul told her. "He's my partner here in the business."

He gave her a dazzling smile. The air suddenly seemed too steamy in the greenhouse. He seemed too close.

"How's the birch tree?" he asked when her silence extended to a full minute.

"It's fine." She raised her chin in a posture of courage, but tilting her head only forced her gaze into alignment with his. His eyes were so profoundly dark, so spellbinding. She lowered her gaze to his throat and found herself equally taken by the harsh lines of his jaw, the powerful width of his shoulders.

She was so overwhelmed by his masculine presence that she had to struggle to remember why she'd come here— the memorial.

"I should have telephoned you to thank you for dinner the other night," he said before she could state her purpose. "It was nice of you to invite me."

"It was nice of you to bring me the tree," she countered, chastising herself inwardly to get on with it, to say what she'd come to say. If only his gaze wasn't so penetrating, if only he wasn't standing so close, if only the golden skin of his arms and face wasn't so damp. If only the atmosphere wasn't so steamy, the ceiling so low, the air so redolent with the aromas of fertile soil and budding life.

He took an unnecessary step closer to her and rested his hand against the table, his fingers curled. Bonnie glanced at the thick ridge of his knuckles. She resented him for being able, without any effort, to stir awake desires that had been lying dormant in her for years. Her resentment directed her thoughts back to the issue of the memorial, and she said, "Look, Paul, the reason I came here is—"

"Because we left things hanging last Saturday."

She shot him a nervous look. "What things?"

He mulled over his words. "Well, you were crying and everything—"

"Crying?" *Don't,* she silently implored him. *Don't say anything too personal.*

"When I was at your house," he pressed on, disregarding the frantic message in her eyes. "I probably shouldn't say anything—I probably shouldn't even think about it. But I felt, maybe there was a possibility...." He shook his head. "I should just forget it. There are too many hang-ups...." He turned to stare through one of the sun-filled panes of glass.

It dawned on Bonnie that he was as tense as she was, as sensitive to the undercurrent pulsing between them. She wanted to warn him away, to steer them both back to solid ground before either of them said or did something they'd regret. But her gaze fell to his hand again, taking note of the scar on his pinkie, the masculine bones and sinews of his wrist. She watched him with a strange, almost detached fascination as he lifted his hand, bringing it to the soft skin of her throat and then around, beneath the heavy blond fall of her hair to the nape of her neck. She felt his thumb stroke along the delicate protrusion of her vertebrae, felt the compelling pressure of him drawing her to himself, felt his breath dance across her upper lip an instant before his mouth covered hers.

His kiss unleashed a deluge of sensation through her body, hot and fluid. She moaned slightly, knowing she ought to pull away at once yet not wanting to. Not wanting the tender friction of his lips on hers to end, not wanting his fingers to stop twining through the silken locks of her hair, not wanting to lose the contact of his firm, lean chest against hers, and his knees, and his hips. Not wanting to deny him—or herself.

With a tiny sigh, partly in resignation and partly in pleasure, she opened her mouth to welcome the gentle invasion of his tongue. The irrationality of this kiss didn't matter; the fact that, as Paul himself had just said, there were too many hang-ups between them was irrelevant. What counted right now was that Bonnie was being kissed more passionately than she'd been kissed in a long time, and that her entire body was throbbing with life. She yearned for Paul as she'd yearned for no other man since Gary's death.

Gary. Merely thinking about him brought her up short. With a gasp, she broke their kiss and jerked her head away. ''We shouldn't,'' she whispered.

Although the kiss had ended—*because* it had ended, perhaps—Paul tightened his hold on her. He splayed the long fingers of one hand over the back of her head and molded the other around the flare of her hip, refusing her the chance to escape. Reading her panic-stricken expression, he offered a crooked smile. ''Glass houses aren't exactly private, are they?'' he muttered.

It hadn't even occurred to Bonnie that she and Paul might have been putting on a show for Peeping Toms outside the greenhouse. Glimpsing the transparent wall just beyond the shelf of seedlings to her left, she shuddered.

Paul refused to relax his embrace. "Can we go out for dinner?" he asked.

"What?"

His smile softened as he took in her muddled state. "Dinner," he explained, brushing his lips lightly against her forehead. "A date."

Say no! her brain shrieked at her. "When?" she responded aloud.

"Whenever you say." He slid his hand forward to explore the hoop of her earring with his thumb.

She gazed into the smoky depths of his eyes. "This isn't why I came here."

"I know."

His thumb wandered into the crease behind her earlobe and she shuddered again, closing her eyes to savor the sudden spasm of desire that racked her body. "Don't, Paul—don't do that."

He traced a line down the side of her neck to the edge of her cardigan, then let both hands fall. Inhaling deeply, he turned away. "I like you, Bonnie," he murmured, more to the fragile infant shrubs than to her. "I like you."

She was touched by his artless words. *I like you.* If only it were that simple.

"The reason I came here," she said slowly, struggling to suppress the tremor in her voice, "was to convince you not to go forward with your memorial."

He turned back to her. As her words sank in, the longing in his eyes faded and his gaze grew hard. "And that's why you won't go out for dinner with me?" he asked, his tone laced with disbelief.

"No. I mean, yes," she stammered.

"You mean no." He rapped his fingers against the table in frustration. "We can disagree on the memorial and still have dinner together. We did it last Saturday at your house. It wasn't so difficult."

"Paul—"

"Tell me the truth, Bonnie," he demanded. The muted tone of his voice only heightened her awareness of his anger and doubt.

"I just did." She averted her gaze.

He assessed her for a long minute, contemplating whether it was worth goading her into giving him an honest answer. Apparently he thought it was—which flattered her, even though she didn't care to be interrogated by him. "What is it? You think I'm not good enough for you?"

"Why on earth would I think that?"

"Beats me," he asked, imprisoning her with his gaze. "Maybe because I'm not a highbrow from Cambridge. Maybe because I work with my hands."

"Don't be ridiculous." If anything, Bonnie had found watching him at work wonderfully appealing.

"If it makes you feel any better, I did graduate from college."

"It doesn't make me feel better," she snapped, exasperated. She forced herself to meet his stare. "You don't have to prove how smart you are to me, Paul. I'm aware that you're an intelligent man."

"Well, thanks," he drawled with spurious gratitude.

She fell silent, lowering her eyes again, gazing at the dainty green leaves sprouting from a baby azalea at her elbow.

"What is it, then? You're involved with someone else?" he asked.

"No."

He scrutinized her, then let out a long, weary breath and bent to gather up the hose. "Liar," he grunted under his breath.

Her heart began a slow, loud pounding, echoing inside her skull in a dirgelike tempo. "I'm not lying," she said, loathing the defensiveness that filtered through her voice. "Unless it's Shane you're referring to—"

"It's not Shane," Paul said quietly. He methodically looped the hose into a circular coil and hung it on a wall hook near the door. Then he twisted off the spigot to which the hose was attached. "I'm referring to Shane's father."

"Gary's dead," Bonnie said tersely, resenting Paul's implication even though she privately acknowledged the accuracy of it.

"Gone but not forgotten," Paul charged, his voice still restrained but simmering with anger. "The amazing man, right? The genius. You live with all his pictures staring down at you from the fireplace—"

"Paul." She didn't want to hear this. She didn't want Paul to do anything that would make her stop liking him.

"Saint Gary," he went on, his fury rising, spilling over. "Saint Gary of the Cambridge Manifesto, with books being written about him. I don't measure up to him, right? I didn't burn enough draft cards for your taste."

"Paul, please—"

"I've got blood on my hands, right? Tell me about it, Bonnie. Your amazing genius husband Gary was safe and sound in Boston, helping his followers dodge the draft, while I was overseas bayoneting babies and hurling grenades into crowded grocery stalls and having one hell of a good time. Is that it?"

"Don't!" She wanted to squeeze her eyes shut and jam her hands against her ears, to block out the vile things he was saying. She listened for a minute to the sound of her own respiration, ragged with fury. Why was Paul doing this? How could he speak so cruelly about Gary? What did he want from her?

"Gary is dead!" she erupted, wishing she could hurt Paul as much as his words had hurt her. "He's dead, Paul. Don't you ever, ever talk about him that way again."

Paul pressed his lips together and turned from her. She saw the tension in his shoulders, in his fingers as they clenched into fists. He let out a long, uneven breath, then muttered, "I've had a lot more contact with death than you, Bonnie. Don't patronize me."

"And don't you insult my husband."

A bitter laugh escaped him. "Your husband, present tense. He's still alive for you, sweetheart. I'm not going to compete with that."

So what if Gary still was alive in her heart? So what if Paul couldn't compete? That was his problem; she wasn't going to apologize for who she was or what she felt or whom she loved. She wasn't going to let Paul put her on the defensive again.

"I came here to discuss the war memorial with you," she said, sounding infinitely more composed than she felt, "but obviously this isn't a good time." Gathering what shreds of dignity she could find within herself, she straightened her shoulders and walked out of the greenhouse.

"DID I EVER TELL you 'bout Jolene?" asked Swann.

They were seated at the side of a rutted dirt road, about a kilometer northwest of camp. A clammy drizzle was falling and the low-hanging clouds gave off eerie purple reflections of moonlight. Once the patrol got close to the village, maybe another kilometer north, they would have to cut the chatter. But here in the middle of nowhere, as they took five minutes for a rest and a smoke, Swann's bright, cheerful voice was a welcome sound in the night's misty gloom.

"Yeah, you told us about her." Rigucci took a sip from his canteen. "The one with the beaucoup big boobs."

"She sent me this love letter today," Swann boasted, leaning his head back against the trunk of the tree under which he was sitting. "She says she just about can't live without me. Says no man can satisfy her like I do."

"I take it she's speaking from experience," Paul teased.

Swann gave him a sharp glance, then threw back his head and guffawed. "I don't care how many men she experiences, so long as I'm the one she comes home to. I ain't one of you jealous white boys, Tremaine. I know I'm good. I'd just as soon she played the field a little. That way, she'll appreciate me more."

"You let that head of yours swell any bigger," Macon warned, pausing to relight his soggy cigarette, "and your helmet's not going to fit."

"She can fool around all she wants," Swann insisted, "so long as I'm over here. What's a hungry little girl like her gonna do, you know? Let her snack around. Soon as I'm stateside, she's gonna enjoy the main course."

"You're making me hungry," Rigucci complained. "You bring along any food, Macon?"

"When I get off that big silver bird in San Diego," Swann went on, "I expect Jolene is gonna be standing right there on the tarmac, just waving those great big—" he paused for effect "—hands at me. And then we're gonna go to the nearest motel and not come out for three days."

"Unless she finds herself another main course some-where," Rigucci taunted.

"Don't be so negatory, man," Swann chided him. "She'll be waiting for me. I'm waiting for her. Ain't I, Tremaine?"

Paul smiled reflexively, but his mind was elsewhere. For some reason, he no longer felt like joking with the others. In the distance he heard the cawing of a crow, and it made him envious. The crow was free, soaring through the sky, flying away, away from this place. He wished he could be that free, could spread his wings and rise up above the twisted branches of the trees, above the rain, above the monsoon clouds and into the ozone. He wished he could smell air that didn't reek of wetness and death.

Listening to Swann brag about his girl back home only made it worse. Paul didn't dare to say what he was thinking—not that Swann's girl might not wait for him to come home, but that Swann might not make it home himself. He hated getting into that kind of head—it made for bad days and worse nights—but he couldn't help himself. He'd cut his girlfriend loose when he left Northford for Basic last fall. He didn't want anyone waiting for him. He didn't want any torches burning. Hoping for too much could be dangerous.

The way he figured it, he'd be lucky to survive, to get himself back home in one piece. Once there, he'd start all over. No loose ends from the past, no memories of who he used to be.

"Let's move," Macon said, glimpsing his watch and then snubbing out his cigarette in the soggy soil at his feet. "We've got another couple of kilometers to cover before we call it a night."

"We going north of the village?" Swann asked.

"That's the plan."

Paul felt something twist tight inside him, momentarily blinding him, depriving him of breath. Rigucci might be satisfied by food, Macon by a smoke, Swann by dreams of sex. But for him, for Paul . . . The only thing that would satisfy him would be a crow's broad black wings, something to carry him away from this, something to keep him from losing whatever was left of his soul.

A part of him had died a long time ago—the day he'd seen a woman and her baby lying dead at the side of the road, the day he'd seen body bags being loaded into a cargo transport, the day he'd heard a grown man scream in pain, the day he'd carried a wounded comrade to a medic at the rear and then discovered the poor bastard had died sometime between when Paul picked him up and when he laid him down. A vital part of Paul had vanished the day he'd set foot inside this godforsaken country.

He didn't want some lover from the past throwing that up to him, reminding him of who he once was and would never be again. He didn't want to go home to find the people he used to know and love staring at him in confusion, wondering who the hell he was.

The only thing worse than that, as far as Paul could imagine, was not going home at all.

Chapter Five

Bonnie braked to a halt in the middle of her driveway and gaped at the dark-haired, mustachioed man lounging in one of the porch rockers, his feet propped up on the railing and his arms folded behind his head. Despite his dapper attire—pleated khaki trousers, a crisp oxford shirt, tasseled leather loafers—and his short, well-tailored hairdo, she recognized him at once. The mustache, though less shaggy than she remembered it, still drew attention to his smirking smile, and his eyes still reminded her of a hound's, moist and beseeching.

"Tom?" she called, climbing out of her car and using her hand to shield her eyes against the sun's early-evening slant. "Tom Schuyler? Is that you?"

He grinned, swung his legs down from the railing and stood. "In the flesh," he said, spreading his arms as if to display himself to her. "I hope you don't mind my dropping in on you like this."

Bonnie did mind. Even under the best of circumstances she would mind. Now, when she hadn't yet had a chance to recover from her cataclysmic encounter with Paul, was hardly the best of circumstances.

Needing time to compose herself, she turned her back on her visitor and busied herself with the garage door, jiggling her key in the lock until the latch gave and then heaving the door up along its tracks. She got back into her car, coasted into the garage and remained seated behind the wheel, cocooned within the garage's shadowed interior, taking deep, regular breaths and trying to regain her composure.

During the entire trip home from the nursery she'd tormented herself with thoughts about how glorious it had been to kiss Paul, and how much better it would have been if she hadn't enjoyed his kiss so much. She'd felt guilty for losing track of her purpose in visiting him, for abandoning the cause she'd gone to the nursery to fight for...and most of all, for allowing him, during those few heated moments when his mouth had united with hers, to obliterate every thought of Gary.

Then she'd felt guilty for flying off the handle when Paul accused her of still being in love with her late husband. What he's said had cut close to the truth, and she shouldn't have blown up at him. But she'd lost her temper because she'd been ashamed that, for those few heavenly seconds when she stood in the circle of Paul's arms and let his kiss transport her, she'd stopped being in love with Gary.

Guilty, ashamed and frightened. That about summed it up.

And then, to drive home and discover Tom Schuyler, Gary's old cohort from the Cambridge Manifesto days, his closest friend and political ally, the man who'd knelt beside him as he lay dying in a parking lot in California... To find Tom, whom she hadn't seen in five years, making himself right at home on her front porch was unnerving, to say the least.

Letting out a small, tremulous sigh, she pulled the key from the ignition, gathered her briefcase from the seat beside her and climbed out of the car. She scanned the garage briefly, noticed that Shane's bike was missing—which confirmed that he wasn't home—and braced herself to contend with Tom Schuyler alone. Emerging from the garage, she closed the door and then turned to confront her uninvited guest.

"You're wondering what I'm doing here," he guessed.

She kept her eyes on him as she walked across the lawn to the porch. She supposed it had been simple enough for him to find her. Her address and telephone number were listed in the phone book, and as far as she knew Tom still lived in the Boston area. The last she'd heard, he was teaching mathematics at Boston University; when she and Shane were living in Cambridge her path had occasionally intersected with Tom's. But for all Gary's reliance on Tom and rapport with him, Bonnie had always felt uncomfortable around the man. She'd never been able to shake the suspicion that, even after she became Gary's lawful wife, Tom was checking her out as a possible sexual conquest.

He made no bones about checking her out now, as she warily approached the porch. "You look fantastic, Bonnie," he declared. "You still have the figure of a college girl."

"I never was a college girl," she retorted, just to be contrary. "I was a college woman." She made an effort to swallow her anger. Tom had traveled here from some distance; she supposed she owed him a modicum of hospitality. "You aren't looking so bad yourself," she said, even though she found his yuppie polish not to her taste. "Are you still teaching at B.U.?"

"An associate professor," he said with a grin. "Tenured, as a matter of fact."

"Congratulations." She really ought to offer him a drink—and if he weren't looking so damned proud of himself, she would. Instead, she said, "You're right—I'm wondering what you're doing here."

"Have you got any beer?" he asked, compensating for her shortcomings as a hostess by taking over. "I've been lecturing all morning and talking on the phone all afternoon. I'm a mite parched."

A mite parched. Bonnie suppressed a grimace at his pretentiousness and headed into the house, not bothering to comment when Tom trailed her indoors. She would be courteous to him out of respect for Gary's memory. Perhaps that would help to alleviate her sense of guilt.

"I see you still have your little exhibit set up, just like at your place in Cambridge," Tom noted, lingering in front of the fireplace mantel. Admiring the photographs in which he appeared, Bonnie thought with a scowl.

"Some things never change," she said dryly, referring more to Tom than to her home's decor. She continued into the kitchen, and Tom followed. She pulled a bottle of beer from a shelf in the refrigerator and handed it to him. Then she filled a glass with apple juice for herself. "Let's go out on the front porch," she suggested. "It's a pleasant afternoon, and I'd like to keep an eye out for Shane." She refrained from adding that she couldn't bear the thought of being alone in the house with Tom, especially when she was so keyed up about what had happened earlier that day. She hoped the balmy breezes would help to dissipate her nervousness.

"Shane!" Tom exclaimed, as if the mere mention of Bonnie's son sent him into orbit. "How is the little blond bambino?"

"The little blond bambino is thirteen and taller than I am," Bonnie informed Tom. "Right now he's probably riding his bike all over town, courting a flat tire." She led the way out to the porch and gestured toward the rocker on which Tom had been sitting. She sat in the other one and took a sip of her juice.

"If he's anything like I was at that age, he's courting something much more interesting than a flat tire," Tom said with a wink.

God forbid that Shane would be anything like Tom, Bonnie thought, although she hid her sentiments behind an impassive smile. "So, what brings you to North-ford?"

"Well, as I said, I was on the telephone for much of the afternoon." He took a long draft of beer, then settled more comfortably in the chair and propped his feet on the railing again. "I was conversing with one Kevin McCoy, on leave from the Boston *Globe*. It seems he's writing a book about Gary."

"With my permission," Bonnie confirmed. "I hope you don't mind that I gave him your name. I want him to write a well-rounded biography. That entails talking with as many of the people from the Cambridge Manifesto days as possible."

"So he told me." Tom took another drink of beer. "I assume this means he'll be speaking with Marcie, too?"

"Of course. Marcie was in at the beginning," Bonnie pointed out. Indeed, it had been at Marcie's urging that Bonnie first attended one of Gary's campus rallies. Marcie had been involved in the movement even before Bonnie—although Bonnie had often suspected that Marcie's participation was based less on her political views than on her desire to be a part of the action, to re-volt against her conservative parents and to feel impor-tant. And, of course, they'd all been close friends—Bonnie, Marcie, Gary, Tom and the others.

Marcie had continued working part-time with Gary even after the war had ended and the rest of the Manifesto gang had left Cambridge for other pursuits. She'd been on Gary's doomed trip to California, she and Tom both, while Bonnie had stayed at home with Shane. They'd been at the auditorium with Gary when he was heckled; they'd been with him when he was struck down by the hit-and-run driver. They'd been at the hospital when the emergency room physician declared him dead. They'd been the ones to telephone Bonnie with the news.

"I want Kevin McCoy to talk to the people who knew Gary best. That certainly includes you and Marcie," she said, trying to chase away the mournful memories before they overwhelmed her.

"You should have notified me," Tom reproached, "just to give me some warning. I didn't know whether I was supposed to talk to this guy or not."

Bonnie smiled in spite of herself. "Obviously, that didn't stop you from talking to him for much of the afternoon."

A flicker of indignation passed across Tom's face at her subtle dig. Then he relaxed and took another sip of beer. "Anyway, I tried phoning you as soon as I got off the phone with this McCoy character, but you weren't home. And then I thought, say, why not drive out and see the old girl in her new environment? We could do dinner, reminisce about old times . . . whatever feels right. I don't have any classes tomorrow morning."

"I do," Bonnie said laconically. She wasn't sure whether she was misconstruing Tom's friendly invitation by viewing it as a come-on. But even if his motives were pure, she wasn't in the mood to share a dinner and an evening of nostalgic chitchat with him. If she wanted to go out for dinner with anyone, it certainly wasn't Tom Schuyler.

She wished she could convince herself that it wasn't Paul, either.

"Still teaching the little kiddies?" Tom broke into her thoughts. His arrogant tone implied that he considered college professors vastly superior to elementary school teachers.

Why should he feel superior? she thought bitterly. The only reason he'd managed to become a professor was that, unlike Gary, he hadn't sacrificed his graduate studies to devote himself full-time to the goals of the Cambridge Manifesto. Political demonstrations were fun—and groupies even more fun—as long as they didn't interfere with the completion of his Ph.D.

"Yes," she said coolly. "I'm still teaching fourth grade."

"Aren't you bored to tears out here?" he asked, surveying the front yard and the surrounding forest. "I mean, what does one do here for stimulation?"

"One reads," she answered, mimicking his stilted phrasing. "One talks to other people. One takes long walks and meditates. I've been living here for three years, Tom, and I haven't gotten bored yet."

"What do you do for a social life?"

"None of your business," she snapped. If it weren't for what had occurred in the greenhouse a half hour ago, she would have been able to handle Tom's nosy questions with aplomb. But right now the mention of a social life led inexorably to thoughts of Paul, troubling thoughts of everything that was wrong between them, and everything that could have been right if not for the long, grim shadow history cast over their friendship. "How's *your* social life?" she asked, not because she was interested but because she was tired of Tom's one-sided interrogation of her. "The last time I saw you—outside Grendel's Den, wasn't it?"

Tom grinned. "You were with a bunch of school-teachers, weren't you?"

Tom had been with a woman, of course. "You told me that your life was going to remain unsettled until you got tenure," Bonnie reminded him. "Well, now you've got tenure. When are you going to settle down?"

"Settle down?" he repeated, wrinkling his nose. "You sound like my mother."

"I *am* a mother."

"Well, I have no intention of becoming one myself," Tom quipped. "You know me, Bonnie—I'm an alley cat. Always was, always will be. I have the feeling I'm much better as a boyfriend than I'd ever be as a husband."

"In other words, you still aren't ready to grow up."

Tom eyed her skeptically. "And you're still the Grand Domesticator," he shot back. "I warned Gary, way back when, that if he married you it would put a real damper on his social life. Fortunately..." He drifted off and sipped his beer.

"Fortunately, he was in love with me," Bonnie completed. "I don't condemn you, Tom, but...I mean, come on. You're in your forties, and you're still running around like a kid."

"Most men in their forties are running around like kids, marriage notwithstanding," he said. "Marcie's divorced, by the way."

"Oh, that's too bad," Bonnie said genuinely. "I'm sorry to hear it." She'd lost touch with Marcie after Gary's death, but she'd heard through the grapevine that her old friend had gotten married a few years ago and moved to Phoenix. "What happened? Did her husband run around like a kid?"

"Not all alley cats are male," Tom commented, winking again. "Marcie's an ardent believer in equal opportunity. Don't shed any tears for her, Bonnie."

"Have you got her address?" Whether it was a result of Tom's unexpected appearance, the news of Marcie's divorce or simply the fact that Kevin McCoy's book had gotten her to reminiscing about the past a great deal lately, Bonnie suddenly felt the urge to touch base with her former classmate. "I'd really like to talk to her."

"I . . . don't know," Tom hedged.

"But I want Kevin to interview her about Gary. You said you wished I had warned you before he contacted you. Maybe I ought to warn her."

"I'll warn her," Tom promised. "And if she wants to talk to you, I'll give her your number."

"Why wouldn't she want to talk to me?" Bonnie asked, bewildered.

Tom shrugged. "You had the good marriage, Bonnie. You and Gary had a son. She was a flop as a wife. Maybe she's jealous."

Bonnie could hardly believe that. She and Marcie might have lost contact over the years, but there were still so many bonds that tied them together, so many shared experiences. So many afternoons at the old house on Avon Street, sipping herbal tea and proofreading conscientious objector petitions, so many marches through so many cities, so many late nights listening to Joni Mitchell's *For the Roses* album and trying to imagine their futures when they should have been studying for their midterms.

Before she could question Tom further, however, she was distracted by the sound of a truck bumping along the last few yards of Pond Road where it ran into Fair Hollow Lane near her house. She glanced toward the corner in time to see a green Tremaine Nursery pickup steering into her driveway.

FOR NO GOOD REASON, Paul decided to drive down Pond Road. It wasn't on his way home, and the last thing he wanted to do was run the risk of seeing Bonnie. But he doubted that she'd just happen to be standing across the street from her house at the junction of Pond and Fair Hollow when he cruised by. And right now, he felt the compulsion to conquer something, even if it was only a decaying back road. He was anxious and angry and frustrated in all sorts of ways. He was hoping that a good, hard drive would help him to unwind.

He cruised to the eastern border of the town green and then south, watching for Pond Road. As soon as he made the turn, his front tires dipped into a deep pothole, tossing him unceremoniously up and down on his seat. He jiggled the steering wheel and leveled the truck, then smiled. One obstacle down, a few million more to go.

Damn her. Damn Bonnie. It bothered the hell out of him that, according to her son, she had no difficulty navigating this road in her car. It irritated him that she could have walked out of the greenhouse after a kiss like that. He wasn't going to let her get the better of him, not when it came to his memorial or romance or the history of the past twenty years. Or this damned obstacle course of a road, he thought, bouncing in and out of another pothole.

The dense canopy of leaves overhead darkened the road. Paul waited until his eyes adjusted to the gloom, then forged ahead, circumventing a large rock and then a stretch of crumbling asphalt. At the sight of a car approaching from the opposite direction, he almost steered off the narrow road into a shallow gully.

A short distance farther along he spotted a mysterious movement, a gliding figure in silhouette. Driving closer, he discerned that it was someone riding a bicycle; closer yet, he noticed the mop of pale hair crowning the rider's head, and the bulky high-tops on his feet. Paul bumped the truck over a fallen branch and then slowed to a stop alongside the cyclist.

"Shane," he called through the open passenger window.

Shane had coasted to the eroding edge of the road to leave room for the truck. When he saw who the driver was, he halted and planted his feet on the ground. "Hey, Paul! What's happening?"

"I've decided it's time to come to terms with this road."

Shane grinned and shoved his hair out of his face. "It's nasty, isn't it?"

"In every sense of the word." Paul gazed through the windshield at the rubble ahead, then turned back to the boy. "I'm sure with practice I'll get the hang of it."

"So, like, am I supposed to start working for you this Saturday?" Shane asked.

"Unless you've got a problem."

"No problem." He eyed the truck. "I could work after school, too, if you want."

"No. After school you should be doing your homework."

"I don't get much homework," Shane declared.

"Yeah, sure," Paul said, his knowing smile contradicting his stern words. "I went to the same school you're going to, and I remember exactly how much homework the teachers gave."

"Yeah, well..." Shane shrugged. "Me and Matt get it all done in study hall."

Paul laughed in disbelief. "Are you coming from Matt's house now?"

Shane glanced around him, weighing his answer. Then he leaned toward the open window, letting his bike tilt between his legs. "Don't tell my mom," he whispered conspiratorially, "but me and Matt were down at Breaker Gorge."

"Why shouldn't I tell your mom?"

"That's where I got my flat tire last week. I was real careful this time, though. We parked our bikes up near the top and went down on foot." Shane studied Paul curiously. "Did you used to go climbing down there when you were my age?"

Paul nodded. In truth, his most vivid memories of Breaker Gorge involved descending to the mossy bottom with Denise Franklin and exploring, in the relative privacy of the culvert, the secrets that lurked beneath her clothing. "Would you like a lift home?" he asked, feeling generous in the mellow afterglow of that happy recollection.

"Yeah, that would be great." Shane swung off his bicycle and lifted it into the empty truck bed.

As soon as Paul issued the invitation he realized it was a mistake. But he couldn't very well retract it. Maybe it was for the best that he drive directly to the Hudson house. If Shane was going to be working at the nursery for the next several weekends, Paul was bound to run into Bonnie. He might as well get used to seeing her.

"You aren't going to tell my mom, are you?" Shane asked nervously, climbing onto the seat beside Paul and shooting a quick glance at his bicycle through the rear window of the cab.

"About Breaker Gorge? No."

"It's just—I mean..." Shane shrugged again. "She doesn't understand stuff sometimes. She's a lady, you know?"

And how, Paul muttered under his breath.

"So, you used to hang out at the gorge, huh," Shane said once Paul had resumed driving.

"Sometimes."

"Did you bike?"

Paul tossed him a quick look. "Mostly I walked down with friends," he said carefully.

"Girls?"

Paul looked toward his passenger again. He wasn't about to lie to Shane. "Yeah, sometimes."

"Did you mess around?"

Paul mulled over his response. "Why do you ask?"

Shane squirmed in his seat. "I don't know. Just curious."

Paul knew there had to be more to his questions than simple curiosity, and he waited patiently for Shane to elaborate. After they'd passed a fallen log blocking part of the road, he did. "Matt told me this girl at school told him that this other girl likes me."

"Do you like her?"

"I don't know. Like, I hardly know her. And even if I did, I wouldn't know what to do with her."

"You could always follow her lead," Paul suggested.

"Yeah, I guess I could. She's real foxy, you know? It's like, she knows how to walk."

"How to walk," Paul repeated, uncertain he'd heard Shane correctly.

"Yeah. I mean, some girls, they walk sort of funny, you know? Like, they're always looking over their shoulder, making sure someone's watching them or something. Not Melinda. It's like she doesn't care who's watching. She's always got someplace to go."

"She sounds pretty special," Paul remarked, because Shane seemed to expect him to say something.

"Yeah, she is. For a girl, that is." He shrugged. "So, like, did you used to mess around with girls?"

Paul's mind filled with a vision of Bonnie, of her lips so soft against his and her silky hair spilling through his fingers. Shane's question had centered on girls, not women, and he pushed away all thoughts of Bonnie.

"I messed around some," he admitted. "I was a little bit older than you, though."

"How old?"

"I don't know—fifteen."

"So, like, when you were my age, you didn't care about girls at all?"

"Oh, sure, I cared about them," Paul conceded. "I spent lots of time thinking about them. I just didn't mess around much with them."

"Right turn over here," Shane reminded him when they reached the intersection at the end of the road. "But, like—did you notice the way they walked?"

"Definitely," Paul reassured him. "Some of those girls really knew how to walk right." He steered around the corner and into Bonnie's driveway—and cursed the woman under his breath. There she was, sitting on the porch and entertaining a man. Who the hell was this one? Paul wondered irately. Another reporter writing a book about her famous husband?

"Hey, I know that guy!" Shane jerked on the door handle and shoved open his door as soon as Paul brought the truck to a halt. "He's one of my dad's old friends. We've got pictures of him in the living room."

Great, Paul thought, slumping in his seat and wondering if there were any way for him to drive away without acknowledging Bonnie or her guest. He found a certain grim humor in the fact that the old friend—undoubtedly a self-righteous draft-card-burning radical in his prime—now wore his hair shorter than Paul did. His amusement faded, though, when he considered that the old friend was sitting comfortably at Bonnie's side, on her porch, closer to her than she would ever allow Paul to be.

Before he could figure out a way to make a discreet escape, Bonnie came charging across the lawn. "Were you hitchhiking again?" she assailed her son.

"Uh-uh," Shane said, shaking his head for emphasis. "I swear. I was just riding on Pond Road and Paul came along and gave me a ride."

Bonnie glanced at Paul. He imagined she was searching for confirmation, but the minute her enchanting hazel eyes met his, his body responded all over, tensing in desire and frustration and no small measure of anger.

"It's the truth," he said, aware that she suspected him of ulterior motives.

"That's Dad's best friend, isn't it?" Shane asked, pointing toward the man on the porch.

"Yes, that's Tom Schuyler. You can go say hello." She watched her son lope across the lawn to the porch, then turned back to Paul. He sensed more than suspicion in her gaze, more than resentment, but he couldn't guess what it was. She opened her mouth and then closed it without speaking.

Her silence made Paul even tenser. "I've got to go," he said abruptly. "You have company—I didn't mean to barge in on you." He glanced past her toward the porch, where the man and the teenage boy were sizing each other up.

Bonnie hesitated an instant, then lowered her eyes. "I'll get Shane's bike," she mumbled, closing the passenger door and walking around to the back of the truck.

As awkward as they felt in each other's presence, Paul wasn't going to let her hoist a dirty, heavy bicycle out of the truck, not when she was wearing an attractive skirt and blouse outfit, nylons and sandals and her neat cardigan sweater. After turning off the engine, he jogged to the rear of the truck. "Let me get it for you," he said, gently urging her aside.

The feel of her shoulder under his palm provoked another surge of emotion inside him, arousal at war with resentment. He grabbed the bike by the crossbars and lifted it over the tailgate. Once the tires touched down Bonnie gripped the handlebars and held the bike upright.

"I don't suppose you'd care to stay for dinner," she said, her voice rising questioningly at the end.

As invitations went, this one was hardly enthusiastic. It was also utterly unexpected. "While you and your husband's best friend sit around the table reminiscing about the good old days? I'll pass, thanks."

"I didn't invite him," she said, her voice quiet but oddly imploring.

He peered at the man on the porch, who had apparently lost interest in Shane and was watching Bonnie. Paul wasn't sure whether she meant that the man would be leaving, or that he would be staying even though he hadn't been invited.

Whatever her invitation meant, it was too complicated, too unfathomable. The man on her porch was as significant as the photographs on her mantel, as vital a part of who she was and what mattered to her. There was no room on her porch or her mantel for Paul. He didn't belong here.

"Thanks, anyway," he declined, faking a smile. He nodded at the man, waved to Shane and got back into the truck.

Backing down the driveway, he paused to scrutinize the birch tree he'd planted the previous weekend. Seeing that it occupied such a prominent place on Bonnie's property heartened him. Not only had he managed to conquer Pond Road, but he'd also conquered Bonnie's front yard. The tree was his. It would always be his, in some small way. He might not belong on her porch, but she would never be able to rid herself of him completely.

Permitting himself a small, vindictive smile, he turned the wheel, shifted gear and drove off.

"FRIEND OF YOURS?" Tom asked as Bonnie joined him on the porch.

Shane had already disappeared inside. She leaned his bike against the porch railing before climbing up the steps. "Actually, he's a friend of Shane's," she said, then crossed to the screen door and hollered, "Please come back out here and put your bike in the garage!"

"A friend of Shane's, is he?" Tom repeated, obviously unconvinced. He didn't bother to wait for Bonnie to return to her chair before he resumed his own seat. "I'd say your taste has changed, love. A man like that, a good-looking rustic laborer—"

"Get your mind out of the gutter, Tom," Bonnie snapped, her nerves frayed. "He's an acquaintance of mine, and Shane is going to be working for him on weekends." She bit her lip to silence herself. She didn't owe Tom Schuyler any explanations.

"Shane's grown up to be quite a young man," Tom remarked in a transparent effort to mollify her by praising her son. "I remember when he was just a little baby."

Bonnie softened, her lips shaping a tender smile at the memory of Shane's infancy. Before she could descend completely into sentimentality, her gangly adolescent son came bounding out of the house, nearly knocking her over as he sprang across the porch to get his bike. "Sorry about that, Mom," he said as he wheeled the bike across the lawn to the garage, leaving a track of flattened yellow grass in his wake. "What's for supper?" he called over his shoulder from the driveway. "I'm starved."

She hadn't yet decided on what to fix but she *had* decided that she would be cooking only for two. Turning back to Tom, she offered an apologetic grin and said, "I'm afraid I can't ask you to stay, Tom. It's a school night, and..."

He regarded her for a minute, then reluctantly took his cue and stood. "I guess I'll be hitting the road, then. It was good seeing you, Bonnie."

"Good seeing you, too," she said automatically. "And congratulations, again, on getting tenure."

He shrugged, falsely modest. "So, you have no objections to my telling this McCoy fellow everything I know about Gary?"

"Of course not. Be totally honest with him. I want his book to tell the truth."

"If you say so."

"And talk to Marcie, would you? Ask her to give me a call. I'm sure she has some important insights to contribute to the book."

"I don't doubt it." Tom extended his hand to Bonnie for a farewell shake, and when she took it he pulled her toward him and gave her an unwanted but relatively painless kiss on the cheek. "Take care, Bonnie. I'll be in touch."

"Drive safely."

She watched Tom stroll down to the street, where a midnight-blue BMW was parked. He got in, revved the engine a few times and drove away.

Sagging against the railing, Bonnie shut her eyes. It was easy enough to rationalize her refusal to invite Tom to stay for dinner—he was as smug and presumptuous now as he'd been twenty years ago, when she first met him. Less easy was trying to figure out why she'd invited Paul.

It didn't matter why—he'd said no. He'd turned her down, just as she'd turned him down in the nursery. Now they were even, the score all tied up. No winners.

The sound of Shane's footsteps plodding toward the porch prompted Bonnie to open her eyes and straighten up. He vaulted up onto the porch and swung into the house. "Come on, Mom," he demanded. "I'm hungry. Let's get something to eat!"

She caught the screen door before it closed and followed Shane inside. On her way to the kitchen, she glimpsed the mantel full of photos and hesitated. Tom hadn't changed much at all, she realized as she lifted one of the pictures with him in it and studied it closely. His hair was shorter and his attire neater, but his smile and that begging-for-love look in his eyes were exactly the same. He'd been such a good friend to Gary, she really ought to view him more kindly... but while Gary had trusted him, Bonnie had never been able to share his trust completely.

Setting that photograph down, she lifted the one of her, Gary and Shane as an infant. Tom was right about that, at least—Shane *was* turning into a young man. It was hard to believe he'd once been so small. It was almost as hard to believe that she and Gary had once been so deeply in love, so interdependent, so very much a part of each other's lives, a family. To this day, she was still shocked by the realization that, given how deeply in love they'd been, she had managed to survive without him.

"YOU'RE LATE," she said.

Gary closed the door and locked it, then set down his briefcase and loosened his tie. He looked exhausted—as well he should, since it was close to midnight and he'd only just arrived home from the seven o'clock lecture he'd given at Brown University. He dropped his coat on the back of a chair; Bonnie picked it up and hung it in the closet for him. Then he pulled off his shoes, tossed them across the braided rug and collapsed on the couch.

"How did it go?" she asked, shutting the closet door and then crossing the room to him.

"You want to know the truth?" He shoved his hair out of his eyes and sighed with exhaustion. "These are supposed to be bright kids, aware of what's going on in the world. They treated me like I was a relic from prehistoric times. Their ignorance about what happened in this country just five and six years ago is frightening. The questions they asked—and didn't ask—indicated that they believe everything is hunky-dory now that we're out of Vietnam and Nixon's out of the White House."

"They're young," Bonnie reminded him. "They're in college to learn. You should be glad they invite people like you to come and speak on campus. Obviously, they want to learn."

"Given the option, I'm sure half of them would rather have been at some disco somewhere." Gary leaned back *into the cushions and closed his eyes. "Any chance I can get a back rub out of you? I'm bushed."*

Bonnie pressed her lips together. Perhaps he'd just endured an hour-long drive late at night, after delivering a lecture to a restless audience, but she'd had her own rough night. She sat next to him on the couch and leaned her head against his shoulder. *"I'm not feeling too hot myself,"* she said apologetically.

He opened his eyes and squinted at her. *"You look awful."*

Simply hearing how lousy she looked made her feel worse. Her stomach clenched, and she rose on wobbly legs and headed back to the bathroom. Inside, she knelt on the cold tile floor next to the toilet, praying for the feeling to pass but positioning herself to be prepared if it didn't. Her stomach clenched again, and again. Her head throbbed.

She had hoped that Gary would follow her. This was his baby as much as hers, yet she was the only one suffering. She wanted to sympathize with him over his disappointing evening, but she wanted him to sympathize with her, too. She'd been nauseated nonstop for three months. Didn't she deserve a back rub?

What was she thinking? The nausea would pass. According to the doctor, both she and the baby were in excellent health and progressing normally. Let Gary worry about making the world safe for his child; Bonnie could suffer her constant bouts of queasiness without complaint.

Fatigued, she drew her knees up to her chest and leaned back so her shoulders rested against the wall. Beads of sweat formed across her forehead; her mouth tasted funny. She wanted this baby, she wanted it so much. There were things far worse than morning sickness.

"Oh, there you are. I was wondering where you'd disappeared to," Gary said. *Gradually her eyes came into focus on her husband, who loitered in the bathroom doorway.* *"Are you okay?"*

"I'm fine," she said weakly.

"Did Tom call while I was out? He was supposed to have gotten word on our application for a permit to demonstrate down at the naval base in New London next month, when that new nuclear sub is scheduled for launch."

"He didn't call."

Gary shrugged. *"I'll try him in the morning."* *He gazed down at Bonnie, curled up on the cold tile floor.* *"Are you sure you're all right?"*

"I'll live."

"I thought you were supposed to get morning sickness in the morning."

"You learn something new every day, Gary," she said wearily.

"Well." *He hovered in the doorway for a minute longer, then shrugged.* *"If there's nothing I can do for you, I guess I'll hit the sack. I'm really beat."*

Bonnie stared after him, her vision once again blurring. Who said there was nothing he could do for her? He could soak a washcloth in cold water and press it to her cheeks. He could cradle her in his arms. He could tell her that even though she looked awful she also looked radiant and sexy and he loved her.

But maybe he couldn't do those things for her. Not when nuclear submarines were still prowling the earth's oceans, not when more and more Third World nations were developing nuclear capability, not when billions of dollars were being spent by the military while half the world's population went to bed hungry at night.

Gary was absorbed in the big issues. Bonnie couldn't expect him to be absorbed in her petty discomforts, too. She loved him and he loved her. And soon they would have a child. How could she ask for more?

Chapter Six

The storm hit without warning. Around two o'clock in the afternoon, during a vigorous discussion of *Charlotte's Web*, the sky outside the windows of Bonnie's classroom suddenly grew inky. A clap of thunder shook the building, and then the clouds opened up.

Two of Bonnie's students shrieked, scared by the brilliant flashes of lightning and the ensuing cracks of thunder. Several raced to the windows to gape at the slashing rain. Scott Fiore, the class cutup, began reciting the old saw everyone in Massachusetts knew by heart: "If you don't like the weather, wait five minutes and it'll change."

It didn't change, though. As Bonnie made her sluggish way home two hours later, the rain continued to cascade out of the unnaturally dark sky in torrents, flooding her windshield at a faster rate than her wipers could clear it. Cars moved at a crawl; water gathered in the gutters, streamed down hills and pooled into deep puddles. Pond Road was more pond than road.

At least Shane would be home, she consoled herself as she inched along the treacherous road. He would be home, and once she joined him there she'd make them some soup, and they'd ride out this storm as they'd ridden out so many others in their lives.

She was enormously relieved when her driveway came into view. She coasted up it, got drenched in the time it took to climb out of the car and open the garage, and pulled in. After sprinting across the lawn to the porch, she shook the excess moisture out of her hair and peeled off her soggy cardigan. Stepping into the house, she shouted, "Shane? I'm home!"

Silence.

She darted to the foot of the stairs. "Shane?" she called.

Nothing.

Back in the kitchen, she read the wall clock. His school day ended fifteen minutes before hers, and she usually stayed on at the school an extra hour or more, attending to administrative chores. Even if he'd taken the bus, he should have been home by now.

Stay calm, she ordered herself. It was just a windy rain, that was all. Shane could take care of himself. He was probably on his way home right now, or wisely sitting out the storm somewhere nice and dry.

The telephone rang. Hoping that it wasn't bad news, Bonnie answered it. "Hello?"

"Bonnie? It's Janet Molson." Matt's mother. "I just wanted to let you know that Shane's here."

"Thank God!" Bonnie let out a long sigh. She really shouldn't worry so much about Shane; he wasn't a little boy anymore. "Thanks for calling me," she said. "I was beginning to wonder where he might be."

"The boys actually rode their bikes over here in the storm. Can you believe it? They could have left their bikes at school and taken the bus here, but Matt says school buses are for dweebs."

Bonnie laughed faintly. "They must have gotten soaked," she said.

"They're drying off. Shane's wearing some of Matt's old sweats. They think this storm's a gas. They want to build a fire."

"A fire? It's almost summer!" Bonnie shook her head and laughed again. Raindrops spattered from the wet ends of her hair, and she tore a square of paper towel from the roll attached to the wall and wiped it along the dripping strands.

"They're in the spirit," Janet said. "I've already made cocoa for them."

Bonnie glanced at the clock again. "Listen, Janet, would you mind terribly if I wait a little bit before picking up Shane? I'm hoping the rain might let up in a while."

"Don't worry about it. I was thinking, why doesn't he just stay here overnight? Becky's spending the night at a girlfriend's house, so we're down one kid. Shane's more than welcome to stay."

"That's very kind of you. But what about school tomorrow? He hasn't got a change of clothing."

"When was the last time our sons changed their clothes?" Janet said with a long-suffering laugh. "I'm running his clothes through the dryer right now. And he can borrow some clean underwear from Matt tomorrow morning. Really, Bonnie, it's no trouble. Anyway, this storm's supposed to last well into the night."

"No kidding?"

"That's what they said on channel four. We're getting the tail end of that freak tornado system that tore through Ohio a couple of days ago. There's no need for you to go out in this weather. Relax. Take the night off."

"Thanks." Bonnie slumped against the counter and tossed aside the soggy paper towel. "I appreciate it, Janet."

"No problem. To tell the truth, Bonnie, Shane's a lot easier to deal with than Becky. I'll take a fourteen-year-old boy over a twelve-year-old girl any day."

"Shame, shame," Bonnie teased. "You were a twelve-year-old girl yourself, Janet."

"And I was horrible. My mother warned me I'd get my payback someday. Oops—the dryer's buzzing. Gotta run."

"Thanks again," Bonnie said before bidding Janet goodbye and hanging up. She eyed the soggy wad of paper towel on the counter, and then her equally soggy skirt and blouse. Shoving away from the counter, she went upstairs to change her clothes.

At one time in her life, she had hated spending time at home alone. The silence had been too keen a reminder of Gary's absence; the shadows and echoes had seemed to mock her, magnifying her loneliness. But she'd grown stronger over the years, and she'd come to appreciate those rare occasions when she had the place all to herself. Now that she knew Shane was safe, she found herself relishing the prospect of a tranquil evening of solitude. The constant clatter of the rain on the roof took on a soothing quality, and by the time she pulled on jeans and a sweater she was relishing the coziness of being indoors on such a ghastly afternoon.

She gazed out her window at the watery vista. The front lawn was already flooded, the parched yellowish strands of grass floating in dark, swampy puddles. Scores of leaves and several small branches torn from nearby trees were strewn across the road, and an empty trash can had come to rest on its side at the edge of the driveway across the street from hers. The tulips in her flower beds sagged under the weight of the rainwater collecting within their bowl-shaped petals; their season was pretty well spent, and Bonnie didn't hold out much hope of their surviving this storm.

Turning from the window, she sighed and crossed to her dresser to get her hairbrush. She ran it through her damp hair a few times, then scowled. Something besides the scattered tree branches and the drooping tulips was amiss outside. Tossing down her brush, she hastened back to the window and peered out, squinting to see the yard through the sheets of rain.

The birch tree. Its white bark starkly visible in the gloom, it leaned precariously toward the ground, its slender trunk straining, its pale green leaves fluttering raggedly in the wind.

She sped down the stairs and threw on her raincoat. Yanking open the front door, she charged out onto the porch and gaped at the glistening layer of water spreading across her lawn from the evergreen hedge to the driveway. With so much moisture accumulating in the grass, the soil must have become dangerously muddy, leaving the birch's roots nothing firm to cling to.

Her beautiful new birch tree. Seeing it quake pathetically in a rainy gust, Bonnie did something she hadn't let herself do when she'd discovered Shane missing: she panicked.

She hurried inside to fetch an umbrella, then forged back out into the storm. Her sneakers quickly became saturated as she sloshed across the yard to the tree. She gave the trunk a cautious shake and felt the give in it.

The umbrella slipped, and she let it drop. She could survive a soaking, but the birch tree might not. She touched it again and a small cry escaped her as she acknowledged how wobbly it was. Not until a gale caught her umbrella and flung it across the yard did she let go of the tree.

She raced after the umbrella and caught it, then tramped through the spongy lawn, ignoring the branches in her way, the collapsing tulips and daffodils, the mat of azalea petals carpeting the earth beneath the shrubs. Once she was back under the protective overhang above the porch, she shook out the umbrella and turned back to stare at her tree. "Stand!" she shouted, her voice barely carrying through the storm's cacophony. "Stay standing!" As if the tree were Shane, as if a good maternal scolding would be enough to get it straight.

She tried to ignore the fear gnawing at her as another strong gust of wind tugged at the poor birch and caused it to quiver. She couldn't just wring her hands and wait for it to fall over. But she had no idea how to go about protecting it from the weather's ravages. She had to do something. She would never forgive herself if it died.

Pushing her drenched hair back from her face, she stalked inside and into the kitchen, where she kept the telephone book. Paul was an expert when it came to landscaping; he would tell her how to save her tree. Much as she hated having to turn to him for assistance—especially after their last encounter—she wasn't going to risk losing her precious tree on a matter of pride.

He answered after the third ring. "Tremaine Nursery, Paul Tremaine speaking."

"This is Bonnie Hudson," she said in a level voice. "I'm calling about the birch tree."

He didn't speak for a minute. "What about it?" he finally asked.

"Well, this storm has flooded the front yard, and the tree is rocking back and forth." The words came faster as her anxiety rose to the surface. "I'm afraid it's going to fall over, and if it does, it's going to die. I don't want it to die, Paul. It's such a beautiful tree, and I don't know what to do—"

"Calm down," he said quietly. "I promise you, the tree won't die."

Bonnie clamped her mouth shut to silence her babbling. She hadn't intended to let Paul know how distraught she was.

"It hasn't fallen over yet, has it?" he asked.

"No, but—"

"I tell you what," he went on. "I can leave here in about a half hour. I'll drive over and stake the tree for you. All right?"

She took a deep breath. "What should I do in the meantime?"

He chuckled. "You can either stand outside holding the damned thing upright, or you can stay warm and dry inside and pray for the wind to die down. I'd take the prayer route, myself. This storm's no joke."

She was grateful to him for making light of her alarm, and for not embarrassing her by alluding to anything personal between them. "I'll pray," she decided, matching his casual tone.

"I'll be there as soon as I can," he said before hanging up.

Bonnie lowered the receiver and returned to the living room. The sky had grown even more foreboding with the approach of evening. The tree shuddered in every breeze, teetering at dire angles.

She had never suffered such despair over the ill-fated dogwood tree. During the three years she and Shane had lived in this house the dogwood had deteriorated until it was finally, irrevocably dead, and she hadn't experi-

enced the merest bit of sorrow over its demise. As for her
flowers—she'd planted the bulbs herself, and weeded the
beds when Shane neglected to, which was most of the
time. She liked pretty plantings. She'd missed not having a yard during all the years she lived in Cambridge,
and she was glad to have one now.

Yet she wouldn't despair if the flowers drowned, if the
lawn was washed away. All that mattered was the birch
tree. It meant more to her; it was a present from Shane.
He'd bought it with his own money....

Actually, he hadn't quite bought it. The tree techni-
cally still belonged to Paul. Paul had delivered it, dug a
hole for it, molded the soil around its base with his hands.
When she gazed through the rain at the birch she thought
not only of Shane's extraordinary effort to make amends
for having hitchhiked but of Paul's exertion in planting
the tree, his strength and grace when he'd planted it, his
kindness toward her son.

His kiss.

She stood by the window, holding a kind of vigil,
watching as the wind tormented the tree, as the rain de-
luged the yard and transformed it into a sea of mud. She
prayed for the tree, prayed for the rain to let up, prayed
for Paul to arrive. She hated being dependent on him—
but she was depending on him for the tree's sake, not her
own.

After what seemed like an eternity, she saw two white
beams cutting through the rain, the headlights of a truck
turning onto her street from Pond Road. If she'd bothered to think about it, she would have been astonished by
the overwhelming elation she felt at Paul's arrival.
Grabbing her dripping raincoat from the newel post, she
slung her arms through the sleeves and hastened out onto
the porch. She didn't bother with the umbrella, but sim-

ply sprinted across the yard to greet Paul as he rolled to a stop in her driveway. She darted around the front bumper and swung open his door.

"Thank you," she shouted above the din of the rain hammering onto the gravel. "Thank you for coming."

He pulled on a lightweight nylon jacket and climbed out of the cab. "We guarantee our work," he said. "I should've staked the tree when I planted it. I never expected we'd have a storm like this."

"Obviously," Bonnie muttered, frowning at his inadequate jacket. "Would you like me to get the umbrella?"

Sauntering to the back of the truck, seemingly oblivious of the rain as it soaked his dark hair and shoulders, he shook his head. "If you want to help, I'd rather you use your hands for something more important than holding an umbrella." He pulled three pointed stakes from the truck bed, and then some wire and rubber slings. He carried them over to the tree, laid them down, gripped the tree with both hands and yanked it upright with a single powerful jerk. "Think you can hold it steady?" he asked.

She clasped the trunk, which was slippery from the rain, and held it tight. Paul set to work driving one of the stakes into the mushy earth near the base of the tree.

It was too noisy for them to speak, so they didn't. They simply worked together, communicating with hand gestures and nods. Holding the tree erect didn't require too much concentration, and Bonnie was able to observe Paul while he worked. The rain pulled down on his hair, straightening the waves, and it glued the denim of his dungarees to his thighs. Except for an occasional wipe of his hand over his eyes he ignored the downpour, his focus solely on the tasks of securing the stakes and then looping the slings around the tree. Once all three stakes were in place, he gestured to Bonnie to let go of the trunk and then gave the tree a shake to test it. Nodding in satisfaction, he turned to her.

"Thank you," she said, tasting the raindrops on her lips.

He shrugged. "I should have done it right the first time."

Their eyes met. Water skittered down his cheeks and neck and dripped onto his shoulders from the ends of his hair. Bonnie supposed that she must look like a drowned cat. Even so, she was happy to be here with Paul, helping him. No matter what his nursery's guarantees were, no matter that he'd rejected her after she'd entertained second thoughts about having rejected him, no matter that their relationship was doomed for too many reasons, his having come here during a storm to save her tree was uncommonly thoughtful.

"Would you like to come inside and dry off?" she asked, hoping that he wouldn't interpret the invitation as anything more than a friendly gesture.

He glanced over his shoulder at the house, its windows filled with beckoning amber light. Then he turned back to her. His expression was enigmatic. "It's kind of late. I should be getting home."

If she didn't want him to misinterpret her invitation, she couldn't misinterpret his refusal. It *was* late, and he had every right to want to be home by now. "Well, thanks again," she said. "I would have been miserable if anything had happened to the tree."

"It'll be fine," he assured her, giving the trunk a final testing push to make sure it was solid. Then he plodded across the waterlogged lawn to his truck.

"Drive carefully," she called to him.

He responded with a wistful smile, then climbed in and started the engine. The headlights illuminated Bonnie as she stood in the driveway, watching him back down to the street and drive away.

IF ONLY SHE HADN'T LOOKED so lovely, he would have gone inside with her. If only her hair hadn't looked so sleek and slippery in the rain, and her long lashes hadn't been beaded with pearllike droplets of water, and her lips hadn't looked so invitingly moist, he would have done it. He felt clammy and uncomfortable, and the air had cooled enough to impart a chill to his muscles. He wanted desperately to dry off and thaw out.

But not in Bonnie's house. Not when he still desired her so much.

He switched to his high beams as his truck approached the first shadowy obstruction on the road. He shouldn't have taken Pond Road, but he'd steered onto it reflexively, his mind on Bonnie rather than on the route he was taking home. He couldn't stop thinking about how genuinely upset she had been over the fate of a tree. A tree! Paul worked with trees—he knew exactly how much they were worth and how far one should go to rescue them from the elements. He liked domestic plantings but he had no emotional attachment to them. He viewed them as any professional would.

Bonnie had viewed the birch tree as an owner, though—more than an owner. When she'd telephoned him at the nursery, she'd tried gamely, but without much success, to hide the distress in her voice. And when she'd raced out of the house to greet him before he'd even had a chance to turn off the engine, he'd understood how profoundly attached she was to the tree.

If he were a fool, he'd believe she was attached to it because of his connection to it. He'd believe that when she'd curled her slender fingers around the bark, the tree had stood in for him, that when she'd held it so firmly she was vicariously holding him. He'd believe that the tree meant more to her than it ought to, just as it meant more to him than it ought to, because it was something that bound them together.

But he wasn't a fool, so instead of going inside with her, he'd taken his leave.

The truck bounced over a fallen branch, then dunked into a murky puddle, the wheels spraying brown water to either side. He struggled to dismiss Bonnie from his mind and devote his full attention to navigating this hostile stretch of road. But as the headlights of a car traveling the opposite direction cut through his windshield, he found himself thinking of Bonnie's clear eyes, so bright and dazzling in the dim light. He found himself remembering the way her lids had grown heavy when he'd kissed her two days ago at the nursery, the way her arms had closed around him....

And then he heard a *thonk*! The truck veered wildly to the right, then slid to the left, as if it were totally divorced from the steering wheel. He fought it, swearing as it veered toward the right shoulder once more. The other car careered past him, and he detected the rhythmic bumping and shaking of a blowout.

Muttering an oath, he shifted into neutral, tugged on the parking brake and emerged from the truck. His right front tire was flat.

He would have to change it here in the rain, in the dark. He would put on the spare and go home, treat himself to a long, hot shower and then a stiff drink. He would forget about Bonnie's eyes, her invitation, the warm, dry haven of her house. He would forget about the way her hands had looked as she curved them around the smooth bark of the tree.

At the rear of the truck he unhooked the tailgate, lowered it and straightened up just as another car came along the road, jostling around the rocks and ruts and hitting a deep puddle not far from Paul. A tidal wave of murky water surged up at him, hitting him dead-on.

The hell with it all. He didn't want to forget about Bonnie. He wanted to get in out of the storm—and he wanted to be with her.

Chapter Seven

"Can I come in?" he asked.

It had taken her several minutes to answer his knock, during which time he'd considered hiking back to the tree-sheltered stretch of gravel at the side of Pond Road where he'd abandoned the truck. He had intended to drive all the way back to her house, but the shimmying of the steering wheel and his concern about destroying the tire's rim had given him second thoughts, so he'd parked the truck safely out of the path of traffic and left it, confident that nobody was going to steal an undrivable vehicle with Tremaine Nursery painted across the doors in bold letters.

He assumed she would let him inside for a few minutes. She had invited him in earlier, after all, and he hadn't been gone long enough for her to change her mind. Even so, the way she inspected him in the glow of the porch light, the way she ran her gaze down his drenched body and then back up again to his face, gave him pause. It dawned on him that he looked wretched.

"Of course you can come in," she finally said, holding the door open for him. "Do me a favor and take off your shoes by the door. I'll go get you a towel."

Stepping across the threshold, he relaxed. Her words were just right—friendly, considerate but completely devoid of intense emotion. At that moment, as soggy and disheveled as he was, he was relieved that she was offering him nothing more complicated than the opportunity to dry off.

She vanished from the living room, leaving him to unlace his work boots and remove them. He remained by the front door, watching as the hems of his dungarees dripped water onto the hardwood floor at his feet. He took some small pleasure in the fact that his short walk through the rain had helped to wash most of the mud from his trousers.

He was removing his jacket when she returned with two thick bath towels. She started to hand them to him, then thought better of it. "Follow me," she said, beckoning him through the kitchen and into the bathroom. "Why don't you take off your things? I can throw them into the dryer."

"Bonnie—"

"Your pants are soaked."

That was the truth. His shirt wasn't too wet, thanks to the jacket, and his boots had kept his socks reasonably dry. But his jeans were saturated, chilling his whole body.

Still, he wasn't too keen on getting undressed in Bonnie's house.

"Come on," she chided him. "Ten minutes in the dryer and they'll be dry. You can wait in the bathroom." She balanced the towels on the edge of the sink and eyed him remonstratively.

The shiver that rippled through his flesh convinced him. "All right," he said, closing the door. He quickly peeled off his jeans and emptied the pockets, then edged the door open a crack, passed the jeans out to her and shut the door again.

He wrapped one towel around his cold legs. Then he tackled his hair, rubbing the other towel over the limp waves. The towels had a fresh scent that reminded him of the laundry detergent his mother used to use when he was growing up. That seemed appropriate, because at the moment Bonnie's attitude resembled nothing so much as that of a fussing mother.

"What happened to you?" she called through the closed door after a minute. "You weren't this wet when you left."

"I had a blowout on Pond Road," He glanced around the small room, then lowered the lid on the toilet and sat. The aching in his legs began to wane, and he smiled at the thought of donning his jeans warm and fresh from the dryer. "Thanks," he said quietly.

"What?"

He envisioned her standing outside the door, perhaps leaning against the wall, her graceful arms folded across her chest and her hair cascading down her back. Despite his being partly undressed, he sensed nothing particularly erotic in his situation. It wasn't just that a door separated him from her, but that her mood was so downright sensible, so calm and maternal. His doubts about whether to come here for shelter had been unnecessary. He and Bonnie could manage this.

"I said, thank you," he repeated, aiming his voice at the door. "I'm finally beginning to thaw out."

"What on earth possessed you to take Pond Road on a night like this?" she called to him.

"I thought I could handle it."

She clicked her tongue in disapproval, but he could hear the humor lacing her voice when she said, "You and

Shane with your flat tires. It's no wonder you two hit it off.''

"Where is Shane, anyway?" he asked.

"Spending the night at his friend Matt's house," Bonnie reported. "I was just fixing some dinner for myself. Why don't you join me?"

He closed his eyes and conjured a mental picture of her again, first as he imagined her standing outside the bathroom door and then as she'd looked when she helped him with the birch tree. He recalled the anxiety in her eyes when he'd arrived to salvage the tree, the sheer dread that had touched him deeply, even though he'd found it excessive. And then the joy that had brightened her face when he finally had the stakes in place and the tree adequately propped. He'd thought then that the tree meant more to her than he did—and yet now she was taking care of him, drying his clothing and feeding him, rescuing him from the storm as he'd rescued her tree.

The last time he'd eaten dinner with her, he had discovered how much he desired her—and afterward, how committed she still was to her deceased husband and his militant antiwar philosophy. Paul didn't want to spend another evening feeling attracted to her and then listening to her run at the mouth about how amazing and incredible her one true love had been.

But what were the alternatives? To say "thanks for the towels" and then head back out into the storm? To say "you go ahead and eat" and sit by himself in the living room, where he could stare at all the photographs she kept on display of Mr. Wonderful and his fellow rebels? He was in no mood to deal with his flat tire, especially when the storm showed no signs of letting up.

"Are you sure you don't mind my staying?" he pressed her.

"If I minded, I wouldn't have asked. Maybe by the time we're done eating the rain will have let up and you'll be able to change your tire without drowning."

He meditated for a moment longer. It sounded relatively uncomplicated. "What are you serving?" he asked.

She laughed, apparently interpreting his question as an acceptance. "I'm having what Shane would call a lady dinner—soup and salad. But I could fix you something a little heartier if you'd like."

"Soup and salad sound great."

"Fine. I'll turn up the heat under the pot and then go check your pants."

He listened to her receding footsteps and then to the constant rush of rain against the bathroom's tiny window. Standing, he pulled back the curtain and peeked out at the rear yard. The sky was leaden and moonless, the rain unrelenting.

Like the monsoons in Nam, he thought, then shuddered and let the curtain drop back into place. The fabric featured a pattern of dark blue eight-pointed stars against a beige background. There was nothing frilly or feminine about the curtains—or about Bonnie's house in general. Yet the atmosphere was warm and safe, a world away from the battering storms of Vietnam.

He heard a light rap on the door, and then Bonnie's voice. "Paul? Your jeans are dry."

"Thanks." He reached around the door to take them, and quickly put them on. They were slightly stiff and toasty. As soon as he had his wallet, keys and change back in his pockets, he emerged from the bathroom.

He found her standing at the stove in the kitchen, adjusting the heat under a pot of soup. "Help yourself to a beer if you'd like one," she suggested. "I've got some in the fridge."

Bless her for offering. "Do you want me to get you one, too?" he asked as he opened the refrigerator door.

She shook her head. "I can't tolerate alcohol after a day at work," she explained, lifting the lid of the pot and releasing a cloud of aromatic steam into the air. She gave the soup a stir, then turned off the burner and pulled a couple of bowls from a shelf. "I'm usually so pooped, a few sips of beer would knock me out cold."

"Is it really that hard teaching kids?" he asked, genuinely interested.

She served up two portions of chicken-and-vegetable soup, then brought plates and an assortment of salad dressings to the table. After filling a glass with water for herself, she took her seat across from Paul. "It's unbelievably tiring," she told him. "Especially at this time of year, when they're suffering from spring fever and they can't sit still or concentrate."

"What grade do you teach?"

"Fourth."

"What made you decide to become a teacher?" Paul asked as he doused his salad with French dressing. "Were you one of those creepy little girls who always liked to play school?"

She laughed at the image. "When I was a little girl I wanted to be the first woman on the Supreme Court. Thank goodness we didn't have to wait that long for a woman to achieve the honor, but that was my goal: to be a lawyer and then a judge."

A judge? He would never have figured Bonnie for that. But then, when he was a little boy he'd wanted to grow up to play center for the Boston Bruins. Children were entitled to dream big. "So, how do you get from Supreme Court Justice to fourth-grade schoolteacher?" he asked.

She ate some salad and grinned. "When I grew up and started realizing what a mess the world was in, I decided that the best way to improve things was to get to the children while they were still young. If enough children were taught the value of peace over war, and of negotiation and compromise over ego and intransigence... If I could influence them to choose life over death and destruction, maybe when they grew up they'd be in a position to undo some of the damage our society has done and make the earth a better place. I'm sorry," she said, abruptly cutting herself off. "I didn't mean to sound off like that."

Paul understood that she was as eager as he was to avoid an argument tonight. Of course, he couldn't really find much to dispute in what she'd said. What sane person didn't think life was better than death? Her views seemed pretty naive, but he wouldn't point that out to her, not when she'd apologized for preaching at him.

"This soup is delicious," he remarked, partly to let her know she was forgiven and partly because it was the truth. "Tell Shane to stop making fun of your cooking."

"You tell him," she shot back, then chuckled. "Soup and spaghetti I can do. Anything more challenging than that, and I'm a disaster."

Paul leaned back in his chair, sipping his beer and scrutinizing her. "I would have expected you to be a great cook. You seem like kind of an earth-mother type, with all that long hair and your being a teacher and all. I'd expect someone like you to bake bread and homemade cookies and put up your own preserves."

She accepted his observation with a modest chuckle. "I always pictured myself as an earth-mother type, too," she confessed. "That is, once I got over my Supreme Court phase. I wanted to be the ultimate nurturer, in tune with the cosmos, living on a commune somewhere, cooking all sorts of wholesome feasts and raising a tribe of children. Unfortunately, nobody in their right mind would want to eat any feasts I prepared. And it doesn't look as if I'll be raising a tribe of children, either."

Paul noticed the pensiveness creeping into her expression. For a moment, he found himself resenting her late husband not because of the guy's politics but simply because with his death he'd destroyed Bonnie's dream. "Well," he pointed out logically, "if you'd had lots of children you probably wouldn't have been able to become a teacher."

"If I'd had lots of children of my own, I probably wouldn't have felt such a strong urge to work with other people's children," she countered, shaping a bittersweet smile. After a minute of contemplation she brightened. "Not that I'm complaining. I've got Shane. He's the best thing that ever happened to me."

Paul digested the implication underlying her statement—that her marriage *hadn't* been the best thing that ever happened to her—but didn't comment on it. "It must have been tough raising Shane all by yourself," he said.

"I didn't do it all by myself," she admitted. "My parents live right outside Boston, in Newton. For the first year after Gary died, we moved in with them, and they took care of Shane while I got my master's. After he and I moved back to Cambridge, my folks were still available whenever I needed help. They adore Shane."

"I don't blame them," said Paul.

Bonnie smiled. "To tell the truth, Shane and I had a lot of practice at being on our own even before Gary died. For the first two years we were married, I used to travel with Gary wherever his work took him. But then Shane came along and money was tight—to say nothing of the hassles of traveling with an infant—so he and I would stay home while Gary went on lobbying trips and speaking tours. We missed Gary, of course—and it never occurred to us that one day he'd leave on a business trip and never come back—but we always had each other. And we still do.''

Paul observed her carefully. When she'd discussed her husband in the past she had often become defensive or mawkish. Tonight, however, she seemed at peace with herself, able to talk about her loss without going to pieces. He was glad. He didn't like seeing her cry; it made him feel guilty, even though he was never conscious of doing anything in particular to provoke her tears.

Her soup bowl empty, she rose from her chair and peered out the window in the upper half of the back door. ''It's still pouring out,'' she announced, letting the curtain drop back into place. ''Can I interest you in some coffee?''

''Sure.'' He was in no hurry to get home—especially when getting home entailed changing a tire in a downpour. ''I'm sorry if I've disrupted your evening,'' he added, aware of how much of her time he'd already consumed.

''You haven't disrupted anything,'' she assured him, gathering the dishes from the table and carrying them to the sink. ''And I'm sorry I've gone on and on about myself. I must have bored you.''

''Not at all,'' he insisted, helping her to clear the table. He found a dish towel and stood next to her. The last time he'd eaten at her house he'd dried the dishes, too. It had been the ideal task, allowing him to be near her, to admire at close range her clean profile and her tall, slender body.

He was exerting himself not to notice her beauty now, not to focus on the smooth line of her throat, the tempting softness of her lips and the subtle womanly fragrance she exuded. As if she could read his mind, she buried her hands in the sudsy dishwater and said, "I'm also sorry about what happened the other day." She kept her gaze riveted to the bowl she was washing. "I just..." She scrubbed an invisible spot on the bowl with her thumb. "I think we're better off just being friends."

"Friends? Are you sure we aren't enemies?" He sent her a quick smile so she wouldn't take the question too seriously.

She handed him the bowl and pulled a salad plate from the suds. "Let's not talk about the memorial," she said.

"Okay." He dried the bowl and set it on the counter. He wouldn't push her on that subject; he was her guest, and basic courtesy demanded that he respect the limits she set. But his curiosity got the better of him. "Just tell me one thing—are you fighting the memorial for yourself or for your husband?"

She shot him a flinty look. "You might say I'm fighting for Claire Collins."

"Claire?" The police chief's wife? What did she have to do with it?

"I'd rather see the town spend money on books for the elementary school library instead of on the memorial," Bonnie explained. "But really, Paul—" she offered him a hesitant smile "—I don't think we should talk about it right now. If we do, we'll wind up arguing."

"You said you wanted us to be friends," he countered, refusing to back down. "Friends don't shy away from disagreements—although, frankly, I'm not sure

we're really in disagreement. I have no objection to Claire
Collins ordering more books for the school library. I just
don't see what that has to do with the memorial."

"It's a matter of dollars and cents," Bonnie explained, doing a respectable job of keeping her temper in
check. "The town has enough money to spend on a memorial—which means it has enough money to increase
the library budget, if it chose to. It doesn't choose to,
though. It wants to allocate all the money to a memorial
and none to new books."

Paul mulled over her charge as he wiped a handful of
silverware with the towel. Her complaint seemed reasonable, but he couldn't shake the suspicion that more than
merely the library budget lay behind her resistance.
"Suppose the town had enough money for both," he
said. "Suppose they could afford to double the library
budget and also build a memorial. You'd still object to
it, wouldn't you."

She yanked the sink stopper up and let the dishwater
drain out. Then she turned to him. "Yes," she conceded.
"I would. Not because of Gary but because of me and
what I believe in. He didn't do my thinking for me. I
hated the war long before I met him."

Paul wasn't sure what answer he'd expected or hoped
for. What Bonnie said pleased him, however. It had the
strength and conviction he had recognized in her from the
start, the independence and certainty. He could accept
the chance that his relationship with her would never develop beyond friendship a lot more easily than he could
accept the idea of her being her late husband's puppet.

He gave her a tentative smile. "I've been rude," he
apologized, "talking about this after you asked me not
to. If I were you, I'd kick me out into the rain."

She stared at him for a second longer, then broke into a grin. "That would be an act of war." She laughed, taking the dish towel from him and hanging it over a drawer knob to dry.

"Well, you ought to do something to me," he invited her as she filled two mugs with coffee. "Why don't you raise some subject I don't want to talk about?"

She glanced at him over her shoulder, then set down the coffeepot and turned to hand him a mug of coffee. "Are you divorced?"

The question threw him for a loop—not because his divorce was a particularly painful subject but because he was completely unprepared for Bonnie to question him about it. He took a long sip of coffee to buy himself time to recover, then lowered the mug and nodded. "Why do you ask?"

"Well...I was just wondering why you aren't married."

He chuckled. "I find myself wondering the same thing about you. Although I suppose we're coming from two different places. I'm not still carrying a torch for my ex."

Bonnie opened her mouth to protest his assertion, then pursed her lips. Evidently she was aware that he'd meant his comment not as an insult but simply as an acknowledgment of her deep feelings for her husband.

"So, why haven't you remarried?" she asked once they'd both resumed their seats at the table.

From anyone else he'd resent the question. From another pretty single woman he would assume he was being stalked, and from other people—his parents, for instance—he'd assume he was being reproached. But he honestly didn't mind Bonnie asking him. They seemed to be handling the sticky subjects rather nicely, and he was

willing to keep at it, to see how far they could go. "I guess
I haven't found the right woman," he answered.

"How could you possibly find anyone?" Bonnie
challenged him, her pointed words softened by her smile.
"You hardly ever date."

He considered questioning her on her source, then decided not to. That Bonnie had taken enough interest in
him to investigate his social life was flattering. "The last
time I asked a woman out," he returned, mirroring her
smile, "I practically got slapped in the face."

"I would never slap you, Paul. I don't believe in violence, remember?"

He laughed.

She joined his laughter for a second, then grew serious. "I'm not the only single woman in town. I'm sure
you could find someone better suited to you, if you
tried."

"I'm not trying that hard," he said, then drank some
coffee. Talking to her this way, intimately but without
pressure, without worrying about the impression he was
making, was as pleasant as kissing her. Even more pleasant, he thought, because he understood that no matter
what he said she wouldn't push him away.

"It's difficult dating in a place like Northford," he
explained, running his finger thoughtfully over the
rounded handle of his mug. "You haven't lived here that
long—and I guess you're not really into dating, so maybe
you wouldn't be aware of the problems. But in a small
town, it's not just that there isn't a huge variety of available women to choose from, but everybody knows
everybody's business. I never told you I was divorced,
but you knew I was. I don't think I ever told anyone in
Northford I was divorced, but everyone knows. If I dated
a local woman and then we broke up, chances are I'd

alienate half the town. People would drive over to the nursery just to give me grief about it—or else people would want to know whether we'd slept together or whatever. It's all so public.''

"I'm glad you've warned me," Bonnie said with a laugh. "Now I *definitely* won't go out with you."

Paul laughed, too. "I date women in other towns," he said. "It's a lot less tricky."

"But you aren't trying that hard," she reminded him.

He shrugged. "I didn't make a very good husband my first time around."

"Oh?"

She looked not condemning but sympathetic, and he found it easy to confide in her. "I went through the motions," he said. "I got a college degree, I took a desk job with a fancy title, I bought a nice overpriced house in the suburbs. I was faithful to my wife. We owned a cat and two Toyotas. But it never felt right to me."

Bonnie absorbed his words. "Of course it never felt right. Anyone could see you're a dog person, Paul."

He grinned, impressed by her insight and grateful for her ability to leaven the conversation with humor. He'd never really warmed up to the cat the way Kathy had. Nor had he warmed up to Kathy's approach to life. She used to close herself off whenever he wanted to tell her about what had happened in Nam, or whenever he awakened in the middle of the night, sweating and shivering. "It's not healthy to dwell in the past, Paul," she used to chide him. "Put it away. Forget about it."

"If I were ever to get married again," he said quietly, "it would have to be with a woman who could take me as I am. I could never bottle myself up the way I did in my first marriage. My wife would have to take all of me...and that's probably asking too much of any woman.'' He realized he was straying into areas best left untouched, and he silenced himself with a long drink of coffee.

Bonnie looked much too intrigued, and he braced himself for the possibility that she'd ask him exactly what ''all of him'' meant. But before she could speak the telephone rang. ''Excuse me,'' she said, rising and crossing to the wall phone. She lifted the receiver. ''Hello? Oh, hi, Kevin.''

Kevin. A boyfriend, maybe? Or one of her husband's old Cambridge Manifesto pals?

Paul lifted his mug and went into the living room to afford her some privacy. He stared past the star-shaped crystal at the front yard. Night had fallen, heavy and moonless, but the light from the porch illuminated the continuing rain. Parts of Pond Road would likely be washed out if it didn't stop soon.

Well, sooner or later the storm would have to blow out to sea. If it didn't, he'd kiss the truck goodbye and start building an ark.

Sighing, he turned from the window. His gaze took in the photographs on the mantel and he regarded them thoughtfully. He didn't feel animosity anymore toward the long-haired pacifist featured in the photos. The poor guy was dead, after all, and his widow no longer struck Paul as a potential lover. He still found her beautiful, intelligent and generous, but right now he was content to think of her as a friend and nothing more. If he'd been planning to seduce her, he would never have been able to relax so completely with her.

Her voice drifted out to him through the open doorway. ''I don't understand, Kevin. I talked to Tom Schuyler myself on Monday, and he never said anything about that.... Have you checked with the police out there? That was where he died, and I'm sure their records—''

She was silent for a long time. Paul inferred that she was discussing her husband's death. She didn't sound upset, but that could change. If it did, he'd console her. He wouldn't say anything negative about Gary.

"Talk to Marcie, anyway," Bonnie said into the phone. "I have no reason to believe she'd lie. I know she admired Gary. She'd want to be included in the book.... Well, I haven't spoken with her, but Tom may have. He has her number.... Yes. I want the truth in this book. Gary would have wanted it that way.... All right, Kevin. Thanks for calling. Keep in touch."

Paul heard the phone being placed in its cradle, and then nothing but the sound of the rain hammering down onto the porch steps. He considered returning to the kitchen but opted to stay where he was. When Bonnie was ready to be sociable, she'd let him know.

After several minutes she appeared in the doorway. "Sorry about that," she said, offering him a pathetic smile.

Her eyes, he noticed, weren't smiling at all. They were glassy and unfocused, darting anxiously about the room. Her complexion was ashen, and he wondered whether he ought to question her about what her caller had said to upset her. Instead, he glanced toward the kitchen and asked, "Is everything okay?"

"Of course," she said automatically, making another feeble attempt to smile. "That was Kevin McCoy—the *Globe* reporter who's writing the book about Gary. I think you met him the first time you were over here."

Paul recalled the red-bearded young man standing on her porch the afternoon he'd picked up Shane and driven him home. "We weren't formally introduced," he said.

She shoved her hands into the pockets of her jeans. "He's spent a lot of time here during the past few months, interviewing me and collecting memorabilia. Now he's begun talking to some of Gary's associates." She gazed past him to stare at the crystal star and lapsed into a brooding silence.

"What happened?" he finally asked, thinking she'd feel better if she talked out what was troubling her. "Did one of Gary's associates tell this reporter something you didn't want him to know?"

Bonnie flashed him a desolate look, and then she shrugged. "I'm sure it's nothing, really...." Her voice faded and she ran her hands across her eyes. "I'm not going to cry," she promised when Paul took a step toward her.

He kept approaching. "I don't mind if you do," he said, taking her by the elbow and gently leading her to the sofa. He sat beside her, turning to face her, and held her hands in his. "It must be painful, dredging up all those memories."

Bonnie was clearly struggling against the urge to weep. To her credit, she was succeeding. She blinked several times, ignoring the few tears that skittered down her cheeks, and let her hands relax within Paul's. "It's just..." She took a deep breath and gave Paul a limp, heartbreaking smile. "Well, it's just that Kevin talked to the police officer who filed the report on the hit-and-run accident that killed Gary. According to him, the odds are Gary wasn't murdered by some right-wing maniac who didn't like the speech he'd given on campus."

All right. So her husband's death had been a little less sinister than she'd thought. Paul didn't see what the big deal was. "If it was a hit-and-run, how would they know one way or the other who did it?"

Bonnie lowered her gaze to her hands, tucked snugly within his. He felt her fingers tensing against his palms and he gave them a reassuring squeeze. "I don't know," she said, shaking her head. "Marcie Bradley—she was another of the original people from the Cambridge Manifesto. Anyway, she was there that night, too. She swore that the accident occurred right by the campus, and she was positive that she recognized the driver as one of the hecklers. That was what she told me when she called from the hospital. And when I talked to Tom Schuyler, he confirmed everything Marcie had said: that the accident had occurred right by the campus, that the driver had come tearing out of the parking lot next to the auditorium where Gary had spoken, that the driver had deliberately aimed at Gary and run him down, and he'd shouted something nasty out the window as he drove off...."

"And the police have a different version?"

She blinked back a few more tears. "Kevin told me just now that according to police records, the accident happened outside the motel where they were spending the night. Apparently Gary and Marcie were walking back to the motel from somewhere—it couldn't have been from the campus, because the motel was over a mile away and they'd rented a car. The driver came out of the parking lot of a neighborhood bar, so he'd probably been drinking." Her voice started to crack.

"Hey," Paul said, pulling her into a gentle hug. She seemed so fragile, so close to shattering. "It's all right," he whispered, stroking her hair. "What happened to him was horrible. The details don't really matter."

"But here's the strangest part," she said, drawing back once she'd regained her composure. "The police said Tom wasn't at the scene at all. Marcie was the only witness. Tom told me he was there, and Marcie said he was there, too. Why would they have lied about that?''

Paul shrugged. ''I'm sure there's a simple explanation.'' At her dubious frown, he elaborated. ''Maybe he was in the vicinity, close enough to the accident to see but not right at the spot where it occurred.''

''If he was close enough to see he would have been named as a witness by the police.''

Paul puzzled it through. It bothered him to think anyone—even a couple of hippie radicals—would lie to Bonnie, so he scrambled to find a way to prove they hadn't. ''Maybe Tom was there but refused to give his name as an official witness. That kind of thing happens all the time. People don't want their names going down in a police file.''

''Tom would have loved having his name in a police file,'' Bonnie argued. ''He loved notoriety. And besides, Gary was his best friend. He would have insisted on being a part of the report if he'd been there.''

''All right,'' Paul conceded. ''Maybe he wasn't there. Maybe he lied and told you he was because he had something to hide.''

Bonnie's eyes widened in astonishment. ''I hadn't thought of that.'' She considered, nodding, shaping a bitter smile. ''Sure, that must have been it. He was probably off somewhere, trying to score with a girl from the college or something. Though I don't know why he'd want to hide that from me. I've known for years that he's a womanizer. In fact, he always seemed kind of proud of his reputation as a stud. He was always bragging about his conquests.''

''Then maybe he was hiding something else,'' Paul proposed. ''It doesn't really matter, though, Bonnie.

What happened happened. You lost your husband. The details don't change that; they don't change who he was."

"You're right," Bonnie said, giving Paul her first real smile since she'd gotten off the phone. She wove her fingers through his and tightened them, then released him. "Thank you, Paul. I'm glad you were here when that call came. The possibility that Marcie and Tom would have lied to me about Gary's death...it threw me for a loop."

"No problem." He, too, was glad he'd been there to offer his support. He imagined that Bonnie didn't lean on others very often. But if she did need a shoulder to lean on, he was pleased to have been able to provide her with one.

She went to the window. "It's still raining hard."

He joined her and gazed out. "So it is."

"Maybe we should try to catch a weather report."

"Okay."

He followed her into the den and settled himself on the sofa while she turned on the television. "Take notes," she ordered him, gesturing toward the television, "and I'll get us some more coffee."

He put his feet up on the coffee table and sank cozily into the overstuffed upholstery. He couldn't keep himself from listening to the sounds of Bonnie moving about the kitchen. He tried to imagine what a shock it must have been to receive a late-night call with news that her husband had been killed by a political fanatic armed with a car. Had it been even more traumatic to learn, ten years later, that her husband had been killed by a drunk driver and that his friends had lied about the incident?

To Bonnie, who viewed her husband through a haze of myth, it must have been a mind-blower. Gary hadn't died for his principles; he'd died by some anonymous hand, for no reason at all. As Swann always used to say, "It

ain't the bullet with my name on it I'm worried about—
it's the bullet that's addressed, 'To whom it may concern.'"

On the TV a local reporter stood in the rain, looking
bedraggled while she talked about flood warnings and
power outages and the likelihood that the storm would
continue on into the night. When her report ended, Paul
twisted in his seat to find Bonnie entering the den with
two mugs of fresh coffee. "It doesn't look good," he informed her.

"Don't worry." She joined him on the sofa, curling up
against the arm and tucking her long legs under her.
"We're safe and dry in here."

Paul studied her for a minute, observing in the room's
low light the silvery sheen of her ash-blond hair, the
dainty curve of her lower lip, the loose folds of her
sweater draping over her body, the graceful shape of her
hands cradling her coffee mug. Her words gratified him.
Obviously, she felt safe with him.

He felt safe with her, too, safe in her home, in this
dimly lit room, engulfed by the upholstery of this big,
well-worn couch, with her at his side. So safe he almost
hoped the rain would never end.

Chapter Eight

At ten o'clock Bonnie switched off the television. She couldn't remember the last time she'd spent two and a half uninterrupted hours watching the tube—and enjoying it. Actually, it wasn't the programs she'd enjoyed so much as the company. She and Paul had mocked the shows together, outguessed the scriptwriters and critiqued the commercials. He'd told her that his favorite broadcasts on TV were the Bruins hockey games, and she'd told him that she found hockey too nerve-racking, what with the players skidding into one another and slamming into the boards or sprawling across the ice. He'd told her he'd grown up playing hockey with his friends on the frozen ponds of Northford and that the scar on his pinkie was the result of surgery to repair the finger after it had been broken and dislocated during a rough-and-tumble game.

She turned from the television to see Paul rising slowly to his feet. "It's pretty late," she said, trying unsuccessfully to stifle a yawn.

Paul checked his watch and nodded. "I should be going."

"Going where?" she blurted out. "It's still pouring and you've got a flat tire."

As soon as she spoke she realized the implication of her statement: if he didn't go, he'd stay. Yet she couldn't send him out into the storm at this hour, when he hadn't even repaired his tire.

His gaze converged with hers and she discerned the unspoken question in his dark, shimmering eyes. "Do you want to drive me home in your car?" he asked cautiously, reluctant to jump to the wrong conclusion.

"I have a spare room," she said. She wasn't inviting him into her bed, for heaven's sake. All she was doing was offering a friend lodging for the night.

"If you're sure it's no problem..."

Under other circumstances it might have been a major problem. If all they'd had to go on was their previous encounter, Bonnie would never have dreamed of allowing Paul to spend the night under her roof. But this evening had been different. As handsome as Paul was, she'd found herself attracted to him not for his virile good looks but for his honesty, his self-awareness, his humor, his kindness.

Besides, if it hadn't been for his thoughtfulness in coming to her house to prop up the birch tree, he never would have gotten a flat tire in the first place.

"It's no problem," she assured him. "Let me go make up the bed."

He insisted on helping her. Together they unfolded the convertible couch in the small spare bedroom, spread the sheets and blanket across the mattress and stuffed two pillows into their linen pillowcases. "The bathroom's right across the hall," she told him, pointing out the door. "I usually get up around six-thirty. Is that a good time for you?"

"Sure." He surveyed the room for a moment, taking in the cluttered desk in one corner, the dusty sewing machine, the cartons of outdated magazines lining the wall beneath the window. Then he turned back to her. "Thanks, Bonnie."

"I should be thanking you," she said. At his perplexed smile, she sorted her thoughts, searching for the right way to thank him for daring to test the limits of their friendship, for challenging her philosophy without belittling it, for proving to her that they could argue and still like each other. Most of all, she wanted to thank him for his company, his support and his wise, gentle words when she'd been so rattled by Kevin McCoy's phone call. "I— I'm glad you were here after . . ." She hesitated, afraid to come across as overly sentimental. "I mean, when I was so—when I . . ." She faltered again, and gazed toward the rain-glazed window, embarrassed by her inability to express herself. How could she possibly tell Paul how much his presence meant to her? If she tried, he might take it the wrong way. He might feel threatened—or unduly encouraged.

"Thank you for saving my tree," she finally mumbled.

He respected her reticence. "I wouldn't let anything bad happen to that tree," he said with a knowing smile. He looked at her for a moment, then bowed and brushed her cheek with a light kiss. "Good night."

"Good night," she murmured as she left the room. She understood why he'd kissed her. It had been an act of affection and trust, a way of nullifying their last kiss. She appreciated the gesture even though she was disconcerted by Paul's ability to clue into her thoughts so easily, to answer her needs and relieve her of her apprehension.

Nobody had ever read her that clearly. Certainly not Gary. She had never expected him to. He'd been too busy, his attention focused on more important things. She'd dealt with her needs herself, keeping Gary's domestic life as tranquil as possible so he could concentrate on matters of great magnitude.

She warned herself not to compare Paul and Gary. She'd loved Gary—but she admired Paul and trusted him and, for a few anguished minutes earlier that evening, she'd needed him. And he'd answered her needs.

She took a quick shower in the bathroom off her bedroom, slipped on her nightgown and climbed into bed. Shutting off the light, she listened to Paul moving about down the hall. She heard the hiss of the shower running in Shane's bathroom and, a few minutes later, the sound of Paul's footsteps as he returned to the guest room. She heard the click of his door closing, and then nothing but the constant patter of the rain striking the roof above her.

Before long, she was asleep.

"DON'T!" HE MOUTHED. He wanted to scream the word, to roar it through the rain, through the soughing wind, through the slick, overripe vegetation. He wanted to shout until his voice pierced the clouds, until whoever was up there in heaven making such a mess of things below could hear him and stop them.

Nothing would stop them, though. Not fate, not Paul, not the rain or the vines or the macabre purple haze of this dank spring night. If he shouted, he would only bring their doom down upon them sooner. So he whispered the word, choked on it, damn near strangled on that one helpless, useless syllable: "Don't. Don't do it. Don't go."

They went.

Hiding behind a twisted, rotting tree stump and a couple of scraggly bushes, he watched his friends hike up the sloping path toward the hill. He stared after their re-

treating forms, Rigucci moving with a jiglike dancing step, Macon stalking in anger, Swann loose and graceful, probably dreaming about his sweet Jolene. Paul curled his fingers through the mulchy soil beneath him, flexing them into fists, waiting and wondering whether he would be brought down with the others.

He heard thunder. Or guns. Who the hell knew the difference anymore? He pressed his body to the damp earth and peeked around the tree stump. Swann was ahead, almost at the top of the hill. "Oh, God," Paul murmured, squeezing his eyes shut, "don't let this happen."

He opened his eyes and lifted himself up, watching as first Swann, then Macon, then Rigucci vanished over the hill. *No,* he begged the world around him. *No.* And then the shot, an infinitely cruel blast tearing through the thick night air.

Swann cried out—an animal sound, the most basic emotion expressed in wrenching echoes through the forest. Swann.

More gunfire, Macon barking something, a clap of thunder and a muted, guttural grunt. Above Paul the leaves reflected a fleeting glint of white light. He wished he could believe it was lightning, but he knew it wasn't.

Another round of gunfire, the staccato of a semiautomatic. Then silence, then the cough of a pistol. More silence.

I'm dead, he thought. The others are gone. Now they'll come looking for me.

He lay motionless in the mud, hidden by the stump and the bushes, wondering what it felt like to die. Swann had answered that mystery for him, he acknowledged. Swann's rending cry had told Paul exactly what it felt like to die.

He wanted to pray. He wanted to beg God for forgive-
ness, to repent his sins, to say farewell to his parents, to
go painlessly. To find heaven at the end. He wanted so
much before he died—but most of all, he wanted to cheat
death. He wanted to live, to love, to be human. He ached
for it.

Too late for prayers. He was already dead. He knew he
was, because he heard himself moaning, just like Swann.
He heard himself releasing his breath and his soul in that
same endless, agonized cry.

"PAUL."

She shoved open the door and gave her eyes a moment to adjust to the darkness inside. Once they did she
saw him sitting at the center of the bed, the blanket
crumpled around his waist, his head bowed and his hands
covering his face. She ignored his apparent nakedness;
what she noticed most vividly in the faint glow from the
hallway light was the sweat glistening across the smooth
bronze arch of his back, his wild mane of hair, the trembling of his shoulders, the tense clenching of the muscles
in his arms. He was bent forward, nearly doubled over,
and he let loose with a garbled string of curses. His voice
was constricted and his entire body shook.

"Paul." Two steps carried her to the bed. She lowered
herself gingerly onto the edge of the mattress, afraid that
any sudden move on her part might send him into par-
oxysms of terror. When he gave no indication of having
heard her, she repeated his name louder and touched his
arm.

He jerked away and cursed again. *"Don't."*

"Paul, it's me," she whispered. "Bonnie." She
clamped one hand around his shoulder so he couldn't
pull away. Her brain dimly registered the feverishness of

his skin and the adrenaline-fueled muscles beneath it.
With her other hand she pulled his fingers from his face.
His eyes were open, fiery, staring at her without seeing
her.

"No," he groaned, trying to shrug out of her grip.
"Damn it, I'm dying." He shrugged again, this time
freeing himself from her grip, and rolled onto his side,
presenting his back to her. "Don't come closer. It's too
dangerous."

She climbed fully onto the bed beside him and stroked
her hand soothingly along his temple and his cheek,
brushing his sweat-damp hair back from his face. She
thought briefly of the period, just after Gary's death,
when Shane had been besieged by nightmares. Bonnie
had been afflicted by a seemingly chronic case of insom-
nia, herself, and she'd spent night after night in Shane's
bed, stroking his shivering body and murmuring to him,
warding off the demons that beset him.

She would ward off Paul's demons if she could, too.
"Wake up, Paul," she said tenderly. "There's no danger
here. You're having a bad dream, that's all."

"It's not all," he muttered, at last offering proof that
he had heard her. "I'm dying. It's no use . . . oh, God."
His body jerked again, and he buried his face in the pillow.

His position, with his face pressed down and his arms
cradling the back of his head, reminded Bonnie of the
few war movies she'd seen. It was the defensive posture
of a soldier under fire, hitting the dirt.

"Wake up, Paul," she said, firmly now. She rubbed
her fingertips into the knotted flesh of his upper back and
attempted to dig out the tension. "Wake up. You're just
dreaming."

"You don't know," he mumbled into the pillow.

"Paul, I—"

He lifted his head suddenly, and his expression stunned her. It was both accusing and pleading, turbulent and desperate. "You don't know a damned thing," he said with surprising clarity. "I'm dying here, Bonnie. I'm dying!"

She brought her hands forward to his face, cupping his cheeks, wishing she could draw him fully out of his half-awake-half-asleep dementia. His chin was rough with an overnight growth of beard; his eyes were ringed with shadow. Whatever it was, whatever dreadful thing had taken possession of him, she had to make it go away. She had to get through to him. "You're not dying, Paul," she asserted, her voice steady. "I swear to you, you're not dying."

"You don't know." He sucked in a ragged breath as she glided her thumbs consolingly over the hard ridge of his jaw. "You weren't there."

"I'm here," she said. "And you're here, too, Paul. It's just a dream."

"It isn't just a dream," he argued, his voice still strained, his breath harsh and shallow. "It's real. We all died, everyone." He closed his eyes as a tremor racked his body.

"Not you." She comprehended only bits and pieces of his ranting, but she guessed that he was referring to the war, reliving some horrendous battle. Of course she hadn't been there and it hadn't been a dream—but it was over now, over and done. And Paul was alive. "You survived," she reassured him, combing her fingers into his hair and urging his head to her shoulder, wishing she could comfort him as he'd comforted her earlier that evening. "You survived."

"I'm scared." He brought his arms around her and held her tightly, running his hands across her back as if to make certain that she was real. He twined the fingers of one hand into her hair and shaped a fist. With a firm tug, he pulled her down to the pillow and then lifted his head to stare at her. "I'm scared, Bonnie," he confessed, his eyes blazing.

His face was etched with fear. His chest was mere inches above hers, his legs hidden under the blanket. In spite of her prim cotton nightgown and her wraparound robe, she was suddenly keenly aware of the sexual current surging between them. She felt the tension in his muscles, the pressure of his arousal against her belly, the fierce grip of his fingers in her hair holding her immobile on the pillow.

There was nothing even remotely romantic in Paul's attitude, nothing that spoke of love or affection or anything other than dread and a compulsion to prove to himself that he was alive.

"Don't be scared," she said, wondering for an instant whether she was speaking to him or to herself. His eyes were dark, implacably dark, filled with anger and anguish. His hips ground against hers and she felt the hardness of him, the straining hunger of his body.

Tears filled her throat and then vanished, unspent. She was all right, this was all right. Despite Paul's nearness, despite his rage, she wasn't frightened. She belonged here with him now, easing his soul, doing whatever she could for him. He was her friend; she cared too deeply about him to let him face this unspeakable nightmare alone.

He slid one hand forward, over her shoulder and down to her breast. His eyes remained locked onto hers as his fingers moved briefly over the swell of flesh, rough and probing. His hand skidded down to her waist. He didn't caress, he didn't seduce. His motions were abrupt, anxious, groping. He lowered his gaze to focus on the sash of her robe as his fingers fumbled with the knot.

"I need to do this," he moaned, his voice rasping.

She could stop him, she could stop it before it happened. She could do something to bring him to his senses, something to remind him of who they were, where they were.

But the fear, the haunting, frenzied fear rampaging through him moved her to forget about herself, to offer him whatever she could in an effort to bring him peace. She couldn't bear his torment.

A strange sense of calm resolution settled over her as she slid her hands between their bodies, trying to assist him in untying the sash.

"Don't," he groaned, shoving her hands away. He succeeded in undoing the sash and yanked back the robe. His eyes seemed to burn through the soft cotton of her nightgown, until finally he shoved the gown up to her waist and stripped off her panties. His breath came harsher, his chest pumping, his face contorted with an emotion that seemed much closer to despair than anger. He stared at her but she doubted that he saw her. She wished she knew what it was that he did see—and wished even more that what happened next would obliterate the horror he was experiencing.

"I need this," he whispered brokenly.

"I know," she murmured, circling her arms around him and pulling him down to her. "I know."

THE STEAMY NIGHT had reached its saturation point; huge drops of water materialized out of nowhere and gathered on the leaves and the tree stump. Paul held himself motionless, his shirt glued to his back, his helmet weigh-

*ing like a boulder on his head and his feet slick with sweat
inside his boots. The air was redolent with the cloying
smell of rotting plant life and burning sulfur.*

He wanted a woman.

*An hour had passed since the others had disappeared
over the hill. He'd heard the exchange, maybe ten minutes long, maybe less. And now only the sounds of the
forest, birds and bugs and drops of rain slapping against
the earth. He was afraid to move. The enemy was still out
there, and the slightest motion on his part could alert
them that they hadn't wiped out the entire patrol. So he
continued to lie, continued to wait, continued to pray.*

*A woman. He didn't care who—a peasant, a Saigon
bar girl, an American...it didn't matter. If he was
doomed, he begged God to grant him one last, utterly
impossible wish: a woman to wrap him up in her softness and take whatever was left of his life. He wanted her
fragrance to overcome the stench of death and decay
around him. He wanted her to cushion him from the
muck of the forest floor. He wanted to lose himself inside her before he lost everything, to be cared for and held
and loved for the simple reason that he was a human
being, afraid to die.*

*When he opened his eyes he saw the tangled, dripping
vines woven into a web above his head. When he closed
his eyes he drifted back into his dream of a woman, sweet
and accepting, letting him fill her with his life and prom-
ising him that everything would be all right.*

It seemed too real.

HE OPENED HIS EYES. Instead of the vines and the mud
and the humid, smothering, deathly darkness, he saw
Bonnie.

Chapter Nine

Her head was turned sideways, as if she couldn't stand the sight of him. Her hair swirled across the pillow; her breath was shallow, gasping. Her skin was pale and satiny, stretched taut across the delicate edge of her jaw and her slender throat.

His gaze journeyed lower, to her open bathrobe and the nightgown gathered at her waist. One of his hands was frozen into a fist around the bunched cloth. The thin cotton fabric was white, with tiny blue flowers embroidered along the scooped neckline and down the front. The sight of those pretty stitched flowers caused his eyes to burn with tears.

He commanded his fingers to release the nightgown. As soon as they did he slid off her and rolled to the far side of the bed. The memories screeching through his skull were no longer of a gruesome night twenty years ago but of now, what had just occurred between him and this woman. He vaguely remembered the thunder outside, long, sonorous rolls of it like distant fire, and the rain pounding down on him, closing in on him, seeping through him. Water torture, his buddies used to call the monsoons. Water torture.

He remembered tearing off Bonnie's underwear, moving his hands over her long, slim thighs, spreading them and pulling her to himself, half delirious with need. He remembered thinking that something had to stop. The storm outside the house or the storm inside his soul. It had to stop or he would die.

And then he'd taken her. He'd only wanted the nightmare to end. In her arms, in her body, he'd hoped to find a way to make the horror stop.

It hadn't stopped, though. He could still hear the rain beating down on the roof above his head. He could hear the wind rattling at the windows. His mind clarified itself, and he felt the full force of what he'd done.

He'd hurt her. She had stiffened and cried out, not in delight but in shock and pain. He'd done nothing, nothing for her, nothing to make it comfortable, let alone good. "God forgive me," he whispered. There was a greater chance of winning forgiveness from God than from Bonnie, he thought. It was easier to ask God than to ask her.

She said something. Her voice was gentle and he refused to listen. He didn't deserve to hear anything gentle right now, especially from her. He felt vile and repugnant. The kindest thing he could do would be to leave her at once, to keep his distance, to protect her from himself.

His toe snagged on his shorts, which were wadded up in the bed linens, and he rapidly put them on. Taking a deep, shaky breath, he swung out of bed, grabbed his jeans from the desktop on the other side of the room and tugged them on. His fingers shook as he fumbled with the zipper.

She spoke again, her voice clear and pure. "Paul. Don't do this."

He kept his back to her. "Do what?" he asked, searching the room for his shirt.

"Run away."

"I can't stay," he said, hating her for slowing him down by drawing him into a conversation. Hating himself for hating her.

"Paul, please—"

He wheeled around to confront her. She was sitting up, her nightgown smoothed down over her legs and her robe tied loosely, her sharp, steady gaze impaling him. He examined her lovely face, her gemlike eyes glittering with an unnamed emotion, her cheeks pale and her lips bearing the marks of her own teeth, and his rage spilled over. "Damn it, Bonnie—if you want to have me arrested, call the police. If you don't, then let me leave."

"Arrested?" she repeated, her eyes widening in bewilderment. "Why would I want to have you arrested?"

"Because I—" He couldn't say the word. It remained lodged in his throat, hard and ugly. Even if God forgave him, and Bonnie, and the police, he would never forgive himself for what he'd done to her.

Apparently she understood what he couldn't bring himself to say. She shook her head. "No, Paul, that's not what happened. I was willing. You didn't force anything."

He refused himself the comfort of believing her. How could it be anything but rape when he hadn't kissed her, caressed her, done a single thing to make the moment if not pleasurable for her at least bearable? How could it be anything but rape when he hadn't considered her feelings, when he hadn't even been aware of her identity throughout the entire act? She could have been anyone. He hadn't even cared.

He was sickened by what he'd done, and he resented her for not being sickened by it as well, for not screaming and accusing him and hurting him back.

"I've got to go." He yanked his shirt from the back of a chair and shoved his arms through the sleeves.

"Not yet," Bonnie argued, rising to her feet. For a moment she concentrated on tightening the sash of her robe. Paul gazed at her tapered, graceful fingers as they rearranged the knot. She looked so frail to him all of a sudden, so vulnerable. When she lifted her face to him he noticed the unnatural sheen in her eyes and his soul seemed to compress, shrinking until it was a small, dense nugget of self-loathing.

Anything. He would do anything for her, no matter how painful. He could think of few things more painful than remaining in her company right now, but he would do it if that was what she wanted.

Maybe, he thought ironically, her insistence that he stay and receive her mercy was her own perverse way of punishing him.

"I'll make some coffee," she said, gliding past him and out the door. He watched through the open doorway as she walked along the hall to the stairs, her head held high and her bearing dignified. He watched until she vanished down the stairs. Then he turned and finished dressing.

Unable to stall any longer, he went downstairs. Bonnie stood in the kitchen doorway. "The storm has ended," she said.

ONCE THE COFFEE was ready, they went out to the back porch to drink it. Bonnie felt as restless as Paul seemed to be; when he asked if she would mind sitting outside she was strangely relieved to escape the confines of the house.

Faint glimmers of moonlight filtered through the gauzy layers of mist that shrouded the house, giving the rear yard a surreal appearance. Bonnie sat on the porch step, which had stayed relatively dry thanks to the overhanging roof. Paul sat beside her—as far from her as possible, she noticed. She curved her hands around her mug and sipped, wishing that somewhere in the aromatic steam of the coffee, somewhere in the diaphanous haze blanketing her small corner of the earth, she would find a way to justify her feelings.

Perhaps Paul's perception was right. Perhaps she ought to have been furious with him for having victimized her. But of all the emotions churning inside her, fury seemed to be missing. Nor did she feel like a victim. As she'd told him, she had been a willing participant in what had taken place upstairs. She had known what he was going to do and she'd acceded to it. She had expected nothing more than what had happened—and nothing less.

It had hurt a little, at first—but then, as her tension had waned and her body had grown accustomed to him, the discomfort had receded. At least hers had. Looking up into Paul's face, his eyes squeezed shut and the muscles straining in his jaw, his breath harsh and ragged and his thrusts fierce, she had acknowledged the depth of his torment, the complete absence of joy in his soul. At his peak he'd emitted a dark, anguished cry, and she'd realized that what little pain she might have felt was trivial compared to the agony he had endured.

They hadn't made love; she was under no delusions about that. Yet what she'd done—reaching out to someone she cared for, offering him what she could—had been an act of love. Short of giving birth to Shane, it was the most selfless deed she'd ever committed. No man had ever needed her so much; she'd never before felt the longing to give so much. She didn't for a minute regret what had happened.

"Are you on birth control?" His voice was low and rough-edged.

She took another sip of coffee. "Don't worry about it," she said.

Paul swore under his breath. "I *will* worry about it. Tell me the truth, Bonnie."

"The truth is..." She sighed. Illogical though it was, she knew she was safe. "The timing is off, Paul. I'm very regular, and this isn't a fertile day for me."

He clearly wasn't reassured. Muttering another oath, he stared across the haze-shrouded yard and pounded his fist against his thigh. "Why don't you just let me leave? Why don't you do me a favor and hate me?"

"Oh, so now you're asking me for a favor," she teased. "That's a bit much, don't you think?" She knew he was in no mood for humor. Neither was she. But she needed to break through the barrier of self-recrimination he'd erected between them. She needed to reach him again.

"Damn it, Bonnie—" He seemed on the verge of hurling his mug across the lawn. He channeled his energy downward instead, jumping to his feet and pacing the length of the porch. When he reached the far end, he pressed his forehead against the clapboard wall of the house and groaned. Then he turned on her. "Okay, maybe you enjoyed yourself upstairs. Maybe that's the way you like it. Maybe I've got you all wrong."

She gaped at him. What on earth was he talking about?

"It takes all kinds, Bonnie. Maybe this was exciting for you."

This time she was the one who had to fight the urge to hurl a coffee mug—not across the lawn but at Paul.

"Maybe you want to thank me for what I did," he goaded her. "How the hell should I know? Maybe this was the highlight of your life."

"Shut up," she cried, slamming down her mug and rising to her feet. How dare he insinuate such a thing? "Don't say things like that."

He approached her, his eyes shadowed, his lips twisted in a mirthless smile. "Maybe we ought to do it again, sometime. That's what you're thinking, right? You like it mean and cruel, and—"

She slapped him, first with her right hand and then with her left. As she swung back to hit him with her right hand again, he caught her wrist and jerked her arm away, causing her to lose her balance. She fell against him, burying her face in his shoulder and bursting into tears.

"That's better," he murmured into her hair. He closed his arms around her in a hesitant hug as she sobbed into his chest. "I'd rather you fly off the handle, Bonnie. I couldn't stand seeing you so calm and understanding."

"I'm not understanding," she claimed, sniffling away her tears and straightening up. He immediately let his hands fall from her and she searched his face, seeking confirmation that he wouldn't continue with his vicious insults. "I don't understand any of this, Paul. You wanted me to hit you?"

He peered down at her for a moment, his expression suddenly tender, alive with yearning. Then he sighed and returned to the far end of the porch to get his coffee. He remained there, sipping it and staring bleakly at her.

He *had* wanted her to hit him, she realized. He wanted her to hate him as much as he hated himself. But she didn't think she was capable of hating him. Slapping Paul had been utterly out of character for her—perhaps as out of character as what he'd done to her in the spare bedroom.

"I don't understand," she repeated, referring not to now but to then, not to her aggression but to his. "I don't know where you were when we were in bed. You certainly weren't with me."

His eyes met hers and he nodded, conveying that he knew what she was asking. "No, I wasn't."

"Were you in Vietnam?"

"Yes."

"In the middle of a battle?"

He opened his mouth and then shut it. "I don't want to talk about it, Bonnie."

She pressed ahead, refusing him the luxury of evasion. "Do you often have nightmares like that?"

His expression was pleading, but she refused to withdraw the question. He might want her to hit him, but all she wanted was to know him, to know what had driven him to do what he did, to help him—and herself—come to terms with it.

He answered reluctantly. "I don't have the flashbacks as often as I used to. But sometimes, if I'm sleeping in an unfamiliar place..." He shifted his gaze to the upstairs window, then grimaced and glanced away. "You shouldn't have come into the room."

"But you sounded so upset," she explained. "I heard you moaning in your sleep all the way down the hall in my room. All I wanted to do was wake you up—"

He issued a caustic laugh. "And look where it got you."

Undaunted, she took a sip of coffee and sank back onto the porch, leaning against the railing and studying him in the ethereal twilight. "You kept saying you were dying, Paul. But you didn't die. Over there, I mean. You survived.''

''Everyone died a little over there,'' he corrected her, his tone bitter. ''A lot of the men died physically, and the rest of us died spiritually. Even when we were alive we weren't really living.''

She scrutinized him thoughtfully. His body appeared strong to her, his posture proud and sturdy, his gaze firm. He did not seem like a spiritually dead man. ''I thought you were a hero.''

He snorted.

''Tell me what happened,'' she demanded. For all her antiwar sentiments, she realized that she was pitifully ignorant about what the soldiers had actually experienced in Southeast Asia. But now, more than ever, she *had* to know what had gone on there, what men like Paul had endured. If he talked about it, if he explained it to her, perhaps he could explain it to himself, as well. Perhaps by verbalizing the horror of it he could mend his tattered conscience. ''Tell me what your dream was about.''

He eyed her accusingly. ''Why? You want me to confirm for you that you were right about Nam, that it was a lousy war and you and your Cambridge Manifesto chums were on the money? You don't need me to tell you that.''

''No, I don't,'' she retorted, irritated by his derisive attitude. ''What I need you to tell me is what the hell was going on in your head when you were lying in bed with me upstairs. And if you think I haven't got the right to an answer—''

''I don't like talking about it,'' he snapped.

''Well, isn't that too damned bad!''

Her outburst apparently took him by surprise, and he shot her a look of amazement. Recovering, he carried his mug back to the steps and resumed his seat beside her. He struggled with his thoughts, then relented. "I'll tell you what you want to know," he conceded, gazing at his feet to avoid looking at her, "but you've got to promise you'll never call me a hero."

She hadn't realized he'd been reacting to that specific word. "Why shouldn't I?"

"Because..." He addressed his coffee. "If my CO hadn't gotten himself killed, I probably would have faced serious charges. Maybe a court-martial."

"A court-martial? On what charges?"

"Insubordination. Failure to obey a direct order." He drained his mug, placed it on the porch beside him and focused his gaze on a dimly visible pine in the distance. The air vibrated with the deep-throated croaks of frogs celebrating the end of the storm.

Bonnie waited, but Paul remained silent. She looked from his grim face to his hands, his forearms resting across his spread knees, the sleek, supple strength of his thighs visible where the fabric of his dungarees was drawn taut.

She suffered a swift, utterly irrational pang of guilt. She had acquiesced in what Paul did upstairs for the simple reason that she'd wanted to make him feel better. She'd wanted to bring peace to his inflamed soul. But she'd failed. If anything, he seemed tenser now than he'd been before. The tendons in his neck stood out, and the muscles in his shoulders were knotted. He couldn't seem to prevent his fingers from curling and uncurling.

It had been futile. She could no more bring peace to Paul now than she could to an embattled nation twenty years ago. Far from chasing away Paul's demons, she had added to them.

"I'm sorry," she murmured.

"Don't be. The court-martial never happened."

"No—I mean—" She inhaled sharply and shook her head clear. "How did your commanding officer get killed?" she asked, hoping Paul wouldn't detect the tremor in her voice. Perhaps she'd failed him upstairs, but she wasn't going to make matters any better by castigating herself in front of him now.

"He walked into an ambush," Paul said bluntly. His voice was flat, but Bonnie could sense the churning undercurrent of rage inside him.

"Oh, no." She shook her head and sighed. "How horrible. Oh, Paul—"

"He took two of my buddies with him," Paul went on, still laboring to keep any excess emotion out of his voice.

She instinctively reached for his hand and covered it with her own. He flinched and she let her hand drop. "I'm sorry, Paul," she said, referring to his having lost two friends.

He nodded, informing her that he understood what she meant. He gazed into the distance, scanning the early-morning fog as if seeking his past in its translucent layers. "We were doing four-man night patrols. The night it was my turn, the sergeant decided to have us patrol this one area that seemed..." He shook his head. "I don't know. There had been too much suspicious activity over there. It was just north of this village where a lot of VC sympathizers lived. My sergeant was the fool who wanted to be a hero that night. So he decided to take us up north of the village."

Paul's voice grew more distant as he sank deeper into his reminiscence. His dark gaze continued to comb the mist.

"It was a damp night, kind of like this. The monsoons were a lot like that storm we just had. Sometimes at night the rain would let up, but the air was so wet you could almost see the moisture floating in it.'' He closed his eyes for a minute, lapsing into a silent meditation. ''I had—I don't know whether it was a premonition or what, but I just knew we shouldn't go beyond a rise on the trail. I knew there was trouble waiting on the other side. When Macon said we were going to go over, I said no.''

''Just like that?'' Bonnie was stunned. ''You actually refused to go?''

''I'm here, aren't I?'' Paul said tersely. ''If I hadn't refused I'd be dead like the others.''

She heard the anguish and bitterness in his tone—and comprehended it in some subliminal way. If only his friends had listened to him, if only they'd shared his premonition, if only the war hadn't happened in the first place... So much waste, she thought. So much heartache. So much pain.

It wouldn't do to give voice to her own anguish and bitterness. ''So,'' she asked, directing her thoughts back to the actual event he was describing, ''this sergeant threatened you with a court-martial, right then and there?''

''He said he'd bring me up on charges as soon as we returned to camp. And I said, 'Do whatever the hell you want, but I'm not going over that hill.''' He let out a broken sigh. ''Rigucci and Swann tried to talk me into going with them. They said I was nuts. Maybe I *was* nuts, I don't know. After a while over there, everybody was nuts. You'd grab hold of anything, anything that made sense—because so little did make sense. That night, it made sense to me not to go over the hill, and nobody was going to take that away from me.''

For a long moment he seemed unable to continue. When he finally did, his voice was uneven, on the verge of disintegrating. "I stood by a tree, watching them march off along the trail, disappear over the hill. And then I heard the gunfire...." He shook his head, clenching his hands against his knees. "God," he whispered with such ferocity Bonnie understood that he was reliving the incident again, as he'd relived it in his dreams earlier that night, as he had undoubtedly relived it innumerable times in the past. "Macon, Rigucci and Swann came home wrapped in plastic, and I came home with a bunch of damn medals."

"And you never got court-martialed."

He shook his head. "It took me a long time to get back to camp. I didn't move for hours; I didn't want to draw enemy fire. But when the sky started to lighten—like this..." He lifted his eyes to the moon-glazed clouds. "It had been quiet for so long, I took my chances and advanced to the rise. I saw Swann." He stopped, his voice breaking, and pressed his hand to his eyes. For a long time he was silent.

Bonnie waited.

He swallowed, then continued. "I couldn't find the others quickly, so I just got Swann and carried him to camp on my back. I reported..." He drew in a sharp breath. "I lied, Bonnie. I reported that we'd spread out on the trail, and that's why they had all bought it and I hadn't. I covered my ass."

"What else could you have done?" she asked.

"I could have told the truth, damn it. I could have admitted I was a coward."

"A coward! You chose to live. You listened to your heart and chose to live. That wasn't cowardly, Paul—it was wise. It was human."

"Great. I was wise and human, and my buddies died."

"That's not your fault," Bonnie said quickly. For no good reason, Paul seemed to be blaming himself for what had happened to his friends. He ought to console himself with the fact that he'd tried to talk them out of going.

"I should have died with them," Paul muttered, staring at the wooden step between his feet. "They were good soldiers, Bonnie—even Macon was a good soldier. I was a bad soldier, and I lived."

"Well, that certainly proves something," she remarked, realizing too late that she must have come across sounding flippant.

Paul gave her a scorching look. "Yeah," he snapped, turning away once more. "It proves that there's no justice or fairness in this world. It proves that survival is just a matter of luck."

"Surviving isn't a sin."

"Maybe not. But survival and sin have something in common. They both make you feel guilty."

"You have nothing to feel guilty for, Paul."

"Thanks," he grunted. "I feel a lot better now."

Eager to counteract his corrosive bitterness, she dared to touch him again. Before he could pull away she closed both her hands around one of his. His fingers fisted against her palm as he tried to free himself. She didn't care—she held him tightly, refusing to let go. "You weren't just lucky," she said. "You were smart. You deserved to live, Paul."

"And they deserved to die?"

"I didn't say that." She ran her thumb over his knuckles in a soothing caress. "The memorial you want to erect on the town green—it's for them, isn't it?"

His nod was so small she almost didn't see it.

"But it isn't going to have their names on it, Paul," she pointed out, puzzled. "It's going to have the names of some Northford veterans."

"Who cares what names go on it? In my mind I'll know who the memorial is for. One dead soldier or another...does it really matter?" He took a calming breath, then explained, "I made a promise to my buddies that night, Bonnie. I promised I'd see to it that the world never forgot about them. It doesn't matter whose names get carved into the rock. The only thing that matters is that people remember."

"Then why don't you establish memorials in the towns where your friends came from?"

"Because I'm here," he replied quietly. "Because this is my home, and that's the promise I made."

She was moved by the simplicity of his words. She could understand the appeal of such a promise. Perhaps keeping it had given Paul the strength to survive. Much as she despised his memorial in concept, she appreciated his devotion to his fallen friends.

But his dream just hours ago hadn't been about the memorial. More than a promise had evolved from that gruesome night in Vietnam, more than the death of his friends. More, even, than his own fear of being discovered and killed. Bonnie had felt the ferocious hunger in him when he joined himself to her, the savage urgency. She had nothing to do with patrols and snipers, monsoons and promises—and yet, for those few brief, harrowing minutes she'd been as potent a part of his hallucinatory nightmare as anything he'd described.

"Was there a woman that night?" she inquired. It made no sense that there would have been—except that, as Paul himself had said, nothing made sense in wartime.

"No," he answered swiftly. He whipped his hand free of her clasp and averted his gaze.

"Paul...please. Tell me."

"What the hell do you think was going on there?" he shot back, his voice thick with anger. "It was a war, not a party."

"Then why—"

"Because." He cut her off, then let out a long, uneven breath and turned away.

"Paul." Of everything he had told her, this was what she most needed to hear. She would never be able to understand any of it if he didn't explain this part.

"Because," he repeated, his tone hushed. Evidently he believed she deserved to know; the hard part was saying it. "Bonnie, I...I was lying there for hours, waiting to die. I knew the VC were looking for me. If they found three guys they'd look for more, and if they found me they'd kill me. So I just lay there, waiting.... And God help me, I—" He abruptly stopped.

"You what?"

He buried his face in his palms. He didn't speak.

She ached to hold him, placate him, assure him that there was nothing he couldn't share with her. But if she did, he would probably retreat even deeper into silence. So she only watched him, observing his hunched form, the taut muscles of his shoulders, the spread of his fingers across his face as he tried to shut out his terrifying recollections.

The squawk of a crow cut through the fog, and then the energetic chatter of a pair of sparrows flitting from one tree to another in the distance.

"It wasn't you," he whispered, so softly she almost didn't hear him.

"What wasn't me?"

He shuddered. His head was still bowed, propped in his hands. "Upstairs, in bed. It—I didn't even know it was you. It could have been anyone." His voice was hoarse from the effort of containing his emotions.

She recognized that he'd resisted telling her in an effort to spare her feelings. Of course it hurt to know he hadn't cared who was with him. She fought the impulse to take offense. She had demanded that he tell her the truth, and she forced herself to accept it.

"That night, when I was lying there... It was the most—the most *alive* thing I could think of. A man feels so alive then, so alive when he..." He faltered, then tried again. "I just needed someone that night. Anyone. Just a woman. I didn't care.... I lay in the forest, terrified out of my mind and hard for a woman." He drew in a sharp breath and stood. "I'm sorry, Bonnie. I'm sorry you got caught up in it. I'm sorry I'm even telling you this." He crossed to the back door and went into the house.

Bonnie stayed behind, listening to the thump of the door slamming shut behind her and watching the fog drift above the ground. In a few hours her alarm clock would be buzzing; she would have to get dressed, eat breakfast, pack her briefcase and drive to the elementary school, where she would be expected to instruct twenty-six nine- and ten-year-olds on the significance to their lives of long division.

She couldn't do it. Not when her body was still burning from Paul's aggression and her mind was reeling from his heated words. Not when she was confronting so many complex truths, when she was contending with the very real possibility that what Paul had lost in Vietnam was worse than what she had lost when Gary was run down by a drunk driver who might or might not have been aiming at him. At least she'd been left with Shane, a precious life. All Paul had been left with was a promise—and a burden of guilt no sane man could bear.

She couldn't bring herself to follow him inside. His final statement echoed inside her head: *I'm sorry I'm even telling you this.* She felt brutalized by his words, his secrets. If she went after him he might say something more, and she'd feel even more overwhelmed.

What she needed was time alone to sort through everything he had said, everything she had felt, everything they had shared since he entered her house last night. She needed to acknowledge what she'd given to him, what he'd taken from her and what it meant. She couldn't possibly face a classroom full of boisterous youngsters today.

Yet she would. She had to. She had learned, ten years ago, that no matter what horrors you faced or what tragedies you were dealt, you had to keep going. The storm eventually let up, the fog burned away and the sun returned, bringing with it another day.

And life, however incomprehensible, went on.

Chapter Ten

"Gently," Paul cautioned Shane. "Watch the branches— don't let them get snagged on anything. Remember, just because these trees are no longer in the ground doesn't mean they aren't alive."

Shane carefully separated the branches of two slender pear trees and passed them down, one at a time, from the bed of the truck to Paul, who propped them up against a wooden display frame near the parking lot. A day and a half after the storm, the nursery had been pretty well cleaned up. The rhododendrons, which had been planted in a low-lying area, had taken on too much water and needed some nursing, and the wind had hurled a dead branch against one of the greenhouses, cracking a pane of glass. The ground was still soft and strewn with puddles. But all in all, the nursery had survived without serious damage.

Paul wished he could say the same for himself.

In spite of the night he'd spent in Bonnie's house, he and Shane were getting along well. Shane had shown up for his first Saturday of work promptly at nine o'clock, and he'd been running at full throttle all morning. Possibly it was the official Tremaine Nursery shirt Paul had given him to wear that had inspired him to work so hard.

It was equally likely, though, that he was motivated by the trust and responsibility Paul had conferred upon him. As soon as he finished a task, he'd race through the greenhouses or the warehouse in search of Paul, proclaiming, "All done stacking the hoses! What should I do next?" or, "I loaded the fertilizer in the lady's station wagon. Find me something else to do, Paul."

A half hour ago Paul had handed him a pair of heavy work gloves, which seemed to excite him as much as the shirt did, and had driven with him to one of the perimeter fields where some pear trees had been harvested and wrapped in burlap the day before. They'd spent a few minutes clearing out the litter of leaves and branches that hadn't been picked up the day before, then set to work loading the trees into the truck so they could be transported to the lot by the main greenhouse and tagged for sale. They were reasonably light in weight, and Shane had no difficulty lifting them up to Paul, who stacked them in the truck bed.

Back in the lot, they reversed positions. Shane stood in the truck bed, lowering the pear trees to Paul. "Their branches are so, like, tangly," he remarked, less a complaint than an expression of astonishment. Anyone could have guessed that he was a city kid who'd grown up believing pears came not from trees but from supermarket shelves.

"They're pretty spindly at this age," Paul agreed. "Just be gentle when you separate them. Pulling them out of the earth is enough of a trauma to their systems. Right now they haven't got the strength to recuperate if they get injured."

Shane grinned. His hair blew in the sun-warmed spring breeze and his eyes sparkled, alert and inquisitive. "Isn't it kinda weird, worrying over a bunch of trees like they were people or something?''

"They're living creatures," Paul said. "You've got to treat them with respect."

Shane shook his head and adjusted the bright orange gloves on his hands before he reached for the next tree. "It's just . . . I mean, you're making such a big deal over these trees and you've, like, killed people."

Paul went very still. His lungs stopped pumping, his heart stopped beating, and his skin grew cold. He stared at Shane but didn't see him. Instead, he saw a vision of Bonnie, her hair splayed across a pillow beneath him, her eyes unfocused, her lips bitten raw and her nightgown hiked up and wrinkled. The image lasted for one frozen instant, and then his body began to function again in a rush, his vision washed with red and his gut aching from the sudden, searing return of sensation.

"Where did you hear that?" he asked in a deliberately bland voice.

"Well . . ." Shane extricated another pear tree from the stack and passed it to Paul. "My mom told me you fought in Vietnam."

Paul accepted the tree and spent several long minutes balancing it against the frame. What else, he wondered, had Bonnie told her son? That while he was spending Thursday night at his friend Matt's house Paul was wrestling with the sheets in the guest room, screaming in his sleep, delirious with dread? And that when Bonnie had come in to comfort him he'd wound up assaulting her? And that, in some half-crazed effort to atone for what he'd done to her, he had confessed things that he'd never before shared with another soul?

Had she told her son that Paul was dangerous, reckless, certifiably deranged? Had she told the kid that even though she'd done nothing wrong Paul despised her for being too generous, for being somewhere she shouldn't have been, for forcing her way into his wretched dream and becoming a part of it?

"If I did kill anyone," he said slowly, keeping his back to Shane, "it's not something I'm proud of." He pulled off one of his work gloves and rearranged a few of the delicate branches, concentrating on the texture and flexibility of the tree, the tart, fresh scent of its leaves. Then he turned back to the truck, put his glove on again and took the tree Shane was extending to him. "Maybe fighting in a war deepens your appreciation for all living things," he said. "Even plants."

Shane's eyes shone with curiosity. As similar in shape and color as they were to Bonnie's, Paul detected none of her condemnation in them. "What was it really like over there?" he asked as he delivered the tree into Paul's waiting hands. "I mean, like, was it exciting?"

"It stank," Paul said tersely, then stood the tree against the frame and rethought his answer. "I suppose it was exciting," he added, determined not to be brusque with Shane. "Not in a pleasant way, though."

"My mom, everything with her is black and white," Shane remarked. "But it's like, well, you watch shows on TV and stuff, and—I mean, yeah, I'm sure war stinks, but it looks exciting, too. All that life-and-death stuff, it really gets you kind of pumped up, doesn't it?"

Paul swore under his breath. When Bonnie had warned him that Shane would want to discuss certain subjects with him, he had assumed the specific subject she'd had in mind was sex. He'd never guessed that Shane would want to grill him about his experiences in combat.

"There are much healthier ways of getting pumped up," he said quietly. "Pass me that last tree, Shane."

Shane appeared about to continue questioning Paul, but he read the tacit request in Paul's expression and held his words. Paul didn't like having to silence Shane, but he preferred that to the alternatives—lying to the boy, telling him things his mother would disapprove of, or ordering him to leave the nursery and never come back.

"So," Shane said brightly, leaping down from the tailgate and latching it shut. "What do we do now?"

"We attach price tags," Paul answered. "Do you want to help me with that?"

"Sure." Noticing that Paul had removed his work gloves, Shane did, too. He fell into step beside Paul as they headed for the warehouse.

Halfway there, Paul spotted Bonnie standing near the entrance to the parking lot, engrossed in a conversation with a gray-haired, bespectacled man. She had on evenly faded blue jeans, a short-sleeved white shirt and brown leather sandals. Her hair hung loose, fluffing in the breeze that swept across the parking lot. Paul observed the graceful length of her bare arms, the peach-toned hue of her complexion, the sleek line of her chin, her slender build, her narrow waist, her attractively proportioned legs.

Tearing his eyes from her, he took note of the man with her—Edwin Marshal, from the town council. Ed was showing her some documents; she studied them intently while she talked, her lips moving with a sensuous fluency that lured Paul's attention back to her. He was too far away to hear what she was saying, but not too far to recall the way her mouth had felt one afternoon in the greenhouse, seemingly ages ago, when he'd stupidly believed a relationship could develop between her and himself. The kiss they'd shared had been so dazzling, so rich with promise....

Why did she have to be so damned desirable? Remembering that kiss put Paul in mind not of what had actually occurred at her house a couple of nights ago but of what he wished had occurred. He wanted to make love to her, properly, sensitively, passionately. He wanted to love *her*, not some undefined fantasy figure in a flashback nightmare. He wanted her to give herself to him not in charity but in ecstasy—and he wanted to give her everything she gave him, and more.

Conceding the impossibility of that, he wanted to flee. But it was too late. Shane had spotted his mother. He waved at her and yelled, "Hey, Mom!" before breaking into a run. Paul lagged behind, fighting the temptation to run in the opposite direction.

Hearing Shane's voice, Bonnie looked up from the papers and smiled at her son. Then she saw Paul and her smile faded.

With Shane and Ed Marshal as witnesses, he had to try to behave normally. "Hello, Bonnie," he said, doing his best to filter the emotion out of his voice. "Ed," he went on, quickly turning from her and extending his hand. "What brings you here? Don't tell me Celia's ruined all her daffodils again."

"She didn't plant any bulbs this year," Ed responded with a chuckle. "I wouldn't let her. She's massacred them every year she's planted them, and I just couldn't stand the carnage anymore." What he'd intended as a joke struck Paul like a blow. Glimpsing Bonnie, he saw her wince at Ed's ill-chosen words.

"Truth is, Paul," Ed went on, oblivious of the impact his remark had had on two of his listeners, "I came by because we've received some design proposals on the memorial and I wanted to show them to you. I was just letting Mrs. Hudson have a look at them."

What could be better? Paul thought with a bitter smile. Here was Bonnie, sandwiched between a man who'd attacked her and a man who would be instrumental in constructing a war memorial she despised on principle, getting stuck looking at the designs when all she wanted was to pick up her son. This must be her red-letter day.

Shane did Paul the favor of breaking into his dismal thoughts. "Hey, Mom—check out this shirt, huh?" He struck a pose. "Paul said I could keep it. And these gloves, too. Check them out, Mom—they've got genuine suede palms and everything!" He wagged the work gloves under her nose. "Are these nasty or what?"

"I think you ought to leave them here at the nursery," Paul suggested, happy to focus on Shane instead of Bonnie. "That way you won't run the risk of forgetting to bring them with you next week. I can put them somewhere safe for you here."

Shane shrugged and gave him the gloves. "How about my shirt? Should I leave that here, too?"

"No. You should take that home and run it through the washing machine," Paul advised. "You worked up quite a sweat today."

"Yeah," Shane boasted, turning to his mother. "I worked real hard, Mom. You wouldn't believe how hard I worked."

"You're right," she said, attempting a grin. "I wouldn't." She glanced at Paul, discreetly keeping her gaze level with his chin. "Did he do all right?"

"He did great," Paul said, obeying her unspoken plea and not allowing his eyes to meet hers.

"Well...I'm glad it worked out." She nodded toward the mud-splattered Subaru parked in one of the spaces near the entrance. "I guess that's it for today,

Shane. You'll get another chance to work up a sweat next Saturday."

"Yeah, okay." Shane turned to Paul, his eyes still bright and shining, poignant in their youthful enthusiasm. "I'll see you next week."

"Take it easy, Shane." He watched as they strolled across the lot to the car, Shane's self-importance evident in his strutting gait and his satisfied grin. In contrast, Bonnie's steps were slow and cautious, her gaze on the gravel a few yards ahead of her and her arms crossed in front of her, each hand gripping the other elbow. She was hugging herself, holding herself in, and Paul felt another stab of guilt.

Too much, he thought grimly. He was carrying too much guilt: about the people he might have killed in Nam and about the friends he'd lost, about the marriage he'd failed in and the career he'd abandoned, and now Bonnie. Most of all Bonnie.

"Anyway, I'll just let you look at them without comment," Ed Marshal was saying. "I'll tell you later what the members of the council thought of the designs. If you haven't got time to look them over now, I can leave the folder with you. Just drop it off at town hall later. I won't be in, but one of the clerks can take it."

"All right," Paul said, accepting the folder from Ed. "Thanks." The nursery was swarming with customers at the moment, but he would somehow find the time to examine the designs. He'd make the time if he couldn't find it.

Paul was not going to break his promise to his friends. He was not going to give himself another reason to feel guilty.

BONNIE SAT under an oak tree on the town green, across the street from the school yard. The tree cast a broad shadow over the grass; its trunk was straight and sturdy, surprisingly comfortable against her back. She gazed from the vacant school yard to the stark granite war memorial on the other side of the green, and then to the thick manila envelope in her lap. She'd stayed up half the previous night reading its contents. Now, having completed her grocery shopping, housecleaning and classroom preparation for the following week, she intended to read the manuscript again.

She had just driven Shane and Matt up to Lowell to see a movie—why they wanted to spend a warm, sunny afternoon shut up inside was beyond her, but Shane deserved to celebrate his first day at his first real job any way he wanted. Janet Molson was going to pick them up afterward, so Bonnie had the afternoon pretty much to herself.

She opened the envelope and pulled the manuscript out. Kevin McCoy had clipped a note to the top page: "Bonnie—here's a rough draft of the first section of the book. I'd appreciate comments and corrections. I'm sure this will undergo alterations, but I thought you'd like to see what I've done so far." Nothing about his conversation with the police officer who'd filed the accident report on Gary's death, nor about any discussions he might have had with Tom or Marcie. Nor was there anything about Gary's death in the section he'd sent her.

While perusing it last night, she'd jotted down a few notes: an incorrect date on page fourteen, a misleading implication in a reference to Gary's parents at the end of chapter one. But she'd been distracted, constantly searching for some mention of the circumstances surrounding Gary's death.

It would be stupid to become obsessed with it at this late date. Nothing Bonnie could possibly learn about the accident would change its outcome; nothing would bring Gary back. Whether or not he died a martyr's death couldn't affect the meaning of his life.

And yet it did, somehow. Dying for a cause was far different from getting run over by an intoxicated barfly. One was noble, the other prosaic. Thousands of people were killed each year by drunk drivers. Few were slain for their principles. If Gary had to die, he should have died for his views.

"I must be insane," she whispered, amused in a horrified way by the bizarre turn her thoughts had taken. She couldn't imagine why Tom and Marcie had felt the need to lie about the circumstances surrounding Gary's death—unless they, too, wanted to fabricate a heroic end for a man who had been so heroic in life. Their deception had been not malicious but merely foolish. As Paul had said, the particulars of Gary's death didn't change who he was.

Paul had been so sensitive to her that evening, saying just what she needed to hear and holding her when she needed to be held. She'd had no trouble accepting what he gave her. Why couldn't he accept what she'd given him?

She ordered herself to stop thinking about him. His behavior at the nursery that morning had announced his feelings eloquently: he would never be able to accept her. He couldn't even accept himself. It had been a marvelous thing to look into his troubled soul, to touch it in some way... but it would never happen again. He would never permit it. They would never be friends.

She directed her gaze to the first page of Kevin's manuscript. *When you know you're right, you're half the distance to winning.* That had been Gary's motto, and it made an effective opening line. But the slogan Bonnie used to find dynamic now struck her as sanctimonious. Gary had always been so confident, so unshakably certain that he was right....

Of course he'd been right. How could she think otherwise? The war in Vietnam had been an appalling misadventure. Gary had been absolutely correct in protesting it.

She recalled the doubt and fear she'd seen in Paul's eyes, not just when he'd been caught up in his dream but afterward, when they'd gone to the back porch and talked. There was something so human about Paul, something so very strong about his willingness to expose his weakness.

Why hadn't Gary ever let Bonnie glimpse his weakness? Why hadn't he shared his doubts with her? Probably he'd never had any doubts. Gary had been a paragon, a visionary, a genius.

Paul, on the other hand, was a man.

When you know you're right... Why did Gary's words now sound so insufferably complacent, so downright arrogant?

"This is ridiculous," she muttered to herself. If she spent all afternoon mulling over the first sentence she'd never get to the second. Determined to plow ahead in the manuscript, she opened her eyes—and saw Paul.

He was standing no more than fifteen feet away from her on the green, staring at her with a directness he hadn't dared to indulge in at the nursery earlier that day. His dark hair was blown back from his brow and his eyelids were lowered against the sun's glare. His feet were planted firmly on the ground and his expression was oddly accusing. Tucked under one arm was the folder of designs for the memorial that Ed Marshal had shown her when they'd happened upon each other in the nursery parking lot a couple of hours ago.

"What are you doing here?" he asked.

"I'm reading," she answered, returning his steady gaze.

He regarded her for another minute, then relented and looked past her. "Sorry to interrupt," he mumbled, then sighed and turned to leave.

"Paul—wait!" She had no notion of what to say to him, but she didn't want him to go, not until they had established a truce. She was going to be bringing Shane to the nursery every Saturday for the next few weeks; she couldn't avoid Paul. There had to be some way to reduce the friction between them.

He stopped but didn't turn back to her.

"Which was your favorite design?" she asked, for want of a better idea.

He gave a curt, humorless laugh. "Do you care?"

"As a matter of fact, I do. I'm going to have to look at the thing from the school yard every day. I'd rather look at something aesthetically pleasing." At his continuing silence, she added, "I live in this town, too, Paul."

She could discern the tension in Paul as his shoulders shifted beneath his shirt, as his muscles flexed in his forearms. She could feel it emanating from him in hot, angry waves. "This is hard for me," he whispered, so softly she had to strain to hear him.

"What's hard?"

At last he rotated to confront her. "As if it's not enough, what happened between us, what I did . . . As if that wasn't bad enough, now I'm going to cram this memorial down your throat. I almost wish—" He sighed and glanced away. "I wish I didn't have to build it, Bonnie. I wish I could do that for you. But I can't."

After what he'd told her on her back porch the other morning, she understood what he meant. She didn't like the concept of the memorial any more now than she had when he'd proposed it at the town meeting a month ago, but at least she now understood how essential it was to him.

"Sit down, Paul." Her tone was quiet but firm. "Please talk to me."

He hesitated for a minute. Then he reluctantly lowered himself to sit next to her, bending his knees and resting his forearms across them. The oak's shadow softened the harsh features of his face, making his eyes appear more deep-set, his jaw less rugged.

"Where's the memorial supposed to go?" she asked.

"On top of the hill," he explained, angling his head toward the grassy rise behind him.

"Which design did you like best?"

He opened the folder and flipped through the sketches. "I don't know," he said. "They're all so . . . so gloomy. Ever since they built the national memorial down in D.C. out of black granite, that's what everyone associates with Vietnam memorials. Look at this." He handed her a photograph of a huge stone V in a waterside park. The V was constructed of what appeared to be black marble, with names carved into its sides. "It's a picture of the memorial they recently put up in New Haven. One of the designers sent it along with his proposal, for comparison's sake. Look at it, Bonnie—a V. What the hell is it supposed to stand for, victory?"

She stared at the photograph of the austere sculpture. "Maybe it stands for Vietnam, or veterans," she suggested. "Then again, where I come from, if you shape your fingers into a V it means peace."

"Yeah." He slid the photograph back into the folder, then showed her a few sketches of tall, pointed, four-sided obelisks that bore an uncanny resemblance to the war monument already standing on the green. "Look at these. It's like they're saying, 'Vietnam was just a war like any other.'"

Vietnam hadn't been like any other war—even Bonnie knew that. "What sort of memorial would you like?" she asked him. "If you designed it, what would it look like?"

"I'm not a designer," he said. "I don't know. But it wouldn't be so damned...morbid."

"It's supposed to commemorate those who died," she reminded him. "How can it be anything but morbid? War is about death, isn't it?"

Paul cursed under his breath. "I really don't want to have this argument," he snapped, starting to his feet.

She reached out and clasped his forearm. His skin was warm beneath the wiry dark hair. Although there was no force in her touch, he sank back down onto the grass. She let her hand linger on him for as long as she dared. When he directed his gaze to where she was touching him she sensed his uneasiness and returned her hand to the safety of her lap. He lifted his eyes to her face and then looked away abruptly, before the distress in his eyes could register fully on her.

"Are you okay?" he asked, addressing the grass more than her.

"Yes."

"I mean..." He drew in a deep breath, then exhaled. "I don't have the right to ask anything of you, Bonnie, but promise me you'll let me know if you—if it turns out you're..." His voice drifted off.

Bonnie had no trouble finishing the sentence. "I'll let you know."

"What were you reading?" he asked, gesturing toward the manuscript.

She gave him a curious look. A minute ago he'd seemed desperate to get away from her, and now he was starting up a conversation. "It's a section of the book about Gary," she replied carefully, trying to gauge his reaction. "Just a rough draft. Kevin McCoy wants my input."

Paul eyed the manuscript pages stacked neatly in her lap. "Is it good?"

"Yes," Bonnie said automatically, then reconsidered her answer. "I don't know, Paul. I'm not sure what I think of it."

"Isn't that something," he muttered wryly. "You don't like your husband's book, and I don't like my memorial designs."

"Maybe we're just hard to please." Bonnie smiled tentatively. It gratified her to think they had something—no matter how inane—in common.

"Maybe." For a while he sat silently, observing the sporadic flow of traffic on the road bordering the western edge of the green. Bonnie studied him in profile: his high forehead, the clean, sharp slope of his nose, his stubborn chin, the protruding bone in his neck, the smoldering darkness of his eyes.

She suppressed the impulse to touch him again, to gather him into her arms. If he'd needed her two nights ago, he was apparently trying very hard not to need her anymore. He wasn't Shane; she couldn't kiss his bruises and make them better.

"How's the tree?" he asked.

"What tree?"

He shot her a quick glance, then focused on the street once more. "The birch tree."

"Oh." She had nearly forgotten that the birch tree was what had brought him to her house Thursday night—and, indirectly, what had brought her to his nursery today. "It's fine," she told him. "By yesterday evening the front yard was pretty well dried out, and the stakes are holding."

"Good."

"It's a beautiful tree."

Paul's gaze seemed to drift to some faraway place. "You've got to treat it with respect," he murmured, half to himself.

"What? The tree?"

"All trees. I tried to teach that to Shane today."

Bonnie contemplated him, surprised that he should have espoused such a philosophy—and then, as she thought about it, not so terribly surprised at all. He was a nurseryman, a farmer. It was only natural that he would respect trees.

Silence stretched between them for a few seconds. "How long should I keep the stakes propping it up?" she asked.

He gave her a sidelong glance. "As long as the tree needs them. Once it's strong enough, you can pull them out."

"How will I know when the tree is strong enough?"

"By the way it looks and the way it feels. You check it, you get a sense of how secure it is. When it's strong enough you'll know it."

"What if I don't? I'm not an expert, Paul. I couldn't save that sickly dogwood tree."

"This tree's different. Your son gave it to you. You aren't going to let it die."

His confidence in her seemed totally misplaced.
"Maybe…maybe you could come and check on the tree
every now and then?"

His eyes met hers. "No, Bonnie. I can't do that."

"But if it starts wobbling or something, if there's another storm—"

"No."

"Then *you'd* be the one to let it die," she accused, her
frustration bubbling over. No matter how bad Paul felt
about Bonnie, he owed her birch tree something. He was
the one who'd just declared that trees needed respect.
"It's me, isn't it? You'd rather let my birch tree die than
have to deal with me, right?"

"Bonnie—"

"Am I right, Paul, or aren't I?" She was running the
risk of pushing him too far, but at that moment she
didn't care. "What's more important—keeping a tree
alive or running away from me?"

She detected the fury burning inside him, the rage and
resentment. All he said, though, was "I've got to go"
and started to his feet again.

Bonnie gripped his wrist and yanked him back down,
refusing to let him shut her out. "Why are you punishing me?" she demanded. "What the hell did I ever do to
you?"

He slid his wrist from her grasp and stared at her, his
gaze impenetrable. "I'm not punishing you," he said in
a low, hoarse tone. "I'm trying to protect you, damn it."

"What if I don't want to be protected?"

He shook his head and stood. "I'd protect you anyway," he insisted, smoothing out the papers inside the
folder. "That's the way it is with us Nam veterans, Bonnie—we fight wars no one wants us to fight, and we protect people who don't want protection. Only this time…"

He favored her with a wistful look. "This time, maybe I'm doing the right thing." His gaze grew icy and he turned from her.

She watched as he moved in long, measured strides across the green in the direction of the town hall, as he opened the door and vanished inside. She watched, feeling a chill overtake her, sensing that something vital had slipped away forever.

Chapter Eleven

"Let's run through it one more time," the captain said. "I'm still not clear on how you became separated from the others."

Paul glanced toward the window. Morning was creeping up on the camp, but no sunlight penetrated the dense, slate-colored clouds that hovered low overhead. He was tired but unable to sleep, hungry but unable to eat, half-mad with grief and fear but unable to cry.

"I didn't become separated, sir," he explained, turning back to the captain. He lowered his eyes, and they came to rest on his hands. A trace of Swann's blood was still on his wrist. For a brief, insane moment, Paul imagined that it would be there forever, a permanent mark. "It was more a deliberate thing, sir," he elaborated. "We...kind of made a decision to split up."

"Nobody ever splits up night patrols," the captain said. He didn't sound critical; rather, he seemed curious that this time a patrol happened not to follow standard procedure and as a result wound up not getting completely wiped out. "What made Macon decide to do that?"

Paul almost blurted out that Macon hadn't decided to do anything, other than threaten Paul for his disobedience. He wanted to come clean, to tell his story with candor. But what would honesty get him? A clean conscience, perhaps, but a dishonorable discharge. A purged soul and two years in the slammer. What had happened on a dirt road in the woods last night had been pointless. Opening himself to disciplinary action would be even more pointless.

"We thought we might pick up a little more action if we spread out, sir," he said, taking no comfort in the realization that what he'd said was essentially the truth. They'd spread out and caught action, all right.

"And you personally didn't return fire?"

"I couldn't, sir. I would have had to fire blind or else walk into the ambush. Macon and Rigucci returned fire from where they were. Swann had been hit almost immediately."

"How many enemy troops were there, Tremaine?"

"I don't know, sir."

"And even though you didn't know, you went in in an attempt to rescue Private Swann?"

Paul closed his eyes. His wet fatigues seemed to have shrunk against his skin. His feet were numb and his head pounded with echoes of the firefight. The muscles in his abdomen clenched, making him nauseous. "Yes, sir," he said, his voice betraying nothing of his emotional state. "Not that it did any good, sir."

"I'd say that took a lot of guts, soldier."

Oh, God, Paul thought. If he'd had guts he would be telling the captain what had really gone down last night. If he'd had guts, he would have been with Swann when he died. They would have died together.

"Go get yourself cleaned up," the captain commanded. "I'll send Markey and his men to recover Macon and Rigucci. The map you drew will get them there—

*they won't require your escort. You look like you could
use a shower and some rest."*

"Yes, sir."

*"It was a tough one, Tremaine. You did good. If you
feel the need to talk about it, I'm sure the chaplain—"*

"Thank you, sir. I don't think I'll feel that need, sir."
He stood, saluted and left the room. Outside, his knees
began to buckle and he sank onto the wooden steps. He
couldn't throw up, not here, not on the front steps of
HQ. He had to get himself to the latrine. Once he washed
off Swann's blood he'd feel better.

*A low moan wrenched free from the deepest part of his
soul. He feared that no amount of washing would ever
remove Swann's blood from him.*

HE DIDN'T HEAR the knocking right away. He'd put a
vintage Rolling Stones album on the stereo at high volume, and he had just opened his second bottle of beer.
The dishes were done and a Stephen King novel awaited
him on the coffee table in the living room. He enjoyed
reading horror novels. To him, psychotic cars, teleki-
netic teenagers, animal graveyards and the like were a
laugh compared to some of things he'd been through.

It was six-thirty; he wasn't expecting any visitors. As
it was, he had deliberately opted to spend the evening
alone. John Slinger had phoned him at the nursery a
couple of hours ago and asked if he wanted to shoot some
pool down at Max's that evening, but he'd begged off.
He didn't feel particularly sociable these days.

Ever since he'd walked away from Bonnie on the town
green five days ago, his emotions had been in a tailspin.
He'd managed to conduct business with his usual
equanimity, to swap jokes with his customers and offer
the necessary words of praise to his employees. Just that

morning, he'd spent several productive hours at a housing subdivision in Stow, collaborating with the project's landscape architect to put together an extremely lucrative order for the nursery. He'd been able to review the memorial designs with Ed Marshal calmly and objectively over lunch a couple of days back, explaining that while none of the proposals was abominable, none of them thrilled him, either.

But at around five-thirty each afternoon, when his work was done and his daily ration of charm depleted, he'd headed straight for home, choosing to spare the world his wretched mood. He'd turned down a dinner invitation from a woman in Lowell whom he'd dated a few times, and he'd passed on an evening of poker at his uncle's house last night and pool with John Slinger tonight. He felt as if he had to learn all over again how to live with himself, how to accept who he was and what he'd done and what it had cost his psyche, before he inflicted himself on others.

Part of him—the decent, nice part—knew he'd been right to cut himself off from Bonnie, and another part—his heart and soul—knew that in spite of everything she desired him as much as he desired her. The way she'd touched him, the way her fingers had grazed his arm and then molded to it, the way her eyes had searched his face...

From the moment he and Bonnie had confronted each other in her driveway one balmy late afternoon a few weeks ago, the chemistry had been there, the attraction mutual and strong. It seemed clear to Paul that she hadn't yet figured out how to ignore it.

Neither, he admitted, had he.

In the lull between two songs on the record, he caught the sound of someone banging on his front door. Setting his beer beside his book on the coffee table, he headed down the hall to the door and opened it.

"Hey, Paul," said Shane.

Paul stared in surprise at the lanky young man occupying the front step. Shane was dressed in his usual garb: T-shirt, torn jeans, oversize high-tops, leather necklace. His sandy-blond hair was typically messy. His face, however, was etched in panic, his eyes wild and his smile pleading. "Can I come in?"

"Sure," Paul said, waving him inside and closing the door behind him.

Shane dawdled in the hallway, gazing curiously through the arched entry into the living room. Not that Paul's house warranted curiosity—it was about as exciting as any bachelor's home, with mismatched furniture, trite still-life paintings decorating the walls, curtains that had been donated by an aunt and faded carpet covering the floors. The place was comfortable but not the least bit distinctive. It would never have occurred to Paul to adorn his window with a star-shaped crystal that would spray the walls with rainbows whenever the sunlight struck it.

"Come on in," he urged Shane, who was apparently waiting for permission to enter the living room. "What's up?"

"Nothing," Shane said—which was plainly a lie. His gaze skittered around the room and he shifted nervously from foot to foot.

"Can I get you something to drink?" Paul asked, reaching for his beer. He saw Shane's sparkling hazel eyes grow round and hastily clarified, "Some soda, or a glass of milk?"

"What kind of soda have you got?"

"Coke and ginger ale."

"I'll have a Coke," Shane told him, still rocking back and forth and looking remarkably ill at ease.

Paul considered interrogating him further about his emotional condition, but he checked the impulse. When Shane was ready to state his business, he would. Paul headed for the kitchen.

Returning to the living room with a glass of soda, he found Shane bent over the coffee table, flipping through the book. "Is this good?" the boy asked.

"I don't know. I haven't read it yet." Paul nodded toward the couch. Shane took a seat there, and Paul settled into the overstuffed armchair across the coffee table from him. He lifted his beer in a silent toast, then took a drink.

Shane sipped his soda, lowered the glass and jiggled his knee. He looked around the room in quick, fretful glances. "My mom thinks I don't read enough."

"Then maybe you ought to read more," Paul suggested evenly. If he let his mind wander, even for an instant, it would settle on an image of Bonnie, trying hard to look stern and earnest as she scolded her son while her luminous, lovely eyes radiated the message that, no matter how much or how little he read, Shane was the best thing ever to have happened to her.

Paul willfully blocked the image before it could insinuate itself too deeply inside him.

Shane took another sip of soda and jiggled his other knee. "I bet you're wondering how I found your house," he said, his eyes fixed on the bubbles rising in his glass.

"You looked me up in the telephone directory," Paul guessed.

"Yeah." Shane shot him a quick, half-formed grin. "And then I asked around, and this guy gave me..." His voice drifted off.

Paul scowled. When he'd discovered Shane on his doorstep, he hadn't noticed a bicycle on the front walk or leaning against the side of the house. "Did you hitch a ride?" he asked.

Shane cringed, then nodded. "Hey, look, Paul . . . it's like, I'm kind of in trouble."

Paul refrained from chewing him out about hitchhiking. He'd leave that lecture to Bonnie. "Does your mother know where you are?" he asked.

"Uh-uh. Oh, man . . . She's gonna kill me if she finds me."

Paul wondered whether he should interpret Shane's claim as mere adolescent theatricality or something more serious. "Your mother doesn't believe in killing," he said, trying to keep his tone devoid of sarcasm. "We ought to give her a call and let her know where you are. She's probably worried."

"No way!" Shane shook his head frantically. "You can't call her, Paul! I'm not kidding—I'm in major trouble!"

Paul's instinct was to telephone Bonnie anyway. It was past dinnertime and getting dark; she might be agitated about her son's absence. But he decided to give Shane a little more time to explain what had happened before Bonnie was dragged into the picture. "What kind of trouble?" he asked.

Shane looked toward the window and jiggled both knees.

"Are you in legal hot water?" Paul pressed him. "You haven't been messing around with drugs or anything, have you?"

"No."

"Vandalism? Shoplifting?"

"No."

Of course not. Shane was a good kid. What could he possibly have done that was so terrible he was afraid to face his mother about it?

"You didn't get a girl pregnant, did you?" Paul asked, mostly to jolt a response out of Shane.

The response he got spooked him. Shane flinched, turned ashen and gasped. "Uh-uh! It wasn't like that at all, Paul—I swear. We didn't even take all our clothes off—I swear to God we didn't."

Okay. Whatever had happened, it had something to do with a girl. Paul experienced no small amount of relief to know that Shane hadn't messed around with drugs—and to know that, in the context Shane apparently *had* messed around, he hadn't been totally naked.

On the other hand, Paul was hardly qualified to advise anyone—let alone Bonnie's son—when it came to sexual activity.

"Did you keep your pants on?" he asked, figuring the best strategy was to find out precisely what Shane had done.

"Yeah, well...I mean, I didn't take 'em off, you know?"

"I don't know, Shane. I wish you'd tell me, so I could figure out what the hell's going on."

Shane took a deep breath, fortified himself with several noisy gulps of soda and then sank into the sofa cushions. "It was, like... See, there's this girl at school, Melinda Garrison, and she's really foxy, you know? And she told Jennifer Lash that she thought I was cute, and Jennifer told my best friend Matt, and he told me...."

This rang a bell. "I think you mentioned her to me," Paul said.

Shane nodded. "Well, anyway, she invited me over to her house after school today, so I went. And, like, her mom wasn't home." Petering to a halt, Shane lifted his glass to his lips and drained it.

"And then?" Paul prompted Shane when his silence extended beyond a minute.

"Well, it was kind of her idea."

"What was her idea?"

"That we should, sort of, like, touch each other. But that's all we did, I swear. If she's pregnant, it's not my fault. I didn't do anything!"

"If you didn't do anything," Paul reasoned, "then there's no reason to be afraid of calling your mother. Just to let her know you're safe," he added when his simple suggestion caused Shane to blanch.

"She'll kill me," Shane insisted. "I'm not supposed to go to a girl's house when there aren't any grown-ups around. And besides . . . I mean, like . . . we *touched* each other."

"All right, so you touched each other. It's not the end of the world," Paul assured him. If Shane had forced himself on this girl, if he'd acted like a maniac, the way Paul had with Bonnie—that would have been different. But this sounded like a rather innocuous episode, all told. "Boys and girls do that kind of stuff sometimes. It's a part of growing up, Shane."

"Yeah, but . . . I mean . . ." Shane's cheeks darkened from a sickly pallor to an equally sickly flush. "We were on her bed," he explained in a near whisper. "And, man, it felt . . ." He closed his eyes and swallowed. "I mean, I didn't know it was going to feel like that."

Paul glanced away in deference to Shane's obvious embarrassment. His own, too. He could identify with Shane; he knew that, in some ways, men never progressed beyond that glorious fourteen-year-old astonishment that a woman could make you feel so utterly wonderful.

"And then her mom came home and found us," Shane continued.

"Ah." No wonder the kid was so upset.

"The old lady threw a major fit," Shane mumbled. "I thought she was gonna kill me."

"Mothers of daughters can be that way."

"I just ran. I didn't know what else to do."

Right, Paul muttered beneath his breath. Just as mothers were apt to throw fits, men were apt to run away. When things got too intense, when a man went too far and couldn't face up to what he'd done, he ran.

"Did—did you ever get caught, Paul?" Shane asked. "I mean, doing something like that."

Paul reminisced. Once, during his senior year in high school, some of his buddies had shadowed him and Amy Farrell down to the road near Breaker Gorge where they'd gone parking, and bombarded them with catcalls and flashlight beams through the windshield just when they'd started getting it on in the back seat. As humiliating as that had been, however, it wasn't the same thing as getting caught by a girl's mother.

But with maturity came different humiliations. Paul no longer feared getting caught by someone else. What concerned him now was getting caught by himself. Whatever shame he felt these days was self-inflicted.

"Maybe you should give the girl a call," Paul recommended. "Melinda, right? You could check and see if everything's cool at her end."

"No way," Shane groaned. "I'd rather die."

"That's not too mature, Shane," Paul chided gently. "If you were willing to fool around with her, you ought to be willing to talk to her on the phone."

"Yeah, well... It's not her I'm worried about. It's her mom. What if she answers the phone? What if her *father* answers it?" Simply thinking of such a dire possibility prompted another groan from Shane.

"She's at her house facing up to her folks," Paul pointed out. "The least you could do is face up to your own mother. Come on, Shane, I'll show you where the phone is. Give your mom a call and let her know you're all right."

"Uh-uh." Shane looked desolate. "Would you call her, please, Paul? I don't think I can handle talking to her."

I don't think I can handle it, either, Paul responded silently. But if he were in Bonnie's position, he'd be desperate for news that his son was safe, and he wouldn't give a damn about who the messenger was. "All right," he said reluctantly, heaving himself out of the chair and taking his beer with him. He had a feeling he might need it to get through the conversation. "Don't go anywhere. She's probably going to want to talk to you."

"Tell her I can't talk," Shane implored him. "Tell her I got laryngitis or something."

Paul gave him a reproving look and then trudged out to the kitchen. "What's the number?" he called to Shane. Shane shouted the digits and Paul pushed the buttons.

Bonnie answered on the second ring. "Hello?"

For a woman whose son was unaccounted for, she sounded surprisingly placid. "Bonnie, this is Paul Tremaine," he said, keeping his voice impassive.

She said nothing for a minute, and then, "Oh. Hello, Paul."

"I'm calling to let you know that Shane is here."

Another pause. When she finally spoke, she sounded confused. "He's where?"

"Here with me, at my house."

"I thought—no, that can't be. I spoke to his friend Matt Molson a while ago, and he told me Shane was with him. I thought he was supposed to be staying for dinner."

Evidently Shane's best friend had covered for him. "Well, Bonnie," Paul said, hating to have to reveal Shane's deception to his mother, "the fact of the matter is, he's sitting in my living room right now, listening to Mick Jagger on the stereo. I asked him to call you himself, but he . . . he got himself into a little scrape this afternoon, and he's afraid you're going to come down hard on him."

Again, Bonnie took her time before answering. "I probably will. I don't understand any of this, Paul. What kind of scrape did Shane get himself into? Was he hitchhiking again?"

"Well, that's only part of it. It seems he got caught making out with a girl from his school."

"Oh, Lord." Bonnie sounded both annoyed and relieved. "What happened, did he get detention?"

"He wasn't caught making out with her at school. He was caught at her house, by her mother."

He heard a noise that could have been a curse or a bark of laughter. "I hope the woman gave him a good swift kick in the pants," Bonnie muttered.

"I don't think she had the opportunity. According to Shane, he bolted at the earliest opportunity."

"Then I guess I'll have to do the kicking. Could you please put him on?"

"He's not really eager to talk to you right now," Paul warned her. "He thinks you're going to kill him."

"And I thought the terrible-twos were rough." Bonnie sighed. "Well, I'll come over and pick him up. You'll have to tell me where you live."

Paul thought for a minute. Although she kept her anger under wraps, he could sense the exasperation in Bonnie's voice. She'd been lied to and disobeyed. And then, to add insult to injury, her son had sought haven with Paul. She shouldn't have to drive through town to fetch the kid.

If he drove Shane home, he could drop him off and split before Bonnie had a chance to engage him in a conversation, before she had a chance to curve her graceful fingers around his arm and gaze into his eyes. He would be in control of things.

"I'll bring him to you," Paul said. "It may take a while, though. He needs to build up the courage to face you."

Bonnie didn't respond directly to Paul's offer. "He didn't by any chance fill you in on any of the details about this tryst, did he?"

"He claims they kept their clothes on."

"Thank God for small blessings," Bonnie grumbled. "Please bring him home as soon as you can, Paul. It's a school night, and he and I have some talking to do."

"I'll do my best."

"Thanks. I'll see you later." She hung up.

Paul stared at the dead receiver in his hand, then slowly placed it in its cradle. He wasn't exactly thrilled at the prospect of seeing Bonnie. If her brusque farewell was anything to go by, she felt the same way about seeing him. But it would be over with quickly enough. Maybe he wouldn't even get out of the truck. He'd keep the engine running, shove Shane out the passenger door and speed away.

He'd do what he had to do, and then he'd run. That, after all, was what men did.

THE TREMAINE NURSERY TRUCK turned onto the driveway, its heavily treaded tires spraying loose pebbles in all directions. Bonnie had spent the entire half hour since Paul's telephone call seated on the porch, watching for Shane and Paul and trying to sort her thoughts.

When had Shane started noticing girls? He and Matt had taken a rather lusty interest in the *Sports Illustrated* swimsuit issue last winter, but that was a far cry from being caught necking with a female classmate. Who was the girl, anyway? And when had Shane learned how to kiss?

The particulars of his escapade provoked a certain degree of maternal chagrin on Bonnie's part. But what bothered her went beyond the fact that Shane had spent an unchaperoned afternoon at a girl's house and arranged to have his best friend lie about it. Her little boy was growing up fast, and she wasn't sure she was ready for it.

Oddly enough, she was consoled by the fact that after leaving the girl's house Shane had gone to see Paul. Hitching there had been stupid, but his destination had been a sound choice. When it came to advice about sex, Paul could—

What? What on earth could Paul tell him? That if your relationship with a woman reaches a dangerous degree of intimacy, you ought to beat a hasty retreat?

She remained on the porch until Paul turned off the engine. Then she stood, swept back the stray hairs that had unraveled from her ponytail and sauntered across the lawn to the driveway, her hands on her hips and her mouth twisted into an appropriately severe frown.

Through the open passenger window she saw Shane shrink at her approach. Reaching over the gear stick, Paul gave him a nudge and a concise pep talk: "Go ahead, Shane. She's not going to bite."

Sighing dolefully, Shane edged the door open and stepped down onto the gravel. He shut the door behind him and mumbled, "Sorry, Mom."

"I'll bet you are," she muttered.

Paul had made no move to join Shane outside the truck. His gaze met hers and he offered a crooked smile. "He's all yours," he said with mock generosity.

"Don't remind me." Above the rustic symphony of chirping crickets and chattering birds Bonnie heard Shane's footsteps whispering through the unmowed grass as he trudged across the lawn to the porch and inside the house. She glanced over her shoulder in time to see him slam the screen door shut behind himself, and then she turned back to Paul. His eyes were radiant despite their smoky-brown color; there was nothing evasive in his gaze.

He didn't strike her as someone preparing to beat a hasty retreat. Pressing her luck, she asked, "Are you going to fill me in on what happened?"

"There's really not much to fill in," he answered.

She glanced behind her again and deduced from the illuminated second-floor window that Shane had headed directly into his bedroom—where, no doubt, he hoped to remain safely out of reach until Bonnie's fury burned itself out. Scowling, she spun back to Paul. "You called me over a half hour ago," she pointed out. "You and Shane must have been talking about something in all that time."

"We analyzed the lyrics to 'Wild Horses,'" said Paul.

"I need your help, Paul," she demanded, annoyed at having to ask for it. "Shane will never tell me what he's told you."

"Then I guess he doesn't want it told."

"Damn it, Paul—you don't have to titillate me with all the dirty details. Frankly, I'd rather not know about them. But I do need to know just how far this little fling went."

Paul weighed her plea before responding. "From what I gather, it didn't go very far."

"Paul!" She erupted in full-fledged anger, frustrated by her son's misbehavior, by her insecurities about her skill as a mother and, most of all, by Paul's reticence, by her failure to have established a cease-fire with him.

"What do you want from me?" he shot back. "Shane thought you'd be angry with him—rightly, as it turned out—so he came to me. I didn't give him the third degree, Bonnie. He said he messed around on the girl's bed for a while—"

"On her *bed*?" Bonnie gripped the chrome-trimmed edge of the sill and prayed for strength. "I thought they were just holding hands under an apple tree or something."

"I think kids are a little more sophisticated these days," Paul observed. Taking note of Bonnie's apparent distress, he added, "Filling in the blanks, I'd say it was mostly an I'll-show-you-mine-if-you-show-me-yours type thing."

"How can you be so cavalier about this?" she charged. This was the man who'd gone to pieces after sharing a bed with her—and they were two cognizant, responsible adults. Yet here he was, describing her son's first sexual encounter with a girl as if they were two preschoolers playing doctor.

He appraised her for a long moment, running his hands along the plastic curve of the steering wheel, mulling over his thoughts. "What are you going to do to him?" he asked, casting a quick look toward the lit second-floor window.

"I haven't decided," Bonnie admitted, sounding more helpless than she'd intended. "I don't know how to deal with this, Paul. I wish he'd talked to me about it first, or introduced me to the girl or something. I wish it had happened a little slower. He's only thirteen—"

"He's almost fourteen," Paul reminded her, remaining calm in the face of her obvious panic. "His voice has changed and he's going to be needing a razor soon. He's a good-looking kid. I'm sure girls have been admiring him for months, if not years. It's about time he reciprocated."

She knew that what Paul was saying made sense, but she was too rattled to assess the situation pragmatically. Never before had she felt so inadequate as a parent; never before had she wanted so desperately to lean on a man. "Spell it out for me," she implored him. "Tell me this is normal and I shouldn't go off the deep end about it."

Paul studied her for a minute more, then relented and pulled his keys from the ignition. He climbed out of the truck and ambled around to her side. "Come on," he said quietly, taking her elbow and ushering her across the lawn to the porch. "I'll fix you a drink."

"I told you, I can't drink after a day at work," she reminded him, nonetheless grateful that he'd chosen to stay and offer his support. "I might pass out."

"That's not such a bad idea," he muttered, guiding her into the kitchen. "Maybe when you wake up in the morning, you'll have such a whopping hangover you'll forget all about this other nonsense."

She gave him a vexed look. "I'm glad you think this is so funny."

"It isn't funny," he conceded, leaning against the counter a safe distance from her. "I'll even go so far as to admit it isn't nonsense. But what are you going to do, Bonnie? The kid's got hormones. Something like this was bound to happen sooner or later."

She let Paul's words sink in. She took heart not only in their logic but in the soothing warmth of Paul's voice, in the knowledge that, regardless of what else existed between them, he could still be her friend when she needed him.

"What do you think I should do?" she asked, her anger waning. "Should I ground him for a month, or have a heart-to-heart talk with him, or what?"

Paul shrugged. "You probably shouldn't do anything until tomorrow," he suggested. "That would give you both a chance to cool off."

"I don't know if I want to cool off," she said, even though it was too late. Her nervous system was no longer pumping extra adrenaline; her stomach was no longer tied in knots. "He did so many wrong things, Paul— hitchhiking, running away, lying, going to a girl's house without adult supervision—"

"And if you come down on him, what he's going to wind up taking away from it is that sex is evil. Is that the message you want to give him?"

Bonnie favored Paul with a steady stare. She most certainly did not believe that sex was evil, not when both parties were in agreement about what it entailed and what it implied. She was encouraged to think that Paul was of the same opinion, that perhaps, in time, he would come to acknowledge that what he and Bonnie had experienced together one stormy night hadn't been evil.

Standing in her kitchen with him awakened memories of how many good moments they'd shared, cleaning the dinner dishes, arguing about the memorial, laughing and philosophizing and simply feeling comfortable with each other. She missed his friendship. She missed that warm camaraderie that had flourished between them.

She missed him.

Her gaze traveled from his tousled mane of hair to his high forehead, his piercing eyes, his sharp nose and his thin, sensuous lips. She suffered not the first pang of regret at how dreadfully they'd both managed to botch things. But she wouldn't ask him to erase the past, to give their relationship another chance. She'd come as close as she dared to asking that of him the last time she'd seen him, and he'd firmly rejected her.

"I should be going," he said, glancing away. It dawned on her that he'd been gazing just as intently at her, that his eyes had been journeying over her sun-streaked hair to her lips, to her bare arms and her fine-boned hands and then down her long, denim-clad legs. Had he read her thoughts and shared them, sensed her longing and returned it?

"I'll walk you to the door," she offered, taking refuge in etiquette.

She accompanied him out onto the front porch. "Thanks for talking me down," she said. "I guess I was borderline-crazy for a few minutes, there."

"No problem," he said laconically.

She arched her arm around one of the upright beams and gazed out at the star-dappled sky. The air was warm and breezy; the song of the crickets endured, muted but constant. She waited for Paul to escape back to his truck, but he lingered on the top step, just inches from her, viewing the night sky with her.

"How are you?" he asked after a long silence.

The hushed quality of his voice informed her that the question had nothing to do with her anger concerning Shane's transgressions. "I'm fine," she replied.

"I mean . . . are you—"

"No," she said quickly, aware at once of what he was asking. "I'm not pregnant."

Still he hovered on the top step, neither leaving nor approaching her. "Bonnie . . ." He issued a shaky sigh. "I'm sorry. But we both know this just isn't meant to be."

"I'm not so sure I know that," she retorted, even though she was aware that arguing about it was futile.

"It's just . . ." He sighed again. "It's just that I can't go forward with anything when I'm still so tangled up in the past. You can understand that, can't you?"

"Paul—"

"And I won't be able to untangle myself from the past until I build that damned memorial—which you hate, and your husband would have hated—and you still love him, anyway. Don't you see? It's a mess."

His statement made clear, perfect sense. So why, when Bonnie was more than willing to acknowledge the logic in everything Paul had said, did she find herself letting her arm fall, and turning to face him, and taking one small step into his outstretched arms? Why did her head fall back just as his mouth came down on hers, hard and hungry, and why did she moan with joy the instant his lips took hers?

Sometimes logic had to be defied. Sometimes one had to shut out the questions, the doubt, the words of wisdom, and listen only to one's heart.

Tightening her hold on him, parting her lips and drawing him in, Bonnie listened to her heart.

Chapter Twelve

Kissing her felt too good. The texture of her lips, the smooth ridge of her teeth, the erotic motions of her tongue luring him deeper... He felt bewitched, beyond thought, unable to resist. There was something about Bonnie that made him want to relinquish control and let his instincts take over.

The last time he did that, he'd experienced nothing but terror and guilt. This time, despite the warning signals his brain was sending out, he was experiencing only desire, the glorious ache of wanting her. Not just any woman—he wanted Bonnie. He wanted her delicate floral scent to envelop him and her warmth to permeate him. He wanted to drink her in, absorb her, become one with her. He wanted to feel her around him, responding, cresting. He wanted her to gasp with ecstasy this time.

This time. That nagging alarm sounded in his skull, reminding him of what had happened the last time. Chastened, he pulled back and gazed at her. Her lips were moist, her eyes glittering beneath heavy lids. "Don't stop," she whispered, sliding her hands up his spine to the nape of his neck and weaving her fingers together.

His back flexed in the wake of her sweeping caress, and he instinctively leaned into her hands. She twirled her thumbs through his hair and he groaned softly. "We shouldn't," he said without much conviction.

"I think we should," she countered, her voice low and hoarse.

"Great. Now we've got something else to disagree about."

"We don't disagree about this," Bonnie murmured, pulling his mouth back to hers.

He could have prolonged the debate. He could have pointed out that they didn't even agree on whether they agreed. But once again his emotions overruled his mind and he gave himself over to the pleasure of kissing her. His hands journeyed along her back, her sides, the sleek curves of her hips. He dug his fingertips into the flesh of her bottom. Arching against him, she made a soft, purring sound at the back of her throat.

"I can't," he groaned. It was almost as if someone else had spoken, some other voice, distant and disembodied. His actions contradicted those two clear, dispassionate words: he continued to massage the round flesh of her bottom with one hand while the other roamed up to her ribs and forward, teasing the underside of her breast. His lips grazed from her mouth to her cheek and then her brow. "This is a mistake, Bonnie," he whispered into her hair.

"It's not a mistake." She brushed her lips against his chin, then lifted her eyes.

He pulled his hands from her. The loss of contact hurt, but if he touched her any more, he'd never be able to stop. "You love Gary," he reminded her—and himself.

"Gary's dead," she said with a finality that surprised him.

"Not in your heart, he isn't. Not in your thoughts. You've got a million pictures of him on display in your living room, Bonnie. You still worship him. He's the one you love.'"

Her gaze narrowed and she jutted out her chin pugnaciously. "Since when do you know everything?" she asked hotly.

"Damn it, Bonnie—I *don't* know everything, but I *do* know I'm not right for you. Maybe at this moment it feels right, but..."

"But what?" she challenged, her eyes blazing with anger. "But I'm not allowed to care for you because we were on opposite sides of a political conflict twenty years ago?"

"We're on opposite sides today," he noted quietly.

"Opposite sides of what, your stupid memorial?" She broke from him and stormed the length of the porch, giving free vent to her rage. "Go ahead, build the damned thing. Build your silly heap of granite. See if I care!"

Her raving was obviously a result of frustration. Paul was frustrated, too, his body still burning, his mouth still tingling with the taste of her. But beneath her frustration lay an undeniable truth: she *did* think his memorial was stupid, silly, a damned thing, a heap of granite. She and Paul *were* on opposite sides.

He cared for her, too. He cared too much to take advantage of her. If the only thing he felt for her was desire, he'd gather her back into his arms and contrive a way for them to spend the night together. Instead, he was trying to figure out a way to leave, to get away before he wound up hurting her again.

"I'd better go," he said, wincing inwardly at how blunt he sounded.

She glowered at him from the far end of the porch. He detected sorrow and bitterness in her expression. Even when he was trying so hard not to hurt her, when he was willingly sacrificing his own yearning in order to protect her, he seemed to have scored a direct hit. It didn't matter what he did; he was obviously fated to cause her pain.

Sighing, refusing to give lip service to yet another empty apology, he stepped off the porch and jogged across the lawn to his truck. Before he climbed in, he turned back to the house. He saw Bonnie pivot on her heel and stalk inside. Through the screen door, he heard the sound of something shattering against the hardwood floor in the living room.

SHE PICTURED Jacqueline Kennedy, Coretta Scott King, Ethel Kennedy—those fine brave women, never allowing their grief to erode their dignity, never going crazy, howling, kicking walls or tearing at their hair. Their husbands had been not just murdered but martyred, and as the widows of martyrs they had assumed a special function, a heroic demeanor. They couldn't just fall apart and leave it at that.

Bonnie wanted to fall apart—and she ought to have been able to, once Shane had been safely installed at her parents' house in Newton. But the airplane was too public, and Tom and Marcie were flanking her, fussing over her every time she let the merest whimper escape. She felt so self-conscious, so utterly exposed. So unnaturally grown-up.

"I'm going to the lavatory," she told her companions.

Tom immediately rose to his feet to let her out into the aisle. Marcie rose, as well. "I'll come with you," she offered solicitously.

"You will not," Bonnie said, managing a feeble smile. "I'll be back in a few minutes." She edged past Tom into

the aisle and strode toward the back of the plane. A flight attendant gave her a compassionate look as she stepped aside to let Bonnie pass.

Everybody knew. Gary's death had received some coverage in the press: "Well-Known Peace Activist Struck Down by Hit-and-Run Driver During College Campus Tour." Even if the flight crew hadn't read about it in the newspapers, they knew that this plane was transporting his body back east for burial, accompanied by his widow and his two associates. Bonnie supposed that such a cargo wasn't all that unusual for airlines, but whenever she thought of herself as "escorting the body" she felt squeamish.

Once inside the lavatory, she locked the door, lowered the seat lid and collapsed onto it. The past few days had been a blur, from Marcie's hysterical 3:00 a.m. long-distance phone call to this plane trip back to Boston. "There's been an accident, Bonnie," Marcie had choked out. "I'm at the hospital. It's Gary...." And then Tom's voice replaced Marcie's on the line: "I'm sorry, Bonnie. I don't know how to say this any other way. It's really bad. You're going to have to fly out here."

She had arrived in Fresno late the following day. Tom had been waiting for her at the local airport. Driving into town in his rental car, he'd told her what had happened: "The speech went down weird, Bonnie. There were hecklers in the crowd, a really savage gang that kept trying to shout him down. Vietnam veterans, I think, California rednecks. Every time Gary said something bad about the war they shouted threats. They were macho hotshots, you know the kind—they don't feel like they're real men unless they're carrying a gun. Usually hecklers add some spice to a lecture, but these guys spooked me, Bonnie. They spooked Gary, too. When we left the au-

ditorium, he said he had a feeling we'd be hearing from them again.''

They'd run him down. They had run her husband down and killed him, simply because he believed in peace.

At least he'd died for something worthwhile, she thought, propping her elbows on her knees and resting her head in her cupped hands. At least he hadn't died in vain. Like the soldiers who hadn't survived their tours of duty in Vietnam, Gary was a casualty of war. But his war wasn't about American imperialism and the support of unpopular foreign rulers; it was about nonviolence, about the respect for life and the necessity of finding nonmilitary solutions to the world's problems. Gary had died for a cause—and somehow, that made his death a little easier to accept.

Easier, but not easy. No matter how he'd died, or why, he was gone. Bonnie and Shane were alone now. Gary had left them forever.

The tears welled up and spilled over, streaking down her cheeks and leaving damp spots on her Indian-print skirt. The sound of her muted weeping echoed in the tiny enclosure, but she didn't care. She would allow herself one minute to cry, and then she'd wash up, collect herself and return to her seat between Marcie and Tom for the remainder of the trip home. She'd be a fine, brave, dignified widow once more.

"YOU SURE I'M NOT in trouble?" Shane asked meekly.

Bonnie shot him a quick glance, then turned her attention back to the road. "Why should you be in trouble?" she asked. "Your report card was fine, all except for history. I would have liked to see better than a C-plus for the quarter."

"My final grade was a B-minus," he reminded her.

"It would have been a B if you hadn't slacked off this spring. History is important, Shane. It's impossible to know where you're going if you have no idea of where you've been."

"Looks to me like where I'm going is exactly the same place as where I've been," Shane quipped, slouching in his seat and propping one sneakered foot against the glove compartment.

Bonnie gave him another swift look to make sure he had on his seat belt, and then shook her head, envious of the physical elasticity of youth. If she'd attempted that position, the police would probably have to come and cut her out of the car with the Jaws of Life.

It was a summer-warm morning; the sky was scattered with puffy white clouds and the route heading southeast into Boston was relatively free of traffic. Yesterday had been the last day of the school term. Bonnie would be teaching an enrichment reading course over the summer, but the next two weeks were hers to do with as she wished.

What she'd wished was, as Shane had said, to go back to where she'd been. Her justification for the trip to Boston was to deliver Kevin McCoy's manuscript to him in person, to explain her scribbled corrections and comments. But deep in her heart, she knew that Cambridge was really where she wanted to go.

One week ago she'd taken one of the framed photographs of Gary and hurled it to the floor, shattering the glass front and fracturing the chrome frame. It was a photo of Gary and Tom Schuyler with their arms around each other's shoulders. When Bonnie had flown into the living room that night, smarting from Paul's rejection, she'd discerned something annoying about the two men in the photograph, something taunting and cocky. There they'd stood on the steps in front of the Radcliffe Library, sneering down at the photographer.

That night, they'd been sneering down at Bonnie from the mantel, and she hadn't been able to stand it. So she'd smashed the photograph.

The impact had sobered her. She'd swept up the splinters of glass, and then carried the broken frame and the creased photograph upstairs to her bedroom. She'd lain in bed, staring at Gary's image until she was convinced that he hadn't truly been sneering. "I'm sorry," she'd whispered to the long-haired man in the wrinkled photograph, not at all sure of what she was apologizing for.

Shane broke into her thoughts. "You really aren't mad at me?"

"What are you getting at?" she asked, relieved to bring her attention back into the present. "Have you done something I should be mad about?"

"Not recently," he drawled, shoving his wind-tangled hair out of his face. "Next car you get ought to have air-conditioning, Mom."

Not recently. "You're referring to the incident with Melinda Garrison?" Bonnie had finally wrangled the girl's name from Shane and had a reassuring telephone conversation with Melinda's mother.

Shane fidgeted with his leather necklace. "It's like...I mean, she has nothing to do with my getting a B-minus in history."

"A C-plus, but let's not quibble," Bonnie interjected. "I never thought your interest in girls was causing your grades to drop."

"I'm not interested in girls," Shane insisted. "It was just her. Most girls are weird."

"Shane..." She sighed. Even if he thought girls were weird, he had hormones, as Paul had pointed out. "I just want you to remember, honey, that girls have feelings, too. No matter what you do with them, you've always got to remember that. You should never pressure them or try to get them to do something they don't want to do."

"Yeah, sure," Shane mumbled, sounding both embarrassed and impatient.

If she weren't his mother, if she could get Paul to tell him these things... She could only hope he was taking her words to heart. "And you've got to be honest with girls. They like honesty in a guy, more than anything else."

"Okay," he said defensively. "I'm sorry I didn't tell you I was going to her house. I won't lie again."

That wasn't the message Bonnie had been trying to convey, but she'd take what she could get. "Good. I want you to be straight with me, Shane. We've both learned something from this episode. I'm not upset about it anymore."

Shane eyed her with a gratitude he would never give voice to. "I guess it'll be fun seeing Richie," he said.

Ten minutes later, Bonnie pulled up to the house on Chilton Street where Shane's childhood friend, Richie Wyler, lived. Richie's mother invited her to stay for coffee, but Bonnie begged off with the excuse that Kevin McCoy was expecting her. After issuing the obligatory parental warnings about behaving nicely, she kissed her son goodbye and left, driving directly to Harvard Square.

The change in the neighborhood disconcerted her, even though she'd witnessed much of its evolution during the years she'd lived in Cambridge. She'd seen the city's population transformed from ragtag street people and petition-bearing activists to impeccably dressed young executives armed with leather briefcases. Where posters had once hung advertising peace rallies, there were now fliers advertising cleaning services. Psychedelic shop window displays had been replaced by high-tech arrangements of expensive imported sweaters. Everything looked clean and chic and cold.

Shane was wrong. Bonnie might have come back to where she'd once been, but it wasn't the same place anymore. She probably would have been better off having a cup of coffee with Richie's mother.

Instead, she pointed her car toward Kevin McCoy's office in Boston.

"THANKS," SAID PAUL, accepting the telephone from the clerk. He'd just been summoned to the back office adjacent to the retail greenhouse to take the call. Through the doorway he could see a couple of shoppers browsing among the potted plants; through an open window he could see a row of birch trees lined up against a frame next to the parking lot. The trees reminded him of Bonnie and he turned away. "Paul Tremaine here," he said into the phone.

"Hey, man, it's me," John Slinger greeted him over the wire. "How've you been?"

"Fine," Paul lied. "And yourself?"

"Worried about you. Where've you been hiding yourself, guy? Nobody's seen you for weeks."

"I'm not hiding. You know exactly where I am right now," Paul remarked, refusing to let John put him on the defensive. "If you want to see me, come to the nursery and buy a bush."

"I wanted to see you at Max's later," John suggested. "What do you say we meet for a beer and shoot a few rounds of pool this evening after work? My old lady's been dumping on me lately. I want to spend a couple of hours with someone I like.''

"I'll have to pass. I'm really not—"

"You really are," John cut him off. He sounded solemn; the laughter was gone from his voice. "Listen, Paul, if you're going through a rough one, you've got to let it out. If you don't want to shoot pool at Max's, we'll go somewhere else. But you've got to let it out or it's going to eat you alive. I know, Paul. You know I do. I've been there a few times myself."

Paul didn't bother to argue. He and John had both endured bad spells over the years—John more than Paul—and they'd helped to pull each other out of them. Paul had yet to meet a vet who hadn't been through hell at least a few times since returning to the world.

"This isn't what you're thinking," he began, then hesitated. He'd been about to say that his current situation had nothing to do with Vietnam or flashbacks or any of the rest of it. It had to do with Bonnie, how much he still wanted her and how wrong it was to want her. It had to do with love and responsibility and putting her best interests ahead of his own.

It had to do with the way he'd felt glimpsing her last Saturday when she came to pick up Shane after his morning stint at the nursery. Paul had seen her outside the same window he was gazing through right now, and his heart had seemed to swell inside his chest until its fierce beating bruised his ribs. He'd observed her long, billowing hair and her soft lips and her dazzling eyes, and he'd remembered every bit of anguish he'd ever caused her—wanting her, leaving her, inflicting his madness upon her.

"Everything," John said firmly, "goes back to the same thing, Paul. Whatever's bugging you now, it was born in Nam."

"Yeah," Paul agreed quietly. "I guess it was."

"Meet me at Max's tonight," John urged him. "We'll talk it out."

"All right," said Paul. "I'll be there."

BONNIE FOUND Tom Schuyler in his office at Boston University. A clerk in one of the administration offices had steered her to the building, and a secretary there had directed her to the upper floor office assigned to Tom. His door was open, and Bonnie stepped across the threshold before she realized he wasn't alone.

He was conferring with a student—or, more accurately, flirting with her, Bonnie concluded after a brief assessment of the scene. Tom was perched on the edge of his desk, leaning eagerly over the young lady seated on a chair in front of him, his gaze flickering from her up-turned face to the open notebook in her lap, to her breasts and then back up to her face. He was dressed, as he'd been when he visited Bonnie in Northford, with more sartorial flair than she generally associated with professors—a crisp white shirt, pleated trousers, hand-stitched loafers. His student gazed up at him with awe as he explained, in well-modulated tones, the arcana of advanced differential calculus.

Bonnie wanted to scream. She wanted to interrupt the charming little tableau, to kick the young lady out of the room, grab Tom by the throat and throttle him until he spit out the truth. The hour she'd just spent in Kevin McCoy's office had left her reeling; her only hope of regaining a semblance of emotional balance lay in finding out from Tom exactly what had been going on the night Gary died.

Kevin had tried to soften the impact of his words. "I've tracked down Marcie Bradley," he'd announced as Bonnie handed him the manuscript. "She and I had a long talk, Bonnie. I questioned her about the discrepancies between what she'd told you about Gary's death and what the police report said."

"And?"

"And after some hemming and hawing, well..." He'd given her a smile that struck her as brimming with pity. "She admitted that the police report was accurate."

Bonnie had absorbed his words, mulling over their ramifications. "Gary was killed by a drunk driver?"

"Apparently."

"Not by a right-wing crazy?"

"Apparently not."

She'd stared at the bearded young reporter, trying not to hate him for what he'd just told her. "Did she tell you why she and Tom Schuyler made up this story?"

"No. She didn't want to discuss it. Just a conjecture, Bonnie, but maybe they concocted this story to glorify Gary in death. You can't really blame them, can you?"

"If that was their reason, why wouldn't she have wanted to discuss it?"

Kevin had offered a sheepish smile. "That thought crossed my mind, too, Bonnie. I'd like to keep digging—but I want you to be prepared for the possibility that something negative might turn up. Marcie Bradley definitely seemed to have something to hide."

What? What could Marcie and Tom be hiding? During the drive across town to Boston University, Bonnie had torn herself apart trying to guess. She had been Gary's wife! How could they have lied to her?

Tom must have heard her footsteps as she stormed into the office, because he glanced up before she could speak. His face broke into a broad grin of surprise. "Well, hello, Bonnie!" he said, standing. "What brings you to Boston?"

The girl twisted in her seat to view Bonnie. She smiled timidly. Bonnie didn't bother smiling back; she didn't have it in her to be polite. "It's been ten years, Tom," she said without preamble. "I think you'd better tell me what happened."

Tom's smile faltered. "Umm—" he peered down at his student "—I guess we're finished for now, Andrea. Why don't you go through the rest of the problems on your own, and we can discuss them tomorrow."

"Okay, Dr. Schuyler," the girl said meekly. She gathered up her books, stood and offered Bonnie another edgy smile as she left the office.

Bonnie entered and gave the room a critical inspection. It was small but tidy, decorated with a framed print of a seascape and a few colorful posters announcing mathematics symposia on regional campuses. Steel bookcases were filled with textbooks. Two file cabinets stood next to a large green chalkboard attached to the wall, and a personal computer took up much of Tom's desk. Nowhere could Bonnie find the merest hint of evidence that he had once been an outspoken radical.

"Have a seat," he said, gesturing toward the chair the student had just vacated.

His courtesy aroused Bonnie's suspicions. But then, everything about Tom aroused her suspicions. He'd lied to her, he and Marcie. They'd lied about the single most important event in Bonnie's life, and even as she took her seat, resolved not to leave until she had learned the truth, she wondered whether she would be able to believe anything Tom told her now.

She watched him warily as he strolled around his desk and lowered himself into the upholstered swivel chair facing her. "You know why I'm here, don't you?" she said.

He attempted a casual smile. "Judging by your opening salvo, I don't suppose it's because you want to take me out for dinner."

"I've just come from Kevin McCoy's office," she announced. "He's been doing some digging into the facts surrounding Gary's death."

Tom didn't appear terribly surprised. He leaned back in his chair, gazing enigmatically at Bonnie and tapping his fingertips together. "Facts, huh," he echoed.

"Yes, facts. Do you know what facts are, Tom? They have to do with the truth, with honesty. Just this afternoon I was explaining to Shane how important honesty is."

"I always knew you'd make a good mother," Tom remarked.

She wasn't sure whether she was only imagining the snide twist to his smile. Not that it mattered. "How come you were dishonest, Tom? Did your mother forget to teach you that lesson?"

"Now, Bonnie," he said in an unctuous voice. "Sarcasm doesn't become you."

"Lying doesn't become you," she retorted. "So tell the damned truth already. Tell me how my husband died."

"You know how he died," Tom responded evenly. "He was hit by a car."

"And you saw it with your very own eyes?"

"Come on, Bonnie—"

"Tell me!" she demanded, pounding his desk with her fist. The violence of the gesture surprised her, and she subsided in her chair. "Did you see the accident?" she asked, her tone hushed but no less intense. "Did you see the driver? Did you see his face as he ran down my husband? Were you there?"

Tom glanced away, at last showing signs of discomfort. "Bonnie. Be reasonable. It was ten years ago."

"That's right, Tom. Ten years is the life expectancy of any good lie. Now it's time for the truth."

He tapped his fingers against the arm of his chair. "What did McCoy tell you?"

"Guess."

Tom sighed. "Okay. The truth. I wasn't there, I didn't see the accident. You already know it. Now you've heard it from me. The end."

"It's not the end!" she railed. "I was his wife, damn it! Why are you keeping the truth from me?"

"Nobody's keeping anything from you," Tom argued with infuriating logic. "You saw the police report yourself, Bonnie. You flew out to Fresno and read the report."

"Sure, I read the police report," she said with a snort. "I was grieving, I was panic-stricken, I was jet-lagged, I hadn't slept in days, I was broke, I was frantic about my son back east with my parents—and some desk sergeant shoved a stack of papers under my nose. Do you think I knew what I was reading?"

Tom shrugged. "It doesn't actually make much difference whether I was there to witness the accident or not," he posed. "Either way, the outcome was the same."

"It *does* make a difference," she argued. The muscles in her legs clenched; her throat felt tight. She dreaded the

possibility of what she might hear if she continued her
expedition for the truth. But no matter what awful things
she learned, knowing had to be better than not knowing.
"Tell me why, Tom. That's what I really need to know.
Why did you lie?"

Tom appeared annoyed. "Why do you think? It made
a good story: 'Noted Pacifist Slain for His Beliefs—'"

"Not about that," Bonnie snapped. "Marcie could
have handled that much of the lie herself. Why did you
say you were with Gary? Why did you tell me you witnessed the accident?"

He swiveled in his chair until he was facing the window. He stared out, meditating, offering Bonnie only his
profile. She clung to the hope that his explanation for
having misled her so many years ago revolved around
himself and not Gary. As Paul had observed, on the night
of the accident Tom might have been doing something he
preferred to keep a secret. Maybe he'd gone off with
someone to smoke dope. Maybe he'd been seducing the
dean's daughter.

His lengthening silence wore on her nerves. "A couple of weeks ago, when you dropped in on me in Northford, you told me Marcie didn't want to talk to me,"
Bonnie reminded him, laboring to keep her voice even.
"She and I lost touch shortly after Gary's funeral. I tried
to contact her a couple of times over the years, but I
never was able to connect with her. She was embarrassed
about this stupid lie, right? Is that why she didn't want
to have anything to do with me afterward?"

"Bonnie." Tom sighed and addressed the window. "It
was all so long ago—"

"Ten years, two months and seven days. That's how
long I've been in the dark about my husband's death,
Tom. It's damned well long enough."

"You don't want to dredge up the past." His tone held a warning.

"Too late," she asserted. "When I gave Kevin permission to write Gary's biography, I knew he'd be dredging up the past. I'm not going to let him stop now. I need to know what happened that night—and I don't want to have to find out the truth by reading about it in a book."

"Leave it alone," Tom advised. "It's over and done with."

"This is *my* life, Tom. Gary was *my* husband. The father of *my* son. I want to know."

"Maybe you don't. Maybe you'd be better off—"

She sprang out of her chair, no longer able to contain herself. Circling his desk, she confronted him, gripping the arms of his chair so he couldn't swivel away from her. "I'm an adult, Tom. You have no right to make this decision for me."

"Believe me, Bonnie—"

"Believe you? That's a laugh!"

"Gary died a hero. His death meant something." Tom sounded as if he were reciting a litany. "Just leave it alone."

"I can't. I'll never be able to leave it alone—and I won't leave *you* alone until you tell me."

"I'm warning you—"

"Tell me."

"Marcie and Gary were sleeping together."

Bonnie didn't move. She let each word sink into her like stones sinking into a pond, falling until they reached the very bottom of her soul. Slowly, she released the arms of the chair and straightened up, then spun around and stared out the window, seeing nothing, letting each cold, hard syllable descend through her.

"I'm sorry, Bonnie." Tom's voice seemed to be coming from a great distance, from across a chasm of time and grief.

She closed her eyes, feeling as if the very foundation of her existence was crumbling beneath her feet.

"I shouldn't have told you."

"You should have," she said, forcing the whispery words past her dry, tight throat.

"It's true—I wasn't with them when it happened," Tom explained when she fell silent again. "I had gone out for dinner with some people from the math faculty out there. Networking. I hadn't finished my doctoral thesis yet, but I figured it wouldn't hurt to cultivate some contacts to ease my way into a faculty slot somewhere."

Stop it! Bonnie protested silently. *Don't tell me about your wonderful career. Tell me this is another lie. Tell me it's all a sick joke. Remind me that I can't believe anything you say, anyway.*

"Gary and Marcie went back to the motel for a while. Then they went out for a drink. On their way back to their room—that was when Gary got hit."

Back to the motel for a while. To their room. Bonnie felt queasy; her eyes refused to focus. *Their room.* She could believe this, even though Tom was the one telling her. She didn't want to believe it, but she could.

No. Gary loved her. He'd sworn his love, just as she'd sworn hers. They were married, they'd had a child—

"Marcie begged me not to tell you," Tom went on. "Out of respect for Gary—and out of respect for you, too. She didn't want you to have to know. He was dead. Why trouble you about it?"

"Why trouble me?" Bonnie rasped. Her breath came in spasmodic gulps and her eyes continued to swim in their sockets. "What was it, a fling? Two lonely friends far from home with nothing better to do?"

Tom looked sympathetic, but Bonnie sensed something phony in his expression, uncannily reminiscent of his imperious smirk in the photograph she'd destroyed last week. "It started when you were pregnant," he informed her, measuring each word before he spoke it. "At least, that was when Gary first mentioned it to me. You couldn't travel with him, and Marcie could. And of course, once you had Shane you were so involved with him—"

"Involved with him? He was a baby, for God's sake! How could I *not* be involved with him?"

"I'm not criticizing you," Tom hastened to assure her, although coming from him the assurance was hollow. "You were a mother. You did what you had to do."

"I was doing it for Gary, too!" she thundered. "He was busy being a father to his causes. I was the only real parent Shane had."

"For which you should be commended," Tom said with a patronizing nod.

"I don't want to be commended! I want you to tell me—" She fought back a sob. Bad enough that she was shouting at Tom. She wasn't going to cry in front of him.

"Tell you what?" he prompted her.

"That you've made this up," she said brokenly. "That Gary was faithful to me."

Tom drummed his fingers on the chair again. "I could tell you—and this is the truth, Bonnie—I could tell you that he loved you. He really did. When he told me he was going to marry you, I told him I thought that was too straight a thing to do, too establishment. But he said, 'I love her, Tom, and that's all that matters.'"

"It isn't all that matters." Bonnie struggled to swallow a fresh lump of tears. "If he really loved me he would never have had an affair with Marcie."

"Maybe there was a limit to how straight he could be. Maybe, as much as he loved you, marriage was too confining politically. Maybe he thought that by having an affair he was making an important statement about the sociological implications of monogamy."

"It has nothing to do with politics," Bonnie retorted. "It has to do with making promises and then breaking them. It has to do with being dishonest." A tear slid down her cheek. She hastily wiped it away. "He cheated on me, pure and simple." She despised the tremulousness in her voice. "He deceived me."

"Cut the guy some slack. He was a great leader—"

"He was a bastard." She glowered down at Tom, no longer bothering to conceal her tears. "And you're a bastard, too. You probably rationalized it for him at the time, you probably told him that sleeping with Marcie was good politics and made an important statement. You've covered for him all these years—and you're still covering for him, still justifying what he did. You're a hypocrite, Tom. And so was he."

With that, she stormed out of the office, slamming the door behind her. Sagging against the corridor wall, her fury spent for the moment, she let out a long-suppressed sob. It occurred to her that, as shocked as she was by Tom's revelation, some part of her couldn't refute the inherent truth in what he'd told her. He was hardly a trustworthy person, and even when Gary was alive she'd never thought of Tom as her friend, but he hadn't been lying about Gary right now. She didn't want to believe him, but she knew she had to.

Marcie—Bonnie's old Radcliffe chum, the talented cook, the giggling nineteen-year-old who'd journeyed all the way to New York City for birth control pills . . . Marcie, whose greatest joy in college had been defying her straitlaced parents, whose idealism generally seemed to extend only as far as her infatuation with various good-looking rabble-rousers . . . Marcie, the ultimate radical groupie, had been having an affair with Gary, the ultimate radical.

"Dear God." Bonnie's knees trembled beneath her, and she hurried down the hall in the hope that her forward momentum would keep her from collapsing. She reached the stairwell and started down, not stopping until she arrived at the landing between the first and second floors. There she dropped to sit on a step, wrapped her arms around her knees and buried her face in her lap.

For a long time she remained there, shivering, weeping, wishing she could wake up and find herself somewhere else, living some other, happier life. When her uncontrollable shaking finally abated and she lifted her head, she discovered herself facing a yellow cinder-block wall in an academic building at Boston University.

It wasn't a dream. Her husband, the man to whom she'd devoted herself, body and soul, even after death parted them . . . her husband had had an affair. The man whose fine, noble principles Bonnie had revered had in fact been a two-timing rat. She had loved him for his wisdom, his moral vision, his dedication to peace—and all the while, he had been committing the ultimate act of violence on their relationship. The four years of her marriage and the ten years of her widowhood were nothing but a fraud.

Paul would never have deceived her like that.

Startled, she straightened up and shook her head clear. Her world had just been undermined, her past rewritten. She no longer knew who she was. Why should she be thinking about Paul Tremaine, of all people?

No matter what he'd done in his life, she could trust him. She might not agree with what he stood for, but at least she knew where he stood. She could trust Paul.

She remembered the afternoon of the storm, when her tree had swayed and tilted as the ground melted into mud beneath it. Paul had come and braced the tree. He'd propped it up, kept it stable, given it the support it needed to survive.

If ever she needed someone to prop her up, if ever she needed support as the once-solid earth shifted and heaved beneath her, it was now. But the one man she trusted wouldn't let her near him. He had told her quite clearly that he didn't want to have anything to do with her.

Her own husband hadn't found her worthy of his love; obviously Paul didn't, either. The last time she'd reached for him, he'd run away.

If she reached for him now, he'd run away again.

Chapter Thirteen

"So what's the deal with the memorial?" John asked. "How's that thing coming along?"

Paul shrugged. He and John Slinger were seated in one of the scarred wooden booths lining the outer walls of Max's. The pool table had been occupied when they arrived at the bar a few minutes ago, but Paul didn't mind. Sitting in the shadows and sipping a beer suited him well enough.

He traced his fingertip along the label of the beer bottle. "I don't know," he admitted. "As far as town hall's concerned, it's all systems go."

"And?"

Paul lifted his gaze to his friend. John was four years his senior but looked much older. His face was weathered, his reddish hair thinning on top, his fingers bony and nicotine-stained. He stared at Paul with an intensity that would have made him self-conscious if he and John hadn't known each other so long and so well.

"I'm not so sure it's such a hot idea," he said.

"The memorial? What are you talking about? You've been living and breathing that thing for years, man. You've got to build it."

"Why? Why have I got to build it?" His words were directed more to himself than to John. For days now, he'd been asking himself the same question. Would building the memorial truly make him happy? Would it make his life any easier? Would it change what had happened one rainy night in a forest in Southeast Asia twenty-odd years ago? Would it free him from his past?

"It's been your whole purpose for living," John reminded him. "It's kept you going. When times were bad, you always had that to cling to."

"I know." The trouble was, Paul was beginning to suspect that a war memorial was an absurd thing to live for. His attachment to the idea had given him strength during some rough periods—but maybe there were better sources of strength. Maybe he'd clung to the concept of a memorial because he'd had nothing better to cling to.

"So," John said, snubbing out his cigarette and then shaking another from the pack, "other than the memorial, what've you been up to?"

"Nothing."

"You've been like a hermit, Tremaine. What's going on?"

"Hey, look." Paul attempted a smile. "If I'd known you were going to interrogate me I wouldn't have come here."

"You knew exactly what I was going to do," John claimed as he struck a match. He lit his cigarette and shook out the flame. "What is it, money trouble? Problems at the nursery?"

"No."

"What? A woman?"

Although the question wasn't exactly unexpected, Paul flinched. "Yeah," he grunted.

"The one up in Lowell?"

Paul shook his head, then smiled grimly. "Damn it, John—I think I'm in love."

It was the first time he'd actually spoke the word, the first time he'd allowed himself to consider Bonnie in such terms. Recently his dreams hadn't been about the war; they'd been about the taste of her lips, the sweet warmth of her breath filling him, the exhilarating strength of her arms wrapped around him and the luminescence of her eyes as she gazed at him in desire—and in pain, and hatred.

Ever since he'd walked away from her that evening on her porch, he'd found himself dwelling obsessively not on his memorial but on her. She was his new devastation, the victim of his most recent defeat. Perhaps he ought to build a memorial to her instead of to the others.

"Who's the lucky lady?" John asked, clearly fascinated.

"You don't know her, and she isn't lucky."

"Why? What's the hang-up?"

"The hang-up is, I hurt her. I don't . . . I don't know if I can *not* hurt her. And I love her, John. I can't bear hurting her, so I've got to stay away from her."

John digested Paul's explanation and issued a sympathetic sigh. "How does she feel about it?"

"She's in love with someone else," said Paul.

"Sounds like a soap opera." John contemplated Paul's situation as he puffed on his cigarette. Finally he asked, "How come you're so sure you're going to hurt her?"

"We're coming from two different places," Paul explained. "Her husband—he's dead now, but she's still hung up on him. He used to be this hotshot antiwar activist. Founder of something called the Cambridge Manifesto."

"Oh, jeez." John pulled a face. "Not those loonies."

"You've heard of them?"

"Yeah. They were pretty active in these parts while you were still overseas, and then when you were living out on the West Coast." He dragged deeply on his cigarette. "They were a bunch of self-righteous eggheads who staged peace rallies all around the region. As I recall, they did a big sit-in out at Westover Air Force Base, and one down at the naval base in New London. They threw chicken blood at a submarine or something. Yeah, the Cambridge Manifesto made quite a name for themselves in these parts."

Paul cursed inwardly. More than a saint, Gary Hudson had been a celebrity, a media star. Paul could never compete with that.

Not that it mattered. Even if Bonnie's husband hadn't been the renowned leader of a peace movement, the guy would undoubtedly have been more gentlemanly than Paul. Given the way Paul had treated her, any man dead or alive would shine in comparison.

"It's no big deal," he heard himself say. "I'll get over her sooner or later. But you can't blame me for laying low for a while. I just need some time to work it out."

"I guess," John said dubiously.

"I've survived worse things."

"Yeah." John's skeptical look implied that Paul's bravado wasn't totally convincing, but Paul appreciated his friend's willingness to pretend it was.

He raised his beer to his lips and froze at the sight of Bonnie entering the barroom. Dressed in a casual skirt and blouse, she looked neat and composed—until he focused on her face. Her complexion appeared ashen in the tinted glow from the neon signs hanging in the front windows. Her cheeks were drawn, her eyes marble-hard and cold, her lips pinched. Her hands were hidden in the pockets of her skirt, but Paul could tell from the way the fabric draped that her fingers were balled into fists. He lifted his gaze to her face again, taking heart in the glinting gold of her hoop earrings beneath her hair. They looked normal and familiar, unlike her terrified expression.

John must have noticed Paul's sudden reaction, because he twisted in his seat to view the bar's latest arrival. "Who's that?" he asked, giving Bonnie a cursory assessment before he turned back to Paul.

Paul didn't have a chance to answer. Bonnie's eyes had found his, and he felt a visceral jolt at the anguish in her gaze. Her attempt at a smile was so forlorn it hurt him to see it.

She started toward the table. Paul realized John was awaiting a reply. "A friend of mine," he mumbled evasively. "Her son works for me."

"She's a real looker. If I wasn't married, I'd..." John's voice trailed off at Paul's murderous glare. "She's the one you're in love with?" he whispered.

Once more Paul couldn't answer. Bonnie had reached their table, and he stood and presented a smile as artificial as hers. "Hi," he said. "I didn't know you hung out at Max's."

"I don't," she said, eyeing John.

Paul made the appropriate introductions. "Bonnie, this is John Slinger. John, Bonnie Hudson."

"Gary Hudson," John blurted out, wagging a finger at her. He shot Paul a triumphant grin. "That's the guy,

right? The loony from the Cambridge Manifesto? I remember him!''

Paul ignored John's self-congratulatory cheer. He was
too distracted by the way Bonnie seemed to recoil at the
mere mention of her husband's name. ''John's a veteran
like me,'' he apologized for his companion's lack of di-
plomacy. ''He didn't really mean your husband was a
lunatic. He only meant—''

''That's all right,'' Bonnie said tersely, looking, if
possible, even more uncomfortable. ''I'm sorry to chase
you down like this, Paul, but ...'' She drew in a deep,
bracing breath. ''I stopped by the nursery but you'd already left, and Claire Collins told me you sometimes
hang out here, and when I saw the truck parked outside ...'' She inhaled again, desperately, like a drowning
person snatching her last bit of oxygen before she went
under for good. ''Shane won't be coming to work on
Saturday. He's staying with my parents in Newton for a
few days.''

Paul remained silent, certain she had something more
to say. That Shane was visiting his grandparents wasn't
exactly a crisis worth reporting in person. Bonnie could
have telephoned Paul at home later in the evening, or
stopped by the nursery the following day.

''Did something happen?'' he asked carefully. ''Are
your folks all right?''

''They're fine.'' She shaped another sickly smile.
''Well,'' she said, ''I just wanted to let you know he'll be
missing work this weekend. Nice meeting you,'' she
added to John before pivoting from the table.

''Wait.'' Paul closed his hand around her shoulder,
preventing her departure. Simply touching her forced him
to confront the truth he'd just admitted to his friend: he

loved Bonnie. He ought to let her go, but he couldn't—not when she was so troubled and not when she'd gone to so much effort to find him. She had more to tell him, and despite the risk to his emotional well-being, he wanted to hear what she had to say.

She kept her back to him. "I'm sorry I bothered you here, Paul. It's really not important—"

"Of course it's important," Paul argued, aware that they weren't discussing Shane's upcoming absence from work.

Perhaps to make up for his indiscreet remark about Bonnie's late husband, John exercised uncommon tact by sliding out of the booth. "I gotta split, Paul," he said. "The old lady's burning my dinner right now. Take it easy." He turned to Bonnie. "Nice meeting you, too."

Alone with Bonnie, Paul eased her around to face him. "What is it?" he asked, growing increasingly worried as he absorbed her stricken appearance. "Is Shane in trouble? Is there anything I can do to help?"

"No," she said quietly, struggling to tame the ragged edges of her voice. "He's not in trouble. He's staying in Newton for a couple of days, that's all."

"What is it, then?" he asked gently. "Is the birch tree dying or something?"

"No—I mean, not that I know of. I haven't been home yet. I *can't* go home, Paul..." She shuddered, and he raised his free hand to her other shoulder to steady her. "I shouldn't be bothering you with this, Paul—I shouldn't have come here. It's really nothing...." A lone tear skittered down her cheek, belying her claim. "I just wanted to let you know that Shane..." Her voice cracked.

Paul slid one hand to her elbow and guided her through the gloomy, smoke-filled room to the door.

Outside the sun was low but the sky was bright, the air mild and bracing. He drew Bonnie to a halt on the sidewalk, giving her the opportunity to pull herself together. Even though she showed no further signs of weepiness, he could feel her shivering. "Why can't you go home?" he asked.

She stared across the street to the green. Beyond the grass, barely visible above the rise at the eastern edge, stood the unoccupied elementary school building. An empty flagpole loomed over it; Paul could hear the metal hooks clanking hollowly against the pole.

"I shouldn't have bothered you," she mumbled, bowing her head.

"You aren't bothering me, Bonnie." In fact, he was oddly gratified that she'd come looking for him. No matter what the problem was, if he could do something to make it better he'd welcome the opportunity. He had so much to atone for when it came to her. "Why can't you go home?" he repeated.

"The shrine," she whispered, squeezing her eyes shut for a moment.

"The shrine?"

"The photographs on the mantel above the fireplace. I swear, if I get too close to them I'll smash every last one of them."

Paul remembered the sound of shattering glass that had punctuated his departure the last time he'd seen Bonnie. He hadn't known what she'd broken, but he'd known that her rage that evening was directed at him. Tonight, though, it wasn't—at least not yet. Give him long enough and he'd probably infuriate her again.

In spite of that likelihood, he couldn't abandon her when she was so distraught. "Would you like something to eat?" he asked. "We could grab a bite somewhere—"

"No," she said vehemently. "Just thinking about food makes me nauseous."

"Are you sick? You want me to take you to a doctor?"

"No." She sighed, then shrugged free of his clasp. "I shouldn't have come to you, Paul. You're a good man and this is my own problem...."

"Make it mine," he insisted, grabbing her arm again before she could escape him. One ghastly night long ago, he'd been forced to wait helplessly in the underbrush while his friends lay mortally wounded just beyond his reach, beyond his ability to save them. He wasn't going to stand by this time and watch someone he cared for suffer alone.

He urged her back to him. She peered up at him, obviously struggling to come up with the right words. "My husband..." Her eyes filled with tears and she shut them.

Her lips were trembling, and he longed to still them with a kiss. He also longed to hear the rest of her sentence. He simply held her, keeping a lid on both his passion and his impatience.

"...didn't love me," she concluded.

Paul checked the impulse to laugh. He found it ludicrous that Saint Gary of Cambridge wouldn't love a woman like Bonnie, who had worshiped him in life and in death, who had agreed with his politics and supported him in his vocation and borne his son, who was smart and beautiful and strong.

He slid his finger under her chin and steered her gaze to him. "What the hell gave you that idea?" he asked.

"He was having an affair."

If the guy had been alive, Paul would have volunteered to slug him for Bonnie. But having an extramarital fling, while inexcusable, didn't prove much one way or the other about whether Gary had loved his wife. "You just found this out?" he asked.

She nodded.

"Oh, Bonnie..." He gathered her into his arms, frustrated by the inadequacy of the language. What could he say to prove to her that, whatever the fool might have done, her husband had surely loved her? What could Paul say to reassure her that the world hadn't come to an end?

She hid her face against his shoulder. Her tears burst loose and her body shook, and Paul realized that for Bonnie a world *had* ended: the world in which she'd seen her husband as a paragon, pure and noble and above reproach, divinely inspired and utterly principled. Paul's cynicism notwithstanding, she *had* viewed her late husband as a saint. Learning that he was fallible must have demolished her.

Paul tightened his arms around her. Her tears soaked through the cotton fabric of his shirt to dampen his skin. He stroked his fingers consolingly through her hair, but she kept sobbing. Even holding her, he felt helpless.

A couple of men leaving Max's stopped to gape at them, and Paul realized he ought to take her somewhere more private. She hardly seemed aware of him ushering her down the sidewalk to his truck. He helped her onto the passenger seat, brushed a golden strand of hair from her tearstained cheek and raced around the truck to the driver's side. Lacking a better idea, he drove to his house, accompanied by the heartrending sound of her muffled sobs. She made no acknowledgment of the truck stopping in his driveway; she didn't question where they were. She only huddled within the arch of his arm as he led her up the walk and inside the cozy ranch house.

He sat her on the living room sofa, then went to the kitchen to fetch a box of tissues and a couple of beers. When he returned to the living room he found her still hunched over, shaking with sobs.

He sat gingerly beside her on the couch and handed her a tissue. She dabbed at her eyes and glanced around. When her gaze reached him, she released a soft, tortured moan. "I'm sorry," she said in a hoarse voice.

"Don't be." He took the soggy tissue from her and pressed a glass into her hand. Then he poured an inch of beer into it. "Have a drink."

She took a cautious sip and lowered the glass. When she looked around her again, it was with curiosity. "Is this your home?"

"Yes."

"Thank you," she murmured. "I mean, for bringing me somewhere. I must have been making a spectacle of myself."

Paul gave her a reassuring smile, but she was gazing toward the sunset-filled windows and didn't notice. "Are you feeling better?"

"No. Yes." She turned back to him and her eyes, despite their shimmering layer of tears, looked clear and resolute to him. "I don't feel any better about Gary, but I feel better being with you. You're such a good man, Paul."

"You said that before," he remarked, bewildered. "I don't know what you mean."

"You're honest. You don't lie, even if lying might get you what you want. You've always been honest with me."

Like any human being, Paul had done his share of lying over the years. In Vietnam he'd lied about what happened the night his comrades died, in order to save his neck. He'd lied before then and since, for the usual reasons: to spare someone's feelings, to stave off a fight, to simplify a situation.

But he'd never lied to Bonnie. He simply couldn't imagine lying to her.

"Do you want to talk about Gary?" he asked.

She helped herself to another tissue and dried her eyes. "I'm sure this is of no interest to you—"

"It interests me that you're upset, Bonnie. If you want to sound off, if you want to skewer the bas—"

"Don't," she cut him off. He understood that, while she was clearly incensed about her late husband, she wouldn't permit anyone else to speak ill of him—especially Paul. "He was a great leader, and he accomplished great things."

"Right," Paul said wearily. Even after discovering the jerk's infidelity, Bonnie couldn't keep herself from eulogizing him.

She glanced at Paul, abashed. "I don't belittle what he did with his life," she clarified. "I only wish he'd loved me. Obviously—" she struggled to overcome the quiver in her voice "—he didn't."

"That's not obvious at all," Paul argued. "Lots of men love their wives and cheat on them."

"Lots of men give lip service to love," she retorted. "If you really love someone you don't cheat on them."

Paul felt obliged to defend the guy, if only to inject a measure of objectivity to the conversation. "Some guys think of love and sex as two separate issues. Gary might have loved you but succumbed to temptation. It happens. It's not nice, it's not right, but it happens."

"To some men, perhaps. But I always thought Gary was better than that. I thought he—I thought he loved me as much as I loved him." She seemed in danger of dissolving in tears again, but she fought valiantly to remain poised. "It wasn't just a temptation he succumbed to, Paul—it was a relationship of long standing. It started before Shane was born. They were lovers for years, and he—he died on his way to her motel room. He wasn't killed by a fanatic. He was killed by a drunk driver while he was on his way to her bedroom to make love with her."

"Bonnie—"

"Oh, God . . . I don't know what to say to Shane. After I found out about Gary, I picked him up at his friend's house and dropped him off with my parents and bolted. I think I said something about needing a few days alone to do some extra research for the book."

"That was a good story."

"No, don't you see?" she flared. "Now I've lied to my own son! I've been lying to him all his life, letting him think his father was a great man. I've been telling him he should follow in his father's footsteps, embrace his father's values—"

"You've taught him your own values, Bonnie," Paul murmured. "I'd say he's a lucky kid."

"But someday . . . someday I'll have to tell him the truth."

"Maybe, maybe not." Paul sandwiched one of her icy hands between his and gave it a gentle squeeze. "When he's old enough, you can tell him what he needs to know.''

"I always told him his father died for his beliefs, for his convictions. I thought Gary's death had some kind of meaning, because he'd stood for something. I guess that's the thing about myths,'' she said bleakly, lowering her eyes to her lap. "They aren't true.''

"How did you find this out?'' Paul asked. "From the reporter writing the book?''

She nodded. "He examined the police report of the accident. I had never looked too closely at it. I'd simply accepted what Tom and Marcie told me. It never occurred to me that Marcie had been sleeping with my husband and Tom knew about it. 'The wife is the last to know,''' she quoted bitterly. "What a cliché.''

"They didn't tell you because they didn't want to hurt you.''

"Oh, great,'' she snapped, then sighed again and shot Paul a fleeting look of contrition. "Instead, they let me live a lie for ten years. They let me make a fool of myself.''

"You haven't made a fool of yourself,'' he assured her. "*You're* the one with the beliefs and the convictions. You're the one who stands for something. And that's not foolish, Bonnie.''

"In all the years we were married,'' she said in a tremulous voice, "I never looked at another man. Even after Gary died, for years I didn't . . . And I made a home for him, and helped him in his work, and . . . oh, God.'' Her voice trailed off and she sucked in an erratic breath. "He didn't love me. I was in love with a lie, and he wasn't in love at all.''

"Bonnie—''

"If I'd satisfied him, if I'd tried harder...I don't know...."

Whatever Paul's resentment of Gary might have been based on before, it was nothing compared to what he was feeling now. The man had done more than wreck his marriage—he'd destroyed Bonnie's self-esteem. For that alone Paul despised him.

He grabbed Bonnie and gave her a light shake. "Listen to me," he said, trying unsuccessfully to keep his voice free of indignation. "What Gary did wasn't your fault. He was a jerk, that's all."

"And I wasn't enough of a woman for him."

"You're plenty enough woman for any man who's got half the sense he was born with."

"Oh?" Her eyes blazed, firing sparks of gold and green light at him. "In my whole life," she raged, "I've cared deeply for two men—Gary and you. And you both ran from me. Explain it, Paul. Tell me what it is about me that scares men so much. Do I turn them off? Am I too skinny? Too prim? Do I smell funny? What?"

Her accusation slammed into him with bruising force. He'd run from her in order to protect her, and she'd twisted it all around, viewing his action as proof that she was somehow unworthy of love. He couldn't let her think that. No matter what the danger, he had to set her straight.

Sliding his hands up to cup her cheeks, he pulled her to himself and kissed her.

HIS MOUTH WAS FIRM on hers, brooking no resistance. She couldn't breathe, couldn't think, couldn't do anything but move her lips with his, accepting, allowing the warmth of his kiss to seep down through her body until it permeated every nerve and fiber. She shouldn't want this so much. It would only end. Paul would flee as Gary had, he'd find someone better, more desirable, more ... *something*.

But just for now, for this heavenly instant, she would pretend that Paul returned her feelings, that his kiss was a result of love and not pity. She would let the power of his embrace obliterate her awareness of the heartache she would suffer when he came to his senses and rejected her.

Slowly, reluctantly he pulled back, letting his hands roam into her hair and his eyes meet hers. "You smell like daisies," he whispered.

He looked sincere—but sincerity wasn't what she'd hoped to find in his gaze. She'd been hoping for love, rapture, an acknowledgment that they could share more than a stilted acquaintanceship. Sincerity seemed too much like pity to her. "Don't humor me," she pleaded, dismayed by the passionate huskiness in her voice.

"Humor you?" He let out a sharp laugh. "Bonnie ..." He combed his fingers through the long, silky tresses tumbling down her back and sighed. "Bonnie, I'm so afraid of hurting you—but I can't sit by and do nothing while you hurt yourself. You're an incredible woman. Your husband didn't deserve you, and I'm not sure I do, either. But I'm not going to let you think you aren't lovable." He brushed her forehead with a kiss. "It scares me, Bonnie. It scares me to think that what happened the last time could happen again if I let down my guard with you. But, for God's sake, don't take that to mean I don't love you."

He loved her. His eyes told her, his fingers twining possessively through her hair, the heat of his body hovering so close to hers. His kiss told her. He loved her.

"If you love me," she murmured, her gaze locked with his, "don't be scared."

A trace of uncertainty flickered in his eyes. Then, his smile tentative but brave, he stood and lifted her into his arms. Without a word, without allowing his gaze to break from hers, he carried her to his bed.

He laid her down gently and then sat beside her, stroking her hair back from her cheeks, studying her. She felt a faint trembling in his fingers as they grazed her temple. She wished there was some way she could reassure him, once and for all, that the only way he could hurt her was to lie to her—or to leave her. But that was something he would have to discover for himself.

She gathered his hand in hers and pressed his palm to her lips. Groaning, he drew his hand away and replaced it with his mouth. Shifting to lie beside her, he deepened the kiss, plunging deep with his tongue, pushing past whatever barriers fear had erected in the path of his love.

Bonnie wrapped her arms around him, savoring the rugged strength of his torso. He wasn't a myth or a martyr; he was a man, real and solid, his emotions exposed. She had just learned that when she made love with Gary she'd been making love with a deceitful stranger. But she knew Paul. She knew his scars, his apprehensions, his dreams and his nightmares. She knew who he was and she loved him for it.

With a gasp, he lifted his head and peered down at her. He ran the callused tips of his fingers over the satin skin of her throat and down, tracing the edge of her blouse to the top button. "Are you sure you trust me?" he asked.

"Yes."

He gave himself a moment to let her answer sink in. "I'll try not to let you down."

"That's all I'll ever ask of you."

His lips curved in a smile, brief but resonant, and then he popped the top button open, and the next, and the next, parting the fabric of her blouse. He bowed and touched his lips to her sternum, then nibbled her breast above the lacy cup of her bra. She reflexively arched her back but he resisted what she offered, lifting her from the mattress in order to remove her blouse and bra first. Only then did he obey her unspoken request, sliding his lips down to the peaked red bud and sucking it hungrily into his mouth.

She moaned at the excruciating thrill of his kiss, the sublime friction of his tongue and then his teeth playing over her sensitive flesh. She cradled his head against her, then glided her hands down to his neck and probed the warm skin beneath his collar.

He lifted his head. His hands joined hers at the front of his shirt, yanking the buttons open. He shed the shirt with a swift, efficient shrug of his shoulders and flung it over the side of the bed. Bonnie touched the mat of hair that spread across his chest, twirling her fingers through the dark curls and exploring the supple skin underneath.

When she reached his stomach he inhaled shakily and inched back, wavering. "Don't," he whispered, even though he didn't attempt to remove her hands. She sketched light circles over his abdomen, working her way down to his belt. He emitted a low groan and edged back farther. "Let me love you."

"Yes," she breathed.

He unfastened her skirt and eased it down over her hips and away, taking her underwear with it. His hands swept up along her slender calves and then her thighs, and she briefly recalled the blunt, careless way he'd pulled her legs around him the last time they'd been together like this.

No. They'd been together but not like *this*, not awash in love and tenderness. Paul hadn't touched her with such exquisite care that time. He hadn't bowed to kiss the smooth ovals of her knees, the sleek skin of her inner thighs. He hadn't run his fingertips with such sensitivity over the tingling flesh of her belly and hips and then below, into the downy thatch of golden hair, already damp with desire as he slid one hand down between her legs.

She cried out at his touch, transported with a pleasure that was marred only by the knowledge that he wasn't totally naked, as well. She groped for his belt but he eluded her, sliding back to kneel between her ankles. He kissed her thighs again, first one and then the other, then rose higher and pressed his mouth to her.

The world erupted around her, pounding through her in blissful shock waves. She cried out once more, dazed by the glorious sensation yet not satisfied, not quite. This was rapturous, it was wonderful—but it wasn't enough.

"I want you," she breathed, scarcely able to hear herself. "Paul . . . please."

He sat up. He was breathing heavily, apparently as stunned as she was by the speed and power of her response. Through a blur of ecstasy she saw the doubt in his eyes, the anxiety tearing at him. She recognized his fear, understood and respected it. But there was only one way to overcome it, one way to prove to him that he was not fated to hurt her.

"I trust you," she swore, her voice hushed but firm.

He hesitated a second longer. Then, his gaze fixed on her face, he worked open his belt and trousers and slid them off. She noticed the fierce pumping of his chest as he labored with his breath; the lithe muscles of his arms and legs, the slim contours of his hips, his full arousal. Her hands followed the path her eyes had blazed, touching him, learning him.

He remained still beneath her questing fingers, every so often closing his eyes to center his attention on her light caresses. When she curled her hands around his hardness he emitted a faint gasp, then broke from her and rolled away. He rummaged in the drawer of his night table; when he returned he was holding a contraceptive shield. That he remembered, that he cared, that even at such an intense moment he would protect her...

I trust you, she half whispered, half moaned. *I trust you....* and she opened her soul to him.

Chapter Fourteen

"I'm glad I survived," he murmured, nestling his head into the warm hollow at the base of her throat. He dropped a kiss on the delicate ridge of her collarbone; his breath feathered across her skin. "Oh, Bonnie . . . I'm so glad."

Bonnie knew how much that statement meant coming from Paul. He said it as if it were a divine revelation, a final acknowledgment that, whatever terrifying things he had survived, his survival was ultimately more meaningful than his terror.

"I'm glad, too," she said, recognizing at once how absurd an understatement that was. Her body still throbbed in the afterglow of his lovemaking. When he shifted his leg, which was sandwiched between hers, she was gripped by an echoing spasm of pleasure. When he gently shaped one hand to her breast she experienced another, and another when he touched his lips to her collarbone again.

"You make me feel so alive," he went on. His voice was uneven, the words emerging haltingly, but Bonnie understood that he needed to say these things. She curled her fingers through the dense black waves of hair crowning his head, waiting, listening. "The last time, too—even then I felt so incredibly alive...."

"We don't have to talk about that time," she stopped him. Sex had been so different between them then. She wanted to remember only this sweet union, this bond forged in love and trust. She wanted to remember his masterly control, his sensitivity, the slow, lush completion of each thrust, the way his face had glowed with pleasure when she climaxed around him, and when he'd joined her at that splendid peak.

"We do have to talk about it," Paul disputed her, easing out of her arms and propping himself up so he could gaze down at her. "That's still a part of who I am, Bonnie. I can't make any promises—"

"Then don't make any," she whispered, weaving her fingers through his and giving him a reassuring squeeze. "Except to be honest with me. That's the only promise I need."

He continued to scrutinize her, a shadow passing across his face. "This—what we just did—it wasn't some kind of revenge, was it?"

"Revenge?" She frowned. "What are you talking about?"

He sighed, steering his gaze to her slender, blissfully ravished body sprawled across his bed. "You found out your husband had an affair, so now, to get even with him—"

"No!" She tugged on his hand, drawing his attention back to her. "I wanted this to happen well before I knew about Gary. I've loved you for a long time, Paul."

He examined her face as he mulled over her words. Slowly, the doubt melted from his expression and his lips shaped a vague smile. "All men make mistakes, Bonnie.

Gary wasn't perfect, and I'm sure as hell not perfect, either.''

"Who is?''

"I just..." He paused, his eyes searching, full of questions, full of hope. "I just want to know you forgive him.''

"Forgive *him*?'' Paul had spoken disparagingly of Gary so many times—why was he defending him now?

"I'll never cheat on you, Bonnie, never. But I'll screw up sometimes.'' He drew his fingers tenderly through her hair, measuring her reaction to his words. "I need to know that when I do you'll be able to forgive me. If you can forgive him...then I'll know you can forgive me.''

She peered up into Paul's piercing eyes. Once again she was astounded by his willingness to let her see his vulnerability. It took enormous courage to reveal one's uncertainties, one's fears and flaws. Obviously, Gary hadn't been courageous enough.

"I forgive him,'' she confessed, feeling an overwhelming rush of liberation the moment the words left her. What had happened in the past was done. It was a part of who she was, just as Paul's history was a part of him—but now it was time to look forward, to move on. If Paul could forgive himself for surviving, she could forgive her husband for not having been the idealized hero she'd thought him to be.

Forgiveness, she realized, was as precious as honesty.

"I love you,'' she said, urging Paul back to her. She nuzzled his chin, then cushioned her head against his shoulder and sighed contentedly. She loved him not only for his strength and candor but for the lesson he'd just taught her.

He skimmed his hand down her spine and up again in a tranquilizing pattern. "Even though I served in the war?" he tested her.

"I'll never believe that war was a good thing," she countered. "If it happened today I'd be right at the front lines, marching against it. But I still love you, Paul. I can accept your military service. I can even accept your memorial."

"I'm not going to build it."

She drew back, shocked. "Why not?"

He slid his hand up to the nape of her neck and held her head steady, close to his. "I don't want to remember my friends with a stupid heap of granite. Isn't that what you called it?"

She grinned, sheepishly. "I think I called it silly."

"Stupid, silly, it doesn't matter." He ran his thumb behind her ear, as if unable to stop touching her, caressing her, loving her. "Granite is dead. I want to remember them with something alive."

"Books for the school library?" Bonnie asked hopefully.

He shrugged. "Maybe some books, too. I was thinking of a tree."

"A tree!"

"On the green. I know there are already a few trees there, but—a white birch like the one Shane gave you . . . I was thinking, I could put a plaque at the base saying it was planted in memory of those who died in Nam. And then it would grow. It would be alive for them." He paused, then smiled modestly. "What do you think? Too corny?"

"I think it's wonderful," she whispered, gathering him to herself. "I think you're wonderful." Her mouth took his, and her body, telling him without words how much she loved him.

THE CHOPPER WAS WAITING, the rotors churning the air. Paul had been counting the weeks, the days, the seconds for this moment to arrive. Now that it had, he hesitated.

Behind him the camp buzzed with its usual activity. His captain had already saluted him and wished him well, and a couple of grunts were loitering nearby, shouting words—mostly obscene—of farewell. "Get some for me, Tremaine!" one of them hollered. "Get as much as you can! Make up for lost time!"

Lost time. That was how he would think of these past twelve months: time lost but real, always with him, leaving permanent scars. He was about to climb aboard the chopper, about to return to the world—yet he sensed in his gut that he would never leave this place, never.

His heart told him something else. It told him he would leave Nam, even though Nam would never leave him. He would carry it with him wherever he went—but the key was, he would go. He would continue. He was alive and maybe, someday, he would start living again.

The war was a part of his past. The chopper would carry him to his future. He prayed that in time the past would fade and he would heal, that somewhere in that future something good would be waiting for him.

He allowed himself one final look back, then marched toward the chopper and climbed on.

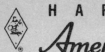
COMING NEXT MONTH

#333 SIGHT UNSEEN by Kathy Clark

It wasn't a whimsical flight of fancy that stable owner Nicki Chandler reported to detective Jake Kelly. Nicki had been visited by a series of waking dreams—dreams she was convinced mirrored a real-life tragedy. Jake never expected that Nicki's dreams held danger—and a direct challenge to a new and fragile love.

Don't miss the second book in the ROCKY MOUNTAIN MAGIC series.

#334 MEANT TO BE by Cathy Gillen Thacker

He was a man with everything—everything but a family. Tom Harrigan, the eldest son in the prominent Harrigan clan, had always won his heart's desire. But now, the surrogate mother of his baby son threatened to destroy his dreams. Cynthia Whittiker, the attractive court-appointed guardian, showed him that love was never a game of lose or win.

#335 NIGHTSHADE by Ginger Chambers

Christian Townsend was rich, handsome, self-assured and smart, and museum employee Sonya Douglas didn't know how she was going to manage him. When Christian probed the unsolved theft of priceless artifacts, he brought the museum close to scandal. But when Sonya finally succeeded in dividing his interest—which then focused on her—the situation got totally out of control.

#336 TALL COTTON by Lori Copeland

Kelly Smith had always planned to follow in her father's footsteps on the horse-racing circuit, but now it seemed those footsteps led to betrayal. Could she prove her father had been innocent of the charges against him? She'd been forced to deceive Tanner McCrey, the man behind the accusations, to find out whether he was ally or enemy. Now would she ever be able to win his love?

HARLEQUIN
American Romance®

Join in the

Rocky Mountain Magic

Experience the charm and magic of The Stanley Hotel in the Colorado Rockies with #329 BEST WISHES this month, and don't miss out on further adventures to take place there in the next two months.

In March 1990 look for #333 SIGHT UNSEEN by Kathy Clark and find out what psychic visions lie ahead for Hayley Austin's friend Nicki Chandler. In April 1990 read #337 RETURN TO SUMMER by Emma Merritt and travel back in time with their friend Kate Douglas.

ROCKY MOUNTAIN MAGIC—All it takes is an open heart. Only from Harlequin American Romance

All the Rocky Mountain Magic Romances take place at the beautiful Stanley Hotel.

RMM2-I

THE STANLEY HOTEL— A HISTORY

Upon moving to Colorado, F. O. Stanley fell in love with Estes Park, a town nestled in an alpine mountain bowl at 7,500 feet, the Colorado Rockies towering around it.

With an initial investment of $500,000, Stanley designed and began construction of The Stanley Hotel in 1906. Materials and supplies were transported 22 miles by horse teams on roads constructed solely for this purpose. The grand opening took place in 1909 and guests were transported to The Stanley Hotel in steam-powered, 12-passenger "mountain wagons" that were also designed and built by Stanley.

On May 26, 1977, The Stanley Hotel was entered in the National Register of Historic Places and is still considered by many as one of the significant factors contributing to the growth of Colorado as a tourist destination.

We hope you enjoy visiting The Stanley Hotel in our "Rocky Mountain Magic" series in American Romance.

RMH-1

Rocky Mountain Magic

The Pirate
JAYNE ANN KRENTZ

At the heart of every powerful romance story lies a legend. There are many romantic legends and countless modern variations on them, but they all have one thing in common: They are tales of brave, resourceful women who must gentle and tame the powerful, passionate men who are their true mates.

The enormous appeal of Jayne Ann Krentz lies in her ability to create modern-day versions of these classic romantic myths, and her LADIES AND LEGENDS trilogy showcases this talent. Believing that a storyteller who can bring legends to life deserves special attention, Harlequin has chosen the first book of the trilogy—THE PIRATE—to receive our Award of Excellence. Look for it now.

AE-PIR-1A